Outside, the storm of firing had settled down

Smoke swirled, and men were shouting at each other, trying to sort out the situation. It sounded as if nobody was too eager to press home the attack.

"Does the expression, 'the devil is in the details' suggest anything to anybody?" Brigid asked. She was hunkered down, clutching a big black 9mm H&K USP in both hands.

Grant tipped his helmeted head to the side. "You're the point man."

"Give me all your grens," Kane said, slinging his scavenged Copperhead, "then grab the chair."

Grant began pulling out microgrens. "This is another classic one-percenter, isn't it?"

Kane tipped a finger off his visor in front of his brow.

"They sure seem to be coming around way more than one percent of the time."

"Think of it as entropy in action," Kane said.

Other titles in this series:

James Axler
Outlanders

SUCCESSORS

A GOLD EAGLE BOOK FROM
W RLDWIDE ®

TORONTO • NEW YORK • LONDON
AMSTERDAM • PARIS • SYDNEY • HAMBURG
STOCKHOLM • ATHENS • TOKYO • MILAN
MADRID • WARSAW • BUDAPEST • AUCKLAND

For the Knappenbergers: Jim, Joan-Mri,
and of course, the excellent and irrepressible Melissa.
With love and gratitude.

First edition August 2005

ISBN 0-373-63847-7

SUCCESSORS

Special thanks and acknowledgment to Victor Milán
for his contribution to this work.

Printed in U.S.A.

"He who fights with monsters might take care lest he thereby become a monster. And if you gaze for long into an abyss, the abyss gazes also into you."

—Friedrich Nietzsche

"[A] rat is a dog is a pig is a boy."

—Ingrid Newkirk, former law-enforcement officer and president of People for the Ethical Treatment of Animals

The Road to Outlands—
From Secret Government Files to the Future

Almost two hundred years after the global holocaust, Kane, a former Magistrate of Cobaltville, often thought the world had been lucky to survive at all after a nuclear device detonated in the Russian embassy in Washington, D.C. The aftermath—forever known as skydark—reshaped continents and turned civilization into ashes.

Nearly depopulated, America became the Deathlands—poisoned by radiation, home to chaos and mutated life forms. Feudal rule reappeared in the form of baronies, while remote outposts clung to a brutish existence.

What eventually helped shape this wasteland were the redoubts, the secret preholocaust military installations with stores of weapons, and the home of gateways, the locational matter-transfer facilities. Some of the redoubts hid clues that had once fed wild theories of government cover-ups and alien visitations.

Rearmed from redoubt stockpiles, the barons consolidated their power and reclaimed technology for the villes. Their power, supported by some invisible authority, extended beyond their fortified walls to what was now called the Outlands. It was here that the rootstock of humanity survived, living with hellzones and chemical storms, hounded by Magistrates.

In the villes, rigid laws were enforced—to atone for the sins of the past and prepare the way for a better future. That was the barons' public credo and their right-to-rule.

Kane, along with friend and fellow Magistrate Grant, had upheld that claim until a fateful Outlands expedition. A displaced piece of technology…a question to a keeper of the archives…a vague clue about alien masters—and their world shifted radically. Suddenly, Brigid Baptiste, the archivist, faced summary execution, and Grant a quick termination. For Kane there was forgiveness if he pledged his unquestioning allegiance to Baron Cobalt and his unknown masters and abandoned his friends.

But that allegiance would make him support a mysterious and alien power and deny loyalty and friends. Then what else was there?

Kane had been brought up solely to serve the ville. Brigid's only link with her family was her mother's red-gold hair, green eyes and supple form. Grant's clues to his lineage were his ebony skin and powerful physique. But Domi, she of the white hair, was an Outlander pressed into sexual servitude in Cobaltville. She at least knew her roots and was a reminder to the exiles that the outcasts belonged in the human family.

Parents, friends, community—the very rootedness of humanity was denied. With no continuity, there was no forward momentum to the future. And that was the crux—when Kane began to wonder if there *was* a future.

For Kane, it wouldn't do. So the only way was out—way, way out.

After their escape, they found shelter at the forgotten Cerberus redoubt headed by Lakesh, a scientist, Cobaltville's head archivist, and secret opponent of the barons.

With their past turned into a lie, their future threatened, only one thing was left to give meaning to the outcasts. The hunger for freedom, the will to resist the hostile influences. And perhaps, by opposing, end them.

Chapter 1

The scattered tar-paper shacks slumped at the far side of an expanse of mud that had fractured into a million angular plates as it dried. The Andean runoff had passed, and summer's heat had driven the Río Marañón from its banks like a defeated army. Thatch roofs seemed bowed beneath the weight of the midday equatorial sun. Around the clearing the forest rose like green cliffs.

The smell was like a blow to the face.

"Is this the bloody place?" MacLean demanded as the party emerged from the brush across the mudflat, a couple of hundred yards away. His coarse straw hair was brushed at a bias across his forehead and clamped in place by a white straw cowboy hat. He wore amber shades and a tan bush jacket. A scoped Savage bolt-action rifle, brushed stainless steel and black synthetic, was slung across his back.

Guinan spoke quietly in Spanish to the guide, Rogelio. The team's sec man, Witcover, thumbed up the front of his boonie hat to scratch where it chafed his forehead. His other hand stayed on the pistol grip of his

M-16 A-2 longblaster, which he held pointed in the general direction of the silent huts. He wore an olive drab T-shirt and camou pants over big boots, as if dressed for a role. He had the size and muscles to carry it off.

"He says it is." Guinan had a nasal voice. She was a wiry woman in her early forties, wearing an electric-green ball cap with a dark green bill over long auburn hair wound into a braid that hung between her shoulder blades. She wore a loose white blouse printed in red-and-blue flowers tucked into khaki cargo shorts and low-topped hiking shoes. A 9 mm Beretta pistol rode in a flapped holster at her hip.

Like MacLean, the little team's leader, she had been born and raised on Earth's Moon.

Señor Rogelio watched with sad apprehension in his dark brown eyes. The whites of his eyes were stained like the teeth of a longtime smoker, and his teeth, such as he had, were stained even darker. His muslin shorts and blouse, stained a uniform dingy brown by jungle slop and sweat, were so baggy his thin red-brown limbs and neck seemed to have been added as afterthoughts. His face was as narrow as a blade. A luxury of black mustache dominated his face the way a pristine satin sofa would have dominated one of the one-room shacks. His general air was that of one who expected little and that not good, and was seldom disappointed.

Except there was a little edge to him, to the way he shifted weight from foot to foot, the way his gaze kept skipping from the brush to the long slow brown slog of river to their left to the abandoned-seeming collection of huts. As if his normal dire expectations had started to be considerably and regularly exceeded.

"Well?" MacLean demanded. "Why are we standing here improving our suntans? Let's get this fool's errand over and done with so we can jump back to Cerberus where it's cool and the humidity isn't at physically impossible levels."

"Come now, Algernon," Guinan said. "We're high up here. The humidity is scarcely daunting."

Witcover scowled. "We should mebbe be a little cautious." He had a mustache of his own, dark brown and substantially less imposing than Rogelio's. It was the only thing about him that was less imposing than the local.

"What? You're afraid?" MacLean sneered. "I thought you Magistrates were fearless."

"Former Magistrate," Witcover corrected evenly. He had come up as a junior Mag about the time the unrest started, a couple of years before. The only way to leave the Magistrate Division, in the normal course of events, was feet first. So it was certain that a termination warrant had been issued on Witcover. Not that he didn't have lots of company these days on the death list. He had been hiding out in the Shens serving as sec man to one of the small-time chieftains who had begun to spring up in the Outlands, in the wake of the civil war among the barons. Then Cerberus redoubt caught wind of him, and its agents invited him to join them in resisting the tyranny of the barons and their black-clad myrmidons, the Mags.

"Cautious," he explained. "That way you're not so likely to find yourself with dirt hitting you in the eyes, you know?"

Witcover looked a typical coldheart, albeit better fed than most. But he didn't lack perception. He had encountered a few fellow fugitive Mags even before being brought to Cerberus where Kane and Grant, the most famous renegade Magistrates of all time, made their lair. He noticed that those who tried to run the standard Mag game of busting any head that didn't bow quick enough to your passing by and kicking in every door that didn't open fast enough at your approach—*without* your body being encased in hard-contact armor and without being backed by phalanxes of fellow Mags—wound up reaching ambient temperature in record time.

"I cannot *believe* it," MacLean said, hunching his shoulders as if he wanted to stamp an athletic-shoe-clad foot for emphasis but didn't quite dare. "A world of chillers and blasters to choose from, and we get saddled with a coward."

"Don't be a twit, MacLean," Guinan responded. "He's got a point. Something out of true is going on down here, or we wouldn't be here in the first place. And our poor local guide is frightened out of his wits."

"That's a short journey," MacLean said. "He's such a rabbit he's liable to bolt if he sees his own shadow sneaking up on him. And if this human thumb has a point, it's on top of his mucking head. Bloody hell."

Witcover knew the female biologist wasn't defending him. She was just arguing with MacLean to piss him off. She was hardly less conceited snot than the team leader, who was an astrophysicist of all things. All the Moon-base emigrés acted as if mere ground-pounding Earthmen were born to fetch and carry for them. That the ground crawlers had given them refuge after they were driven from Manitius Base on the Moon didn't seem to register with many of them, at least to the extent of registering gratitude.

Witcover didn't mind. Any shit they gave him, they dished out with a spoon, whereas any Mag senior to you, even if by minutes, used a fusion-powered bulldozer.

"What we can expect to learn from a lot of superstitious devolved savages is entirely beyond me," MacLean added.

"Dr. Lakesh thinks there's something here," Guinan said.

MacLean grunted. The only terrestrial the Manitius emigrés generally respected was Dr. Mohandas Lakesh Singh, Cerberus redoubt's director. He was a certifiably brilliant scientist from way back in predark days, a freezie, and as high-handed as the worst of the Manitius bunch. His word trumped all of MacLean's misgivings unless the displaced whitecoat cared to try his hand at shifting for himself on the mother planet—something none of the oh-so-superior refugees seemed inclined to do.

"Well, what do you suggest, then, Mr. Witcover?"

"Mebbe try to circle this mud flat and get closer. Stay in the bush instead of just strolling across the open."

"And have every twig jab us with thorns and every branch tip another loathsome bug down our collars? I think not."

"It's the Marañón Valley, MacLean," Guinan said. "It's a major feeder of the Amazon. There are bugs everywhere. As you call them."

"Then let me go scope it out," Witcover said stolidly.

"Not on yours, old chap. Will you make up your bloody mind? First you've got the wind up, next you want to go gallivanting off and leave us to our own devices. Which is it to be?"

"Please, *señores,*" Rogelio pleaded. After the lone English word he continued in quiet but impassioned Spanish.

"What's the dammed coward on about now?" MacLean demanded.

"He doesn't want us to argue too loudly," Guinan said. "He fears the demons who took the ville."

MacLean snorted. "Enough of this bullshit. Come on. Move! Witcover, you can lead the way. The rest of us will follow."

He grabbed Rogelio by an arm like a maroon stick and yanked him in front of himself. "And you, my friend, will walk close behind Witcover. *Capisce?* Or whatever the fuck it is you say."

Rogelio took off his battered hat, ran his hand nervously through his brush of dense black hair, placed the hat and crossed himself. He spoke briefly and without animation to Guinan, and then set off after Witcover—if without eagerness, then without reluctance, either.

"He says he has entrusted himself to the Virgin," Guinan supplied as she and the expedition head set off in the wake of the other two. "He advises us to do likewise. He says we're going to die soon." She spoke with a sort of gloomy satisfaction.

"Bloody bullshit," MacLean said. "You can't take that seriously. It's barking mad!"

Guinan shrugged. "We're down here for a reason."

"A wild-goose chase, more likely than otherwise."

Although it had rained savagely from the time they set out from their camp near the village, the sky was clear, with white clouds shining like hope itself piling up into the blue. The sun stung bare skin.

"Bloody madness not to bring the boat here straightaway," MacLean complained, "rather than nose in and stumble half a klick upriver through the bloody bush."

"We need to show a little caution," Guinan said in her dry and slightly nasal voice. "Señor Rogelio says the demons have been advancing steadily through the forest until they overtook his sister's village as he slept in a hut on the outskirts."

"I know, I know," the leader said sullenly. "He was

awakened by screaming. Clawed black forms attacked him and he barely escaped with his life. Fantastic yarn."

"He still has half-healed scratches on his face, Mac-Lean," Guinan said. "Unless you think they're psychosomatic."

"That kind of story isn't too uncommon down here on Earth," Witcover called softly over his shoulder. "Now, both of you pipe down."

"I will *not!*" MacLean shouted the last word in petulant defiance. "I will *not* pipe down!"

Trudging stolidly behind Witcover, Rogelio cringed at MacLean's outburst.

"Asshole," Guinan said.

No one in Cerberus redoubt, buried beneath a mountain peak high in the Bitterroot Range, had any clear idea what was going on down here, just below the eastern foothills of the Andes. The redoubt's satellite coverage showed a zone of distinct change in the flora. Its thermal signature and even its color to the naked eye had changed, as distinctly as if it were a giant pool of spilled paint: a rudely circular splotch of country that had been various shades of verdancy and brown was now almost uniform bluish green, of a shade that matched no other area of the planet's surface visible from the still functioning or recently repaired satellites under Cerberus's command. Moreover, it had appeared suddenly, between one overhead pass and another two days later.

Worst of all, it was expanding at a pace of several miles a day.

"Still no sign of life," Witcover called over his shoulder as they drew closer to the first of the shacks.

"Well, splendid," MacLean said. "Then you've got nothing to be afraid of."

Guinan had stopped and stood frowning. "There is something peculiar about the vegetation here."

"What? It's all bloody green."

"But it's the wrong green, McLean. It's a shade of blue-green I haven't seen before except in Lakesh's photos from space. Like that creeper there." She pointed with a slim hand at a vine running up the bole of one of the nearer trees like a line of blue-green flame.

"So maybe there's something to find here after all," MacLean said. Witcover had stopped a few paces short of the nearest hut. The ancient advertising logos on its soda-can walls had faded to hieroglyphics. "But I want to find somebody to talk to us who didn't run away."

Rogelio, who cowered behind Witcover, began to shake and babble even before Guinan translated. "He says he can't," she told MacLean. "He says they're all dead."

"How would he know?" The astrophysicist put fists on his hips and smirked. "If he's as accurate as he is brave, the bloody ville must be teeming with informants. In fact—"

He strode to the frightened local and grabbed him by the back of the neck hole of his collarless smock. "I'm going to put an end to this malingering right—"

He frog-marched the frightened man to the hootch.

Its floor was elevated on pilings several feet above the dried mud flat, as a hedge against the river's unpredictable moods. A set of rough plank steps led to the entrance, which was covered by top-to-bottom strings of plastic beads sun-faded to murky purple. Rogelio refused to climb them.

"—*now.*" Showing a strength that belied his skinny arms, the astrophysicist propelled Rogelio up and into the darkness with a slithering rattle of ancient beads.

The villager's knees thumped noisily on the floorboards. For a moment there was rustling as he tried to pick himself off the floor. Then silence.

Half-outraged or at least acting that way, Guinan had marched up almost to MacLean's back. Witcover held out a big bare sunburned arm to stop her. She seemed to accept his intervention gratefully.

From inside came a dry whisper of sounds, as of leaves blown across woven-reed mounting. But somehow sharp.

Then the screaming started.

Chapter 2

"Target acquired."

Oblivious to a light drizzle falling from clouds almost low enough for him to touch, an anchorite sat cross-legged on a gray granite ledge above a nearly sheer drop to the surf churning green on the rocky shore to which the Cific had advanced after Soviet earthshaker devices set off monster quakes during the big nuke two centuries before.

Glowing pale green in the dubious light, the telescopic sight's crosshairs centered on the meditator's head. The pale face was almost obscured by a cloud of wind-wilded black hair and gray-streaked beard. Despite the chill the man wore only a pair of black pants, possibly sweats or pajama bottoms.

"Shall I turn this puke's head to pink mist for him?" asked the man behind the scope. Although the contact patch taped all but invisibly over his Adam's apple would transmit even inaudible subvocalizations as distinct speech, he spoke in normal conversational tones. As measured by the sight's laser rangefinder his target sat over eight hundred meters away to the south, a couple hundred meters below a peak neighboring the one where he lay with his black synthetic-stocked long-action Remington 700 sniper's rifle propped on a pair of beanbags he carried with him for that purpose.

"That's a negative, Kông," came the reply from the erstwhile Lieutenant Colonel William "Wild Bill" Mc-Combs, Team Lazarus's leader. "We need to make sure this one's a step-on."

"What's not sure?" the sniper demanded in outrage. "This rifle's got plenty of legs. And at this range I can put it in his ear hole and not even ruffle all the hairs. Don't forget that shot I made in Mogadishu."

"You never let us forget that shot in the Dish," Mc-Combs said. Attached as sniper to Task Force 160 in Somalia during Operation Gothic Serpent in 1993, Second Lieutenant Raymond Hong had made a head shot from a MH-6B Little Bird "Night Stalker" chopper on a man carrying what an observer using low-light television identified as a possible LAW rocket launcher onto a rooftop at over a mile with a Barrett .50-caliber rifle. "Too bad it turned out your kill was a Nigerian aid worker with a bedroll."

"I made the shot, Chief," Hong insisted. "I sealed the deal. That's what counts."

Wild Bill McCombs's long jaw set in his long craggy face. He stood on a shelf ten yards above the unquiet Cific with the white surf noise clearly audible above the freshening breeze. His Kevlar Fritz-style helmet rested on a rock nearby. The wind wisped a shock of virtually colorless hair across his forehead. His .223-caliber M-4 carbine was slung muzzle down behind his right shoulder.

"Negative," he said to the distant sniper. "Our target's way too slippery and has way too many places to hide if you don't get the control shot. You got your orders, soldier. Do as you're told."

He was a man who knew how to put menace in his voice. His early career as a second lieutenant in the U.S. Army Special Forces had been distinguished by his success in Soviet-occupied Afghanistan. McCombs had gone on to a long career advising Third World forces on advanced coercive interrogation and counterinsurgency techniques, starting in the late 1980s aiding the Iraqis during their war with Iran and wrapping up as an observer with Russian forces during the first Chechen war in 1994. From there, after a stint with LAPD's Ramparts division, he had gone on to enjoy success handling special operations for the DEA until recruited for his present duty.

"Yes, sir," the sniper agreed sulkily.

"Asshole." The new voice belonged to steroid-burly black Master Sergeant Jameel Adams, ex-Marine EOD, ex-ATF. He was positioned below the target. He carried an M-16 A-2 with a 40 mm M-203 launcher attached and a vest with multiple pockets full of launch and hand grenades.

McCombs raised an eyebrow. "You remember to squelch that next time, big guy."

The fourth member of Team Lazarus—hired, trained and frozen two centuries ago by billionaire computer mogul Gilgamesh Bates—showed his team leader a grin full of crooked brown teeth. Former Navy SEAL Machinist's Mate Ricardo "Ricky" Ramírez, formerly of the Los Angeles Sheriff's Department and, like McCombs, the United States Drug Enforcement Administration, was a lanky, good-looking kid, except for the teeth. He wore slung horizontal to his waist an M-249 Squad Automatic Weapon almost as big around as he was.

"Ready to do some climbing, Three Fingers?" he radioed.

Far below them, Adams raised the eponymous left hand in a truncated but still big fist. "Don't ever call me that, cocksucker," he said.

Still scowling murderously, he began to climb.

"NICE PLACE you got here, Kane."

"Storm front coming," the shaggy man remarked without looking around. "Heard you coming the last fifteen minutes. Getting sloppy, Grant?"

Despite the body weight mandated by his breadth of chest and shoulders, the tall black man with the outlaw handlebar mustache framing his long powerful jaw was not breathing heavily. He brushed his palms together. His hands and head were the only parts of his body not encased in a formfitting shadow suit.

"Negative," he said. The scowl creasing his ruggedly handsome face was habitual, not a response to circum-

stances. Mostly. "I know better than to try sneaking up
on you. You're still the maximum point man. Don't
want my last sight in this life to be your ugly mug past
an extra hole in the bridge of my nose."

"What makes you think I'm armed, Grant?" the
bearded man asked as he assessed the ocean and the approaching squall. "I've renounced the world."

Grant made a rude noise. "And my ass has turned
white as Domi's."

Kane emitted a sound that might have been mirth.
"Don't show me."

"You may fool yourself, Kane. Don't try to fool your
old door-busting partner. You can't let it go."

"Watch me."

Kane shifted his butt on the rock, stretched his arms
over his head, then turned his upper torso right and left
to stretch out the muscles of his lower back.

Then for the first time he looked at Grant. The eyes
were wolf-gray and as cold as a dead man's hand.

"We've lost it, Grant. Humanity's run is over, except
for whatever servants the Annunaki might want to leave
to hew wood and haul water and build temples for them.
I'm *tired,* Grant. So yeah, I can let it go."

"It sure as hell won't let *you* go, Kane."

The bearded man shrugged. "We all die sometime."

Grant grunted in disgust. He gestured toward a
shadow visible among the jumbled rocks of the cliff
face a few yards behind Kane. "I can't believe you actually found a hermit's cave to hide out in up here."

"I've always been a resourceful kind of guy."

"Dammit, Kane! Get serious."

"When have you ever known me to be anything else?" Kane asked mildly.

"We've been down before. Down hard. Yeah, things have taken a rough turn. That doesn't give you leave to—to just run off and join the circus."

Kane laughed. He shifted to face his old friend, untied his legs to bring his knees up before him. "Is that what you call it?" he asked. "That's pretty good. What do you call it when you go storming off to Shizuka's island promising never to return?"

Grant's scowl deepened. "I always come back."

Kane shrugged. "Mebbe that's your mistake. Mebbe—"

Off to the north the overcast sky ripped. The late-morning sun sent a shaft of silvery light over Kane's shoulder south along the remodeled coast.

Kane's eyes went wide.

"DAMN," THREE FINGER Adams grunted as the deep ax-blow sound of Hong's big Lapua Magnum rifle lighting off reached his ears. He had already heard the bullet whining off rock scarcely twenty yards over his head, a clean miss. "Stupid fuck's gone and got himself burned!"

"Can the chatter," McCombs commanded via the bone-conduction speaker taped to the mastoid process behind the grenadier's left ear. "Get into position to drop some grenades on that ledge."

Clinging to a swell of gray stone, Adams didn't look down. He was roping his way up a not very difficult climb, but realized if he peeled the pitons stood small chance of holding against his substantial weight and that of all the gear he was loaded down with. He was all alone up here; Ramírez and the team's leader were fifty yards higher than him, trying to drop down on their target from above.

"Hand or 40 mm?"

"You're the grenadier. Do I have to tell you everything? Just do it!"

From above came the snarl of a full-auto burst.

A man fell screaming past him.

"I SEE HIM!" Ramírez exclaimed. He unsnapped his carabiner from his safety line. "Long-hair *cabrón* is mine!"

He stood, bringing the light Minimi machine gun with the ammo box hung to one side to his shoulder as if it were a rifle. Dislodged pebbles bounced away down the rocks toward the sea.

"At ease, Ramírez!" McCombs shouted over the comm link. "Don't—"

ALERTED BY VOICES and the falling gravel, Grant rose from a nest of stone slabs with his Sin Eater extended. The man who had popped up out of the rocks ten yards overhead had a low-slung helmet and some kind of assault-armor vest. The machine pistol's 9 mm rounds would never penetrate it. At that treacherous upward angle not even as skilled and seasoned a gunfighting master as Grant trusted his ability to get a snap shot into the triangle of eyes and nose, where a hit would penetrate the brain to the medulla nerve center and turn off the shooter's central nervous system before he could clench a finger on the trigger and stitch Kane's unprotected back with high-velocity 65-grain bullets moving at a kilometer per second.

So as soon as the Sin Eater's perforated muzzle shroud covered a camou-clad thigh, Grant triggered a triburst.

RICKY RAMÍREZ SCREAMED as two bullets lanced through his leg. He had never been shot before; hurt had always been something he laid on other people. The flash of white-hot agony made his right hand clench in reflex. The SAW went off with a gravel-throated roar.

But the same pain impulse had made him yank the muzzle up. The copper-jacketed bullets—the same diameter as those fired by a .22, but longer, heavier, and very much faster—skimmed right off the top of the rock behind which Kane sheltered from the sniper, like stones skipped across a pond.

Grant's 147-grain hollowpoints had missed his femur. But they blew chunks of muscle out the back of the former SEAL's leg. It buckled.

And the machine gun's recoil, comparatively light though it was, combined with the failure of his down-slope leg to push him into space.

Ricky Ramírez had never flown before—not without a plane or a parachute.

He wasn't very stoic about that, either.

KANE RAISED his own Sin Eater just far enough that the muzzle cleared the top of his shielding rock and loosed a long burst at the sniper—whose position had been betrayed by the chance ray of sunlight reflecting off his scope's big objective lens. His chance of hitting was nil, he knew. At a range of half a mile his bullets would almost certainly fall well short even if he angled the big handblaster up to an optimal angle of about fifty-five degrees. Which he didn't—he aimed pretty much straight for the enemy shooter, hoping to distract him with dancing muzzle-flash.

The longblaster's shot was good anyway. It would have taken Grant through the back of his bull neck if he hadn't dropped as if shot himself the millisecond he eased his own finger off the trigger.

Looking back over his shoulder, Kane could just see Grant through a gap between piled rocks. "You all right, partner?"

"Never better. You're a popular guy, Kane."

Grant nodded his chin at Kane's own Sin Eater. "It real comfortable, sitting on that thing all day long?"

"You weren't the only one I've been listening to," Kane said. "Amazing how keen your senses get after a week or so with no sounds but the wind and the seabirds."

"Storms and screamwings, more like."

"You have no appreciation for the finer points of nature, Grant."

"None."

From below came a thunk. A moment later an explosion shattered rock and air above their heads. Frags whined past as both men ducked.

"Strike," Kane said. "They got us sandwiched."

The gren launcher below them popped off again. Kane curled up with his arms over his eyes.

The 40 mm grenade landed neatly atop the rock chunk sheltering Grant. Fragments raked Kane's right forearm. The high-explosive dual-purpose warhead didn't drop the slab on top of the former Cobaltville Magistrate and master Deathbird jock. But it cracked the stone right across the middle.

"Damn!" Grant exclaimed, seeing his sheltering stone sag toward him.

Grant's shelter failed with a sound like a rifle shot. Two broken ends of stone collapsed into his hiding place.

Chapter 3

An eyeblink before, Grant had sprung from his covert like a bolt from a crossbow. As he crossed the open space where Kane had sat meditating scant minutes before, he flung his right hand upward. Half a dozen matte-silver spheres the size of "boulder" marbles flew from his broad pink palm. As Grant tucked and rolled up alongside his partner, a bullet from the faraway rifleman laid a bright copper smear of jacketing across the rock floor and howled away into the boulders.

Several bouncing like balls, the little spheres disappeared over the cliff edge.

Kane was frowning down at the Sin Eater in his hand as if not sure what it was, despite the fact that it had been his constant companion since his induction into the Magistrate Division. He glanced up at Grant as the big man crouched beside him panting with exertion and emotion.

"Microgrens?" Kane asked.

Thunder rippled up from below. It was followed by screams, wild and shrill and seemingly uninterrupted by the need to draw breath.

Grant smiled a panther smile. "Incens."

The shrieking abruptly began to dwindle. Another explosion. Then a series of blasts ripped like a string of Chinese firecrackers, continuing to diminish in volume as their source dropped away toward the foam.

The screams stopped. The crackling continued for a time.

"I kind of wish I could have watched that," Kane said. "Watch our backs. I'm pretty sure there's one more puke up there over our heads."

Grant nodded abruptly, raised his Sin Eater to aim upslope. He was careful to keep the boulder at his back between his skull and the sniper on the next mountain down the coast.

On his belly Kane crawled along the base of the sheltering stone. Toward the rear it toed into the ground. Beyond it were other rocks of assorted sizes. He found what his memory of the space, which he had surveyed with painstaking thoroughness during the days he had spent here, told him would be present: a niche between rocks just large enough for him to push the Sin Eater into.

He did, sliding forward to put his eye to the small optical sight mounted atop the Sin Eater. He quickly found where memory told him the sniper's nest was. Aware he had been spotted, the enemy was out of sight. He might even have shifted to a secondary firing position.

It didn't much matter. If Kane and Grant could lure him into firing again without getting nailed, he'd give himself away.

For the moment Kane surmised the sniper was scanning Kane's retreat through binoculars. A rifle scope is primarily a sight, not primarily a telescope: and certainly not a spotting device. The field of view is far too small. Although not a sniper himself, Kane knew they were trained and accustomed to work in teams of at least two, with a partner both to seek out targets and provide security when the shooter was focusing his entire consciousness through the glass-ended tube toward his prey—or better, two helpers, a spotter and security, although this was a luxury reality seldom afforded.

If the sniper, or a spotter, was watching through binoculars, he would spot the Sin Eater among the rocks. It would take him key seconds to return to his waiting wep and bring it onto the target. If, on the other hand, he was still in the rifle glass, he would only pick Kane's wep up by sheer accident.

Or so Kane bet his life, as he took careful left-handed aim at the sniper's aerie. At any instant he expected to see the tiny light flare that would presage—by about two-thirds of a second—a high-powered bullet smashing through three lenses, two of glass and one fragile membrane, and a trifle of soft tissue, bone and hair, and spraying the spot he had used for meditation with his brains.

Beside him Grant let loose a triburst. He bared his teeth in a grimace and prayed he hadn't flinched.

"Sorry," Grant said. "Thought I saw movement up above. Want to keep the bastard's head down."

Instinct made Kane snatch his hand back away from his handblaster as if it had heated instantly white-hot in an invisible induction field. An eyeblink later the rear lens exploded with a squealing crunch and tinkle. A heavy bullet burrowed into the accretion of soil where Kane's hand had just been—and not long before, his head.

He yanked out the handblaster. Shooting as accurate as this practically mandated a bolt gun—but even if the sniper was shooting a wizard semiauto longblaster there would be an interval when recoil knocked the wep off-line and the target out of view.

The shot had not been perfect: the top of the optical sight had been cut open for about an inch by the bullet. The wep itself was unharmed.

"Kane," a voice called from the rocks above. He couldn't tell how close. The rocks and sea breeze, blustering now as the lead-colored clouds spit down a few chill gobbets of rain, played acoustic tricks. "Mr. Kane, can you hear me?"

Kane and Grant exchanged looks and both sidled back toward the back of the ledge. There was a slight overhang there that would make it harder for an enemy to drop a gren right on top of them should he have any better luck getting bearings by sound. Kane was acutely aware that if his opponent had the means and willingness to start pitching grens down at random he could quickly chill both him and Grant, the same way Grant had torched the grenadier below them.

Best keep him talking, Kane thought. "Yeah," he called. "Who the hell are you, and why are you breaking in on my meditation?"

Laughter answered him. His interlocutor sounded like a vigorous man of middle years. Of course he's vigorous—he's running around the rocks like a mountain goat.

"I admire your spirit," the unseen man called down. "You talk bravely for a trapped man."

"Trapped, is it?" Kane said. "By my count your side's down two. But math was never my strong subject."

Grant caught Kane's eye. He gestured to the rockpile he'd quitted, including the broken slab, indicating he intended to go that way, presumably first to get out of the sniper's line of fire around the mountainside, then work his way up to take the man above them. Kane shook his head. Don't do it.

Grant darted across the intervening space and dived over the rocks on the far side of the ledge. A bullet kicked chips from the top of a boulder as he vanished from view.

Kane shook his head.

"Yes, you successfully murdered two of my comrades."

The voice was raw with emotion to the point where Kane let himself hope—just a little—the bastard might be about to snap. He couldn't figure why the unseen enemy was talking instead of chucking grens. But he sure wanted to keep things that way as long as possible.

"Castaways like myself from another time," the voice said. "They slept two centuries and then were awakened to restore order to this anarchic world. Only to be killed by a lousy criminal!"

Kane felt a surge of anger, but clamped a lid on it. He was an outlaw in all literal fact, had been since he had helped Brigid Baptiste escape her termination warrant and, with the condemned senior archivist, fled Cobaltville with Grant, and the albino Outlands waif Domi. But he had been literally born and raised into the Magistrate Division—the baronial police force. Reflexes ingrained that long died hard: at heart, in ways, he was still a Mag.

Even as he hated with all his heart everything he once stood for as a Mag.

"You're more of Gilgamesh Bates's freezies, are you?" he called. Keep him talking. Kane hadn't wanted Grant to make a move, but since his partner had taken the bit in his teeth and done so, he hoped to distract the enemy above him from wondering what Grant might be doing. "Just like that Team Phoenix we saw come through a few months back."

"Don't compare us to those traitors! They sold out America."

"Looks to me more like they got sold out by their boss," Kane said. "You might just take that to heart yourself."

Harsh laughter rattled among the rocks. "They were weak-minded and willful. Too steeped in illusions of individualism. We were strong enough to be told the truth from the start. From the start, I tell you! That Americans are never so happy as when they have a boot on their necks."

"Then these last couple centuries should've made them a hell of a lot giddier than I've ever seen 'em."

A rifle shot echoed between cliffs. The sky was overcast now, the light twilight-gray. At the same time Kane heard something heavy tumbling among the rocks up and to his left. Something like a body falling. It came to rest, still high and out of sight, rather than toppling off into free fall. But loose stones clattered over an edge of rock into space.

"Grant!" Kane exclaimed involuntarily.

"He appears still to be alive," the voice called, "according to my cohort who has him in his rifle scope. It's an excellent piece of optical equipment—he can see your Mr. Grant's chest rising and falling. He also has an entirely unobstructed shot at your friend's unarmored head. I suggest you put your handgun away now, Mr. Kane, and step out where I can see you clearly."

"Give me a moment—hey, what's your damned name, anyway?" Kane called up at his unseen tormentor, sidling toward the mouth of his shallow cave.

"I hardly see it matters." A gravelly chuckle. "But then again you're a fellow warrior, and a warrior deserves to know the name of the man who kills him. I'm Lieutenant Colonel William McCombs. My compatriot is First Lieutenant Raymond Hong. A gifted shooter. All my men were gifted, Kane. You and your friend robbed your homeland of invaluable assets when you so callously snuffed them out."

"If they were that invaluable," Kane called, finishing his quick preparations and shrugging a loose jacket on over his bare upper torso, "we wouldn't've chilled 'em half so easy."

"Don't trifle with me, Kane!" McComb called harshly. "I hold your partner's life in the palm of my hand."

"How do I know you won't just have your little bud freeze Grant once I put myself in your sights?" Kane asked.

McComb tittered. He seemed to switch from choking near-rage to near-giggles awful fast. A fusie, Kane thought. Great.

"You don't. But I tell you what. On the one hand, it's you Mr. Bates is interested in. On the other, it appears your friend Grant is wearing some kind of extremely durable and flexible ballistic-armor suit. But it's too flexible, from what Kong—that's what we call my associate Lieutenant Hong—tells me. It may *stop* heavy .338 Magnum bullets—eventually. But how much damage might they do to your friend driving the cloth in spikes deep into his flesh? We can find out: I'm always up for an experiment—aren't you?"

"All right, I'm coming into the open." Kane straightened with his hands clasped loosely above his wild-haired head. He stepped toward the front of the ledge.

Ten yards above him a man stood up from behind a granite boulder like a cathedral gargoyle weathered down to a mere suggestion of its former contours. He was tall and spare, clad in mountain camou. The wet wind stirred an iron-gray brush of hair. He languidly pointed a short black carbine from the hip at Kane.

"We meet at last," McComb said. "You look like a fucking hippie."

"Means nothing to me. It's your move, McComb. Why don't you go ahead and make it so we can get in out of the rain?"

"To begin with, I believe your friend Grant has served his purpose. Kong, if you will…"

"KONG" HONG—a name he'd been given back in his cadet days at the Point for reasons having nothing to do with kindness or gentleness, although his linebacker's size played a role—took up slack on his Remington's trigger. He'd vaporize this guy's head with a 250-grain boattailed buzz bomb and then they could pack it in. He was hungry.

For more than just food. That was one thing about working for Gil Bates. The guy was a whack, seven feet tall and pale as a ghost with his wispy red beard and eyes sunk way back in his head like an old, sick bloodhound's. But he understood a man and his needs. Team Lazarus had been given an open-ended hunting license, even before they'd gone into deep freeze.

Bates had promised them that when the job was done and he was king, they wouldn't have to hunt. That was fine with Kong. The trigger approached its break point of 2.5 pounds of pressure. It would snap like a glass rod at an instant Kong deliberately tried not to anticipate.…

Kong's ears heard no sound. Yet he perceived some-how—a minute change in air pressure, sudden sense of the nearness of warmth, tiny vibration transmitted up through the flat gray rock to which his body was pressed like a lizard's—warned him he was no longer alone on the mountain.

As tankers and other AFV crew have nightmares about roasting alive, trapped in their metal boxes, snipers wake up sweating from dreams of being caught "in the glass," pouring their whole beings through the tube of the scope to project a tiny object at great speed to a point scarcely less small.

Kong didn't even try to wheel around his bulky rifle. Instead he yanked his Beretta 9 mm M-9 from its holster behind his hip and rolled onto his back.

He was already too late. A figure stood wide-legged over him with a cascade of red-gold hair striped across its face by the rain-freighted wind, a handblaster leveled at his head.

"A woman?" Kong gasped, still trying to present his side arm.

"Surprised?" Brigid Baptiste said coolly. As Kong aimed his Beretta, she calmly placed a round right between his eyes.

"KONG!" KANE HEARD McComb exclaim. The colonel's head jerked up. His voice keened with distress.

Kane's snap judgment was that the freezie had heard something bad enough to distract him, if only for a heartbeat or two. He seemed to have taken his eyes off the man he thought his captive. Now or never, Kane told himself.

He unlaced his fingers and brought his hands down in front of his face. As they came down, his Sin Eater slammed into his prepared hand. The guardless trigger hit his crooked forefinger, and he triggered a triburst.

Wild Bill's head exploded like a sledgehammered cantaloupe. Blood geysering from the wreck of his lower jaw, his body toppled off into space. It bounced, once, on the lip of Kane's meditative ledge, and was seen no more.

Kane was standing in pelting rain, blaster in hand, gazing contemplatively at the bloodstain dissolving on dark gray stone and ruminating about broken peace and violated sanctuary, when an outraged feminine voice called down from practically over his head, "You used up all the fun? Selfish sumbitches, you!"

Blinking in astonishment, he raised his head. His long hair was plastered to his face, neck and shoulders by the rain. "Domi?"

"Expecting Baron Beausoleil?" Feigned or real, her anger was causing her to speak in the clipped slang of her Outlander youth. "You come help with Grant. I not lugging his semiconscious ass all by my damned lonesome!"

Chapter 4

Lying concealed in the scrub, Team Phoenix watched a ville die.

"This is some seriously strange shit," Sean Reichert remarked. He was a Latino, young, with that well-packed muscularity characteristic of U.S. Army soldiers of the late twentieth century. Although his mustached face, currently half-obscured behind a set of electronic binoculars, showed a slight plumpness, it was darkly handsome enough to have graced the cover of a movie magazine.

If one had been published in the past two hundred years. Which, of course, it hadn't.

The monolith seemed to be steaming, wreathed with white vapors rising up into a blue Midwestern morning sky swept with white horsetails of cloud. As the three men watched, a chunk burst out one story down from the apex in front of a jet of yellow flame.

"Somebody's not having a good day," Larry Robison said. Like the others, the bearded former SEAL and communications wizard wore what appeared to be conventional BDUs.

But they were anything but standard issue, as the men at team Phoenix were anything but standard soldiers. Blouses and trousers were woven of special synthetic spider silk allegedly derived from gene-engi-neered goats—another black DARPA goodie—with thin Kevlar lining to stiffen them and provide some resistance to impact. Steel-ceramic trauma plates were inserted above the sternum to protect the heart. The uniforms constituted light but highly effective ballistic armor, and were relatively cool, being set up to breathe despite the Kevlar.

The team's leader, burly ex-Marine Major Mike Hays, smoothed his silver mustache with a big scarred thumb. "Not so good for some, but maybe better for others," he said. "From what I've heard about life in those weird sterile fortresses, anyway."

With his other hand he cradled the receiver of his primary personal weapon, hung horizontally at his capacious waist on a long sling. It was as out of the ordinary as the four men themselves, the trio up on the rise and the solitary man, with close-cropped bronze hair and beard, and eyeglasses that were circles of reflected sunblaze, who sat at guard in the cupola of the larger of the two vehicles parked in the draw below. The blaster was a serious machine gun, a Belgian Fabrique Nationale MAG-58 in .308 NATO caliber, with a shortened barrel and a molded synthetic foregrip mounted to the gas tube so it could be fired like an oversize subgun.

"I'd feel better if we had some inkling what this is

about," Robison said. His weapon of choice was a beefy IZHMASH Saiga-20K 20-gauge scattergun: full-auto with a drum mag. "Ever since we woke up we hear nothing but how invincible these nine barons are. Now there's flames coming out their penthouse window— and the penthouse didn't even have a window five minutes ago."

When he said *"woke up,"* he wasn't talking about that morning.

"What are the odds we can get what we came for?" came the radioed voice of the man keeping watch from behind the Mk-19 automatic grenade launcher in the turret of the LAV-25, dubbed Bobzilla.

The men on the rise traded looks and shrugs. "Good question," Major Mike said. It was characteristic of the team's sole lifelong civilian, Joe Weaver, to cut right to the core.

What they had come for was information that might lead them to the whereabouts of their treacherous erstwhile employer, Gilgamesh Bates. In the waning years of the twentieth century he had recruited them to put down into deep freeze, to be reanimated to serve as a special cadre in hopes of catalyzing the rebuilding of America in the wake of the catastrophic war Bates foresaw. The war duly happened, followed by a hundred years of chaos and then almost a century of tyranny under the nine barons. And then, at last, Team Phoenix had been thawed. Their time had come to act.

Only they found—after considerable hardship and

battle—that they were being used, not as angels of mercy, but as pawns in a megalomaniac scheme to conquer an already long-abused North American continent.

And that high among the threats to any prospect of restoring anything remotely resembling a decent life, much less freedom, to the suffering inhabitants of what had once been known as the Deathlands and was now generally called the Outlands, ranked Gilgamesh Bates himself.

"Whoa, wait one," Sean Reichert warned, suddenly tensing behind his binos. "Events."

"I got it," Major Mike said, shifting his own big Zeiss glasses downward. Refugees had appeared, streaming away from the city across the plains. Most were on foot but various wags were visible, some with the battered look of Outlander trade vehicles allowed into the ville under day passes to do business, others clearly ville utility vehicles. At the moment they seemed to be simply scattering, with no apparent destination except to flee.

"Don't get lost in the glass here, guys," Larry Robison warned.

As if in response to his words, from behind the smoke-bleeding tower a black shape appeared. Long and black it was, like an evil insect, with a shimmer in the air above it. Smoke curled toward the rotor as it prowled past.

"Deathbird!" Robison sang out. "We have a bandit."

"Let him come," Joe Weaver said simply. He had a Stinger MANPADS launcher all laid out on the deck in front of Bobzilla's turret. If the enemy attack chopper, a heavily modified Apache, slid their way, he had but to hop down, put the surface-to-air missile launcher to his shoulder and the sighting system to the eye and wait for the friendly tone announcing a lock-on. Weaver was a man seldom taken by surprise.

"Shit." Reichert started backing down off the crest.

"Not so fast, kid," Hays said. "He's not heading this way."

Instead the Deathbird put its nose down. A thin ribbon of smoke trailed back from beneath its drooping snout.

"He's strafing the refugees!" Reichert exclaimed, sitting up now. The snarl of the chin-mounted chain gun reached their ears. It was a sound seemingly more mechanical than percussive.

"Son of a *bitch*," Robison said. His bearded face tensed with frustration.

"We already had a few clues these weren't nice people," Hays said around his stub of unlit cigar.

Robison shook his head. "It's just…we're supposed to be rebuilding America. Just sitting here watching them massacre fleeing people…"

"We don't know the people he's shooting at," Weaver said laconically. "They may be perpetrators, not victims."

Larry Robison's expression suggested he smelled something bad. "I don't like this."

Reichert rubbed the back of his neck. "Not as if we haven't seen worse," he said in a muted tone, "back in the day."

A second Deathbird appeared. The first flying machine broke to its right, out of a firing pass at targets hidden by folds in the ground.

Light flickered beneath both stub wings of the newly arrived Deathbird. Complementary flashes danced across the racing-shell fuselage of the first chopper as a volley of 57-mm Shrike free-flight missiles slammed into it. The Deathbirds were encased in extremely lightweight and extremely durable armor that might have resisted the explosions.

But the rapidly spinning rotor couldn't. It shattered like glass dropped on concrete. The helicopter fell down sideways out of sight.

A yellow dome of flame appeared, turning into a globe born upward on a twisting column of black smoke. Several beats later the *whoomp* of exploding aircraft fuel reached Team Phoenix's hiding place.

"That's what you call your modern-day episode of *Family Feud*," Reichert said as the victorious helo turned away to fire its own chain gun at unseen targets near the outer wall of the monolith. Then it vanished in a bright flash as the Gatling gun in one of the ville's Phalanx air-defense towers caught it with a 20 mm burst.

Larry Robison shook his head.

"It's a brave new world, that's for damned sure," Hays said. He took his cigar from his mouth and studied it. In Indian territory he never lit it, lest its distinctive and penetrating smell, borne far by the wind, betray their presence.

"Anybody still think there's any point in infiltrating the ville?" he asked in a growl.

A beat. "That'd be a big negative," Reichert said.

"We can snaffle a few of the refugees, see if we can get anything useful out of them," Robison suggested.

Hays cocked a brow at him. "And here your heart was bleeding for them poor victims just a minute ago."

Robison shrugged. "So we ask them nicely," he said.

THE BOUND MAN SCREAMED as the lit torch was thrust into his face.

He kicked violently, fell over backward on the packed slightly moist sand of the draw floor. Overhead the Great Plains stars looked down uncaringly on the scene being enacted by the light of a campfire in the dead ground among the small stand of trees.

It wasn't the first time they'd witnessed something like this.

Several of the ragged score of people gathered in the arroyo cheered. Others shouted harsh encouragement: "Worthless tower bastard! Haul him up and give him more of what he's got coming!"

The four remaining captives, and the woman lying on her side with her throat slit, wore finer garments than the others. At least they had been when they put them on at the start of the day.

His face blistering and eyebrows and a hank of hair crisped by the brief exposure to fire, the captive kicked and made inchoate protesting noises when two burly former denizens of Mandeville's Tartarus Pits tried to lay hands on him. The woman with the torch clutched it in both hands. Her thin, hunched body quivered almost to the point of convulsion with exaltation.

"Let's all just back off here now, folks," a voice said from the darkness.

Two men strolled into the circle of firelight. The refugees turned to stare at them with slack mouths. One man was in his late twenties, dark hair and mustache, olive skin, slightly plump but handsome. The other was eight or ten years older and taller, an inch or three above six feet. He had a dark beard and mustache on a square, sleepy-eyed face. They wore camou that looked dappled gray and black in the firelight. Their heads were bare, but they carried longblasters slung in easy reach, and handblasters were holstered on their web gear.

They smiled; and the smiles took in their eyes. There was an attitude about them—even beyond the blasters and warlike gear—that very definitely suggested the smiles could go away most quickly, though.

The bigger guy just stopped and stood, beaming. The younger one walked over to where the tortured man, dropped by his would-be tormentors, lay on his side blubbering and shaking. The olive-skinned young man nodded to the two men who had been trying to haul the victim upright. They backed away quickly as if glad for the chance. Then he gently took the torch—a burning brushwood branch—from the hunchbacked woman who held it, nodded her back until she retreated and sat down among the recent spectators. Then he tossed the branch into the fire, sending up a drift of crackling sparks, and helped the wounded man sit up.

One of the men who had held the victim moistened his lips and found his voice. "Why're you helping them?"

"We help everybody," the bearded man said. "It's our job."

The woman who had wielded the torch batted away the solicitous hand of the man who sat next to her. "Why are you interfering with us?"

"We need information," the olive-skinned young man said over his shoulder from where he knelt examining the captive.

With a flourish he produced a butterfly knife and flipped it open in a quick but elaborate *escrima* pattern. The would-be torturers got quiet. He severed the cord binding the captive's wrists.

"Just lie down here and we'll get some ointment on those burns."

"Mags!" a man screamed. "They're just fucking Mags!" He was big, in torn, grease-stained coveralls. He stormed to his feet and swung a heavy wrench, which had lain unnoticed in the scrub grass by his feet as he hunkered, high over his head. He rushed at the young man bent over the prisoner.

The young man had his back to his attacker. He shrugged, then hunched forward, straightening his left arm behind him as he did so. It held a blocky black Glock 22 handblaster. The .40 caliber pistol was upside down, just like his hand. It cracked twice, slam-ming spent casings straight down into the grass as two 135-grain Triton hollowpoint rounds smacked the wrench wielder in the center of the chest. The holes in his cov-erall were spaced no more than a finger's width apart.

Then a lot more holes appeared in the coverall's right side as the bearded man gave him two 20-gauge loads of Number 4 buck from his Saiga.

The wrench man fell into the fire and began to burn without a sound or further movement. Blood sizzled and boiled with popping noises.

"Somebody want to pull him out?" the bearded man asked mildly. He held his shotgun muzzle-skyward with one hand, letting the barrel cool. "If he starts to stink too badly, you folks might lose your appetites for the MREs we brought you."

The younger man had holstered his handblaster and gone back to his work as if nothing had happened.

"I don't see no MREs," said a little man with a cloud of wiry gray hair, huge bulbous gray eyes and a tuber of nose that dripped clear snot constantly from its red-dened tip.

"Why, that's because we dumped 'em back outside the circle of light from your fires," the bearded man said. "We wanted to come into camp light since we weren't sure what kind of reception we'd get."

Moving as if their boots were cast from lead, the Pit-ters who had recently been picking up the captive for more torture went and fished the chill from the bonfire by his boots. They dragged him off toward the darkness, his body shedding embers and burning twigs. In a moment one raised up a hoarse shout, "Hey! They's crates out here."

The bearded man looked smug. "My name's Larry Robison, by the way," he said. "My partner there is Sean Reichert."

Reichert smiled and nodded. He had finished smearing white zinc-oxide ointment, with antibacterial kicker, on the blistered right side of the tortured man's face. He proceeded to cut the bonds of the other two living captives. Then he sat on the ground next to them.

"Here's how it is, folks," he said cheerfully. "We're not investigators. We're not lawyers."

The ragged circle about him looked blank. The prisoners he had freed seemed to catch the drift of the latter word. He shrugged.

"Anyway, we have no way to know who's right here and who's wrong."

The ragged men and women broke into a Babel of angry expostulation. The tower dwellers spoke up with scarcely less indignation. Still smiling broadly, Reichert drew his Glock again, racked the slide. He caught the ejected .40-caliber cartridge, a yellow glitter in the firelight, before it fell past his drawn-up knees.

Everyone shut up at once. "That's better," he said, tucking the cartridge in a breast pocket. "Not sweet reason, nor emotion, nor sheer volume is going to make any impression on my partner and me. Oh, and I guess we forgot to mention the rest of our team, who're still out in the weeds sort of keeping an eye on things."

"Why should we believe you?" The largest of the group, a hulking grease-stained man with a red face like a collection of poorly matched scar tissue, looked up from the prefab meal he was wolfing down.

Reichert looked at Robison, who shrugged. Reichert sighed.

"We have no reason to lie to you," the young man said. "But to save breath, what's your name?"

"Huh?"

"*Braahh*. Wrong. I'll give you one more try—what is your name?" He said it all in the manner of a television game-show host of the late twentieth century. The jape fell as dead as all the television game-show hosts of the late twentieth century were now.

"Dylan."

"Very poetic." The man continued to glower at him like a colicky boar. "All right, there, Dylan, I want you to pick up the foil you peeled off your rat pack there and hold it up over your head."

"Huh?"

"Dylan, you're trying my patience here. Do it."

Staring at Reichert as if he had fused, the man slowly bent down and picked up the foil sheet discarded by his scarred boots.

"Just use your fingertips," Reichert directed. "That's it. Now lift it up. High, high."

The man stretched his arm up as far as it would go.

A ringing crack burst the night sky. The assembled Mandeville refugees saw a huge hole torn through the center of the foil sheet before it was plucked from Dylan's hands as by a great wind. Dylan fell down and groveled in the dirt, covering his head with his hands.

"Ladies and gentlemen," Robison said, as the crash of a gunshot, distant but powerful, rolled through the camp, "I present to you Little Willi. Little Willi is an antimatériel rifle. The man behind him right now can put a 20 mm projectile straight through your head from two klicks off. Those of you with a working knowledge of the laws of physics already know he's a good deal closer than that at the moment, reckoned by the time it took the sound to reach us."

"Okay, then," Reichert said, rubbing his hands. "We've entertained you all enough. Now we'd like you to entertain us. Tell us what happened in the fortress back there."

"Why ask us?" one of the ragged refugees said resentfully. "We heard shooting and then everything started blowing up. Then they started fighting down in the Pits."

"Who did?" Larry Robison asked.

"The maggots. The blacksuits."

"Ah, Magistrates. They were attacking you?"

"Killing each other. You wanna know more, ask *them*." He jerked his head toward the erstwhile captives, who, like their recent tormentors, were tucking into the food brought by Team Phoenix with a will.

But the upper-level Enclave dwellers, none of whom was connected to the Magistrate Division—at least so they claimed—could tell little more. "We heard a rumor the baron had gone," the thin woman said.

"Gone where?" Robison asked.

She shrugged. "Away. Disappeared. It seemed that the baron's retinue had tried to hide it for a while, but then the word got out."

"One Senior Magistrate claimed to be in charge," a man said. The right side of his face convulsed in a tic at unpredictable intervals, and he kept, in a very low-key way, compulsively scratching himself at various points on his body. "Then suddenly Magistrates started rounding up other Mags, Magistrates who had supported the first one. Then fighting broke out in general."

"And you booked?" Reichert asked. "I mean, you took off then?"

The man nodded glumly. "It seemed like the thing to do at the time."

TEAM PHOENIX DROPPED the Enclave fugitives at a small ville on a stream about twenty miles from Mandeville to keep them being lynched by the Pitters as soon as their temporary guardians pulled out. Just after sunset two days later the four were a hundred miles or so south of Mandeville parting ways with a couple of warriors from the Osage Nation.

"Sorry we couldn't help you boys," said the taller of the two, Jimmy Weasel Bear. Not that either Osage was short: Jimmy had an inch on Larry Robison, tallest of Team Phoenix, and his uncle Frank Feather had a good two inches on him. Both were rangy, with heads shaved to black scalp locks and bands of red paint around the eyes. Both wore buckskin pants and homespun shirts dyed red. Jimmy carried a scoped Savage bolt rifle in .270 on a sling over his shoulder. Uncle Frank carried a heavy bow of what looked like laminated wood and a deerhide quiver of arrows. "We hear all the barons have up an' vanished. Fighting's broke out in a lot of the monoliths, just like Mandy. But that's what we got."

"We keep close track on the baron bunch," Frank said. He had a face that seemed to consist entirely of seams. "Only way we managed to keep the maggots out of our hair. And we trade with them, sure—hard to get by out here if you don't. And the Tartarus Pits were always a good source of intel on what the bastards were up to. But whatever happened in there, happened like—" He snapped his fingers.

"No advance warning," his nephew agreed. "Mebbe the baron and his gang were a little more squirrelly than usual the last few weeks—but that's relative, and they been goin' through shit changes in general the past couple years."

"I hear you," Larry Robison said. He, Weaver and Major Mike stood or squatted out in front of their two vehicles. Reichert perched atop the turret of Bobzilla, the LAV-25 they'd pulled out of a cache on the Colorado River after their first one was destroyed fighting, ironically, the Lakota Indian band of Sky Dog, blood brother to the man named Kane and ally to Cerberus redoubt. Ironically because in the months since then they'd made a point of making contact with Native American tribal groups. Like Sky Dog's band, other Indians tended to be cohesive and skilled at a combination of staying under the baronies' radars and exacting costs when the baronies did manage to detect them and try to bring them to heel. Unlike Sky Dog's bunch, a number of the other tribes, interested in trade and possible allies against the iron rule of the barons, were willing to ask questions first and shoot later, if properly approached.

In the case of the Osage Nation, Team Phoenix had been able to sweeten the pot with weapons taken off a squad of baronial auxiliaries who had no further need of them.

"Word on the trade grapevine is something major spooky's going on," Jimmy said. He rubbed his chin. "There's folks as think things're about to get worse. *Big* worse."

"Worse than the barons?" Reichert called down from the turret.

The Osage warrior shrugged noncommittally.

"Well, thanks for what you could give us," Major Mike said, taking a drag on his cigar. He'd already gifted Weasel Bear and his uncle with a Havana each. "We'll be booking now. Can we give you boys a lift anywhere?"

"Naw," Frank said. "We'll hoof it home."

The two Osage warriors turned and disappeared into the twilight.

Chapter 5

Rogelio, the Spanish guide, reeled out of the hootch. His face seethed with squirming, tiny, maggotlike bodies. His eyes were gone. He fell down and began convulsing. His whole body teemed with the maggot-things and small creatures that seemed a mixture of bat and spider. The female biologist, Guinan, bent over him, batting at the creatures with her white straw hat with the tropic-colored band.

Flying blurs began to descend, and a house-cat-sized shape landed on top of Guinan's head, then stung the biologist three times rapidly in the chest or upper abdomen with a naked segmented tail.

She leaped to her feet, clawing at the winged creature. As Witcover tried to get a shot at the horrific creature attacking the woman, other smaller, winged things flew at her and stuck like handfuls of thrown mud.

MacLean lifted his bolt-action rifle to his shoulder and fired. Guinan's body jerked as the shot struck her in the back. The bullet smashed out through her sternum and clipped the stinger from her attacker's tail. It whipped out leathery wings and rose as the scientist slumped to her knees.

Pale flame jumped from the muzzle of Witcover's carbine as he fired a full-auto burst at a swarm of flying things trying to descend on Guinan. Some creatures disintegrated in a spray of blood, hair and flesh. But they were hard to hit; the only reason any were struck was that they swarmed too thickly for his shooting to make any difference.

Guinan was inundated with furry winged bodies. At the side of the frame MacLean was struggling with his rifle. In his excitement, he had worked the bolt inexpertly, double jacking it and locking it up on an unfired cartridge half-ejected; the pointy bullet protruded from the receiver, copper jacket gleaming red in the equatorial sun. He looked up to see another fox-sized horror flying toward him. He threw the rifle down and fled.

Witcover, turned to fire on the creature pursuing the expedition leader. The creature struck MacLean right between the shoulder blades and clung. Its doglike muzzle snapped at the back of his neck. Its stinger stabbed for his spine, and MacLean collapsed.

In his zeal to cover his teammates, Witcover had neglected to watch his own back. The swarm of creatures attacked from behind. In agony, Witcover twisted and attempted to raise his carbine, but the furry winged creatures overwhelmed him in moments.

ALL WAS SILENT in the Cerberus operations center. The biolink info on the wall display indicated that Guinan,

MacLean and Witcover were dead, and the manner of their deaths had been violent and agonizing.

"Lights, please." The voice of Dr. Mohandas Lakesh Singh was crisp with irritation.

Robison turned to look at the Cerberus contingent: Kane, Grant, Brigid Baptiste and Domi sat on the left side of the room while his three buddies sat on the right. "I hate to play the moron here, but what exactly just happened?"

Lakesh smiled thinly. He was in his element: lecturing. He gestured, and the frozen-frame image of blurred alien ground was replaced by a map of the northern half of South America.

"Satellite observation showed a bloom of what appeared to be anomalous growth in the upper Amazon basin, in what once was Peru," he said. "We decided to investigate."

"Is that the sort of thing you usually look into?" Hays asked.

"It's not 'usual' in any sense," Brigid Baptiste said crisply. She kept glancing at his cigar with tightening around her emerald eyes that indicated disapproval, even though the smoke wasn't lit.

"We don't exactly have a, what?" Kane said. "Written mission statement." He frowned and rubbed his jaw, still not used to feeling bare skin there, and cast a sidelong look at Lakesh. "Sometimes it's a little hard to tell just what the hell we're doing."

"Don't be unreasonable," Brigid said. "An anomalous event on that scale demands our attention no matter who is responsible."

"It's in another hemisphere, Baptiste," Kane said.

"Spreads fast," Domi said with a jerk of her head at the screen, which was showing a loop of an animation showing the observable growth in the past four days. She was chewing happily on jerked meat traded off Sky Dog's bunch. Kane was none too sure he wanted to know what it came from. "Keeps spreading like that, how long till it spreads all the way up here?"

"It's got a hell of a long way to go."

"Not that long if it keeps doubling like that," Grant said. "She's got you there, Kane."

"Not that I want to interfere in a nice, friendly domestic dispute," Reichert said, "but if I can just cut to the chase here, do you fine people think to see the heavy hand of one Gilgamesh Bates, twentieth-century computer mogul, gazillionaire, freezie and all around lying sack of—" He glanced at Brigid, who kept drawing his eyes "—*it* in this particular unexplained event."

Several people tried to talk at once. "Yes," a deep, loud voice said.

Everybody looked at Grant. What the Cerberus bunch knew, as the visitors did not, was that the big black ex-Mag seldom raised his voice.

He seldom had to.

"Kid's right," he said, back in his customary earth-settling rumble. "We got a tendency to bicker like a clan of inbred swampies."

"Like there's some other kind," Domi said.

"During our training," Larry Robison said, "back in the 1990s, we heard rumors about some kind of super-secret biological project Bates was running. Bioengineering. Needless to say the particulars didn't filter down to us, the squaddies in the wadis. At the time we didn't think too much of it—it seemed a natural sort of sideline for a guy with a sci-fi frame of mind like Gil to dump a few of his billions in."

"What's the benefit to Bates if mutant vegetables and flying foxes with stings take over the Amazon basin?" Joe Weaver asked. "Or the whole world, for that matter?"

Robison tipped his head to the side. "That's our Joe," he said. "Always a bottom-line kind of guy."

"Your play-pals the hybrids have access to some pretty alarming technology," Hays pointed out. "Why suspect Bates? Not that I'd put anything slimy past him—but what's in it for him, as our resident machinist so cogently asked? And why multiply explanations? This could be a case for Occam's razor."

"But neither you nor the bishop of Occham has heard all the evidence, gentlemen," Brigid said.

"It was your boy Bates made the play for Kane, here," Grant said laconically, "when he was sitting on a mountaintop growing his hair and contemplating his navel."

The four outsiders stared at him. "We might be getting near too much information, here," Robison said. "What makes you think it was Bates, Grant?"

Domi emitted a snort of laughter. "What makes you think you're his only freezie commandos?"

Reichert stared at her. "You have got to be kidding me."

"What?" She sneered at him. "You wouldn't say *shit* if you had a mouthful? You think I never heard the word before? Or do you just not want to say it in front of a *lady,* meaning Brigid Baptiste?" She spoke the name as if it were one word.

"Take the Fifth, kid," Hays said. "Preferably Beam's Choice."

He bumped knuckles with Larry. Then the two made swooping-rising gestures with their hands, intoning in unison a drawn-out "Smoo-o-oth."

Kane looked at Grant. Grant shook his head.

"They're fused-out," Domi said. "What's new? We're all fusies here, that's for damn sure."

"I don't think any of us has a hard time believing Gil would hedge his bets," Robison said, "but what makes you think the hit team was his? With all due respect, it's not like you guys don't have plenty of other enemies."

"They wore the same outfits you got on now," Grant said. "Also they said they were Bates's boys."

"That was subtle," Robison said.

"At least we can console ourselves we're the first team," Reichert said.

"So, given that Gil Bates has raised his ugly head again," Hays said, "what exactly do you want from us?"

"I've been a bit out of the loop here," Kane said, "but

let me take a wild-ass swing at it. Knowing Lakesh's devious mind as I do, I think he's hoping to get you to help out in his current harebrained scheme by offering you a crack at Bates."

The scientist beamed and nodded. Kane could never, even after all this time, anticipate his reactions, emotionally speaking. On the other hand he never seemed to go wrong banking on Lakesh's deviousness and soft-spoken ruthlessness.

"Leaving aside your gratuitous pejoratives, an admirable summation, friend Kane. It appears to be both in the interests of our Team Phoenix friends and our own to take joint action to counter what certainly appear to be hostile initiatives by Bates."

Grant rubbed his square chin. "Somebody asked a little while ago, what good it did Bates to let loose some kind of bizarre ecological plague in South America. I'm wondering that myself."

"We don't know," Lakesh said. "It is something we devoutly hope to find out."

"We know Bates has some kind of hidden redoubt of his own somewhere," Brigid said. "He trafficked extensively in government contracts, both open and covert, in the years leading up to the nukecaust. The United States government, in turn, had substantial involvement in just the area of South America in which the mysterious outbreak is taking place, under the rubric of its failed War on Drugs. Which, it appears from my readings in the archives, was concerned rather more urgently with manipulating the flow of recreational pharmaceuticals into the then U.S., for the profit of well-placed political interests, than in suppressing the trade."

Major Mike took his unlit cigar stub from his mouth and studied it. "Figures," he said.

"While it's tempting in hindsight to convict Bates of any and all dirty dealing up to and including the Lindbergh kidnapping and the killing of Cock Robin," Larry Robison said, "I'm not sure I see any kind of unbreakable evidentiary chain here."

"Because there is not one, Lieutenant Commander," Lakesh said brightly. "We are doing what is technically referred to as 'grasping at straws.' Do you want in?"

"You'll be sorry," Kane said.

"We're already sorry," Reichert said.

"What's the scam?" Hays asked.

"We transport you to South America to help organize the human residents of the area to resist the outbreak. At the same time you can investigate whether the outbreak indicates Bates's secret base lies nearby, and attempt to track it."

Sprawled in his chair, Grant stirred. "A bug hunt?" he demanded.

Kane shrugged indifferently. "Be a relief to rumble with somebody who can't shoot back."

"Be careful what conclusions you leap to, Kane," Brigid said with what seemed a certain grim satisfaction. "These life-forms are unlikely to be like anything known or even suggested in the literature of cryptozoology before the nukecaust."

"Crypto-what?" Kane demanded. "Baptiste, are you talking dirty?"

"Means 'the study of hidden animals,'" Hays said. "What that means is research into critters unrecognized by science. Ranging from the okapi to the Loch Ness monster. Only one of which had actually been acknowledged by science before we got put under."

"Or anyway they never got around to telling us grunts any different," Robison said. "Seems like there was a lot of that going around."

"The logical inference, I might say the necessary one," Brigid continued, as if Kane and the Phoenix operators were unruly schoolboys, "is that the creatures are either alien life-forms or genetically engineered ones. About which we know nothing for certain except they are alien to *us,* and unquestionably hostile. So how confident are you, Kane, that some of the life-forms have not evolved, or been designed, to employ some sort of ranged attack?"

Kane looked at the outsiders. "Never argue with Baptiste," he said. "If you learn nothing else here in Cerberus, learn that."

Robison leaned forward, resting his forearms on his knees with his big powerful hands dangling between. "Do we need to go off for a private confab here, provided our hosts will be so kind?"

"Make yourselves at home, my friends," Lakesh said grandly.

Joe Weaver, who had sat upright throughout the discussion, slid down in his chair and rested one Popeye forearm on the back of the vacant chair next to his. "I don't see the need," he said. "It's a pretty thin lead to Bates, but it's a lot thicker than anything we've been able to turn up to date. We're just spinning our wheels up here—I just want something to do. Even if we don't wind up with Gil Bates with a noose around his neck."

"I'm with you," Hays said. He looked at the other two.

"I could use a change of scenery," Larry Robison admitted.

"Lock and load," Reichert said. He looked at Brigid, causing Domi to scowl. "Will you be accompanying us, Dr. Baptiste?"

"I'm not really a doctor," she said.

"Certainly your quite intensive training and experience as senior archivist in Cobaltville would serve as at least the equivalent of a preskydark Ph.D.," Lakesh said. He was Mr. Magnanimity today. It made Kane deeply suspicious. "To be truthful, though, gentlemen, I have not decided precisely what allocation of resources would be optimal—"

Grant shifted in his seat and fixed Lakesh with a glare like that of a Kodiak bear awakened from a much needed sleep. "Are you forgetting that you don't run jack around here, Lakesh? We're all volunteers in this chickenshit outfit."

"Ah, forgive me if, in my quite wholly understandable enthusiasm, I misspoke, friend Grant. However I am generally conceded the role of coordinator and chief strategist. Or do you desire a realignment of functions here in the redoubt?"

Grant's heavy, handsome, mahogany-hued face, which scowled at rest, became a giant X of discomfort. "No, not really. I just don't want you getting the notion you can just dictate to the rest of us, is all."

"Admit it, Grant," Kane said. "He's got us by the short and curlies. Neither of us wants the job of running the damned show. And if he really wants to go totally nuke on us he can always threaten to appoint that shit-heel Philboyd his successor and pack it in."

The door to the operations center opened. A slight, short woman with short gray-blond hair and big glasses walked in with a worried expression on her face. Kane understood that was her standard look, but it was more pronounced than usual.

"How may we help you, Sally?" Lakesh asked.

The look of worry deepened. "Our computer projections have come back," she said. She was an analytical whiz Kane and Grant had helped to escape from Snake-fishville some time before.

"And what do they have to tell us?"

She moistened her thin lips with a nearly colorless tongue and looked uneasily around the briefing room. "No good news, I'm afraid, Dr. Lakesh," she said. "Remote observation suggests that not only alien flora and fauna appear to be involved in the expanding biological anomaly. The speed and completeness of the replacement of the existing ecosystem appear to indicate that microorganisms are involved, as well."

"Good news is everywhere," Reichert said.

She looked at him, blinked several times rapidly, then turned back to Lakesh as if shutting the boisterous young man out of her consciousness, possibly forever.

"Go on, Sally," Lakesh prompted. "What do these new data mean?"

"If correct," she said, "this means that the invasion cannot be stopped by any conventional means."

"Excuse me, Ms...." Robison began.

Her eyes, gray and huge behind her circular lenses, flicked to Lakesh as if seeking permission to address the outsider. Lakesh nodded.

"Wright," she said. "Sally Wright."

The big bearded ex-SEAL nodded encouragingly. "Ms. Wright, could I ask what you meant by 'conventional means'?"

She bit her lips. "Guns. Fire. Explosives. That sort of thing. Fire and explosives might work on a purely local basis. That would be all, though."

"How about poison?" Joe Weaver asked.

Sally shook her head emphatically. "That could cause substantial environmental damage."

"Doesn't whatever is happening down there already constitute substantial environmental destruction?" Brigid asked. "Inasmuch as it's supplanting the extant ecosystem?"

The close-cropped head bobbed. "Oh, it is. Altogether. But I was concerned about damage to areas not yet affected by the invading bioforms. In any event, our best assessment is that poisons would not work, either. For one thing, the bloom is so large already that dispersing them as widely as necessary, yet in effective concentrations, would be quite beyond our means even if we possessed or could manufacture sufficient quantities of toxins."

"Provided we even knew what killed 'em," Reichert said.

Sally Wright smiled shyly. "Precisely."

"All right, Sally," Kane said. "You sounded like there was a *but* in that first statement of yours. Do you have some idea what *unconventional* means might do the trick?"

"Yes, Mr. Kane." She looked at Lakesh. "But I don't think you're going to like it."

Chapter 6

"Couldn't we have jumped straight inside?" Kane demanded. He was lying on his belly in the scrub in the dark. Above the whistling wind the full moon laughed down from a vast idiot face.

"That depends," Brigid said, "on whether you're just tired of the world, or of life."

Grant snorted in something suspiciously like half-suppressed laughter. "He just got tired of his job and ran off to join the circus. Ask Bates's goons how ready Kane was to lie down and wait for dirt to start hitting him in the eyes."

"You're a hell of one to talk about running off to join the circus. Who is it who's constantly threatening to run off to the islands to play co-shogun with Shizuka."

"At least there *is* Shizuka. Unless you'd struck up a friendship with a female mountain goat…"

"I'm sure you gentlemen are deriving great satisfaction from your primitive bonding ritual," Brigid said tartly.

Grant grumbled way down in his throat. Kane chuckled softly and pressed the minibinos to his eye.

"Still don't see why we're doing this the old-fashioned way," he said. "Why not jump in?"

Brigid sighed. "I thought Lakesh explained it in sufficient detail—"

"We've been tuning him out," Grant said. "For days."

AND DAYS IT HAD BEEN. While Team Phoenix was off playing hearts-and-minds in South America, Kane and Grant cooled their heels and grew increasingly restive as Brigid, Sally Wright and Lakesh pored through what seemed like every byte of data accumulated in the vast Cerberus database.

Occasionally they had made brief jumps into assorted hellholes seeking new puzzle pieces. Grant still favored his right leg after the last one, and Kane wouldn't be eating any fish for a while, at least until certain memories lost their immediacy.

But at last Lakesh claimed a breakthrough: not the location of the deadly Grail they sought, but perhaps the map to where it lay hidden. And it led them here. Back, as it were, to the source. In front of them the Cobaltville Administration Monolith rose like a white porcelain dildo gleaming in the light of a gibbous moon.

"We're not sure," Brigid said, "who is presently in charge of Cobaltville. To jump directly in could bring the whole place down on our necks."

"That's enough for me," Grant said. "We've done this stuff before. This is nothing special, just another job. What worries me is getting out."

"Tell me again," Kane said, peering down at the

monolith through his miniaturized glasses, "just why it is we want this end-the-world bug, anyway?"

"You heard those briefings as well as I did, Kane," Brigid said, "even if I was the only one paying attention. The irruption in South America itself has the potential to destroy the world. It will take extraordinary means to defeat it."

"I mean, using a thing that could destroy the world in order to save it…maybe it's just me, but that seems more than a bit ass-backward."

"Lakesh believes that he has the capability of altering the self-replicating assembler in such a way that it will attack organisms possessing the gene sequences peculiar to the invader ecosystem, and only such organisms."

"*That's* reassuring," Grant said. He sat in the shelter of an outcrop cradling a G-3 battle rifle with starlight scope. "This wouldn't be the first time Lakesh has overestimated himself—"

"But it sure could be the last," Kane said.

Brigid shook her head. In the moonlight the glory of her fire-gold hair was muted to shades of gray, like the rest of the nighttime world. "You shouldn't malign Lakesh. He has made mistakes, but he does have a great intellect."

"Which he's used to put your nicely turned ass in harm's way about as often as Grant's and mine, Baptiste," Kane said. "But more to the point, if he outsmarts himself this time, zingo! No more world from magma skyward in what, seventy-two *hours,* according to Mustang Sally's little horror show?"

"There'd still be a world, Kane," Grant said. "It'd just be a layer of gray goo twenty klicks thick or whatever."

"And the worst pisser is, it probably wouldn't zero out our new Annunaki pals," Kane said. "Although it wouldn't leave them much to lord it over."

"This is our best chance," Brigid said.

"Don't forget nobody we know of has so much as seen one of these damned things firsthand and lived," Grant said. "We don't even have a tissue sample for Lakesh to match."

"Gathering such samples," Brigid said, "is a primary part of Team Phoenix's mission in the upper Amazon."

Kane dropped the microbinos and tipped his head to the side. "Better them than us."

"How do you figure we get in, Kane?" Grant asked.

"I'm all over it. Like stink on a swampie."

Grant looked at him levelly through the darkness. "No idea, huh?"

"None whatever."

Kane picked himself up from the sandy soil of the ridgetop. "Might as well head in. We want to be dressed out and waiting patiently in line at dawn when the gates open."

The others stood, hefting light rucksacks.

"Baptiste," Kane said.

She looked at him. "What is it, Kane?"

"Can it really do that?" he asked. "I mean, turn the surface of the Earth and everything on it into muck in a couple days?"

"Theoretically," she said, "yes."

Kane grinned. "Then we got nothing to worry about. We all know theory never pans out in the real world."

"Dream on, Kane," Grant said. "Theory only doesn't work when it's on our side."

Kane grunted. "Yeah. You're right. Well, follow me, people. Time to break back into jail."

"HELLDAMN," Domi said, slapping at a paper-white forearm. When her hand came away a scarlet smear was left behind. "I hate bugs. Except the juicy ones."

"Much as I hate to say it," Larry Robison said, "but aren't you a little, well, underdressed for the occasion?"

Walking out through the forest at the head of the small but well-armed group, the slight albino woman stopped and turned back. "Why do you say that?"

They stopped and stared at her out of faces dappled with forest leaf-shadows beneath the brims of their jungle-camou boonie hats. The hats were made of the same stuff as their camou suits, with extra Kevlar lining to stiffen them and provide resistance to impact.

The diminutive albino woman wore a gray-green-black camou-pattern T-shirt that left her arms bare. As were her slim, strong legs.

"Wear a long-sleeved shirt," Mike Hays said.

She stuck out her underlip in a pout. "Point is? It's not cold."

Reichert gestured at her. "Well, bugs for one. Less likely to bite if you covered up more."

"If I get big enough bugs, hey, it's protein."

She gestured at the four men of Team Phoenix. Beneath a heavy encrustation of weapons and gear—inevitable, given how far they were from the caches Gil Bates had salted across North America for them in happier times—all wore camouflage battle dress with long sleeves and full legs on their trousers. It was less hot and humid than they had expected: they were fairly high up here, not far east of the great wall of the Andes. But their faces shone with sweat from exertion, and their tongues hung metaphorically out.

"Is it really worth stumbling around in your own personal saunas to avoid a few bug bites, big brave men?"

"Y'know, hon," Mike Hays said, taking the stub of unlit cigar from his mouth, "if you weren't so darned easy on the eyes a man might be tempted to ask just what you're tagging along here for."

"'Tagging along'? Who's in the lead here, old man?"

"The old men are keeping up with you pretty well," Joe Weaver said, his face splitting in an uncharacteristic broad grin.

"Not that we don't enjoy following you," Sean Reichert said, taking off his boonie hat to wipe sweat from his forehead. For his main weapon he carried a 5.56 mm Kalashnikov AK-108, part of a special lot assembled by Joe Weaver from the pick of the parts in the bins of the IZHMASH factory in the USSR. Although its connection to classic Kalashnikovs was largely cosmetic—it had a similar distinctive profile, being built on a Kalashnikov frame, but the action was all new—it was accurate, smooth in operation and utterly reliable. It was also heavy, as the young former Delta operator was noticing. "But what exactly are you doing, still with us? We could be in Indian country here."

Domi had accepted Lakesh's request she squire the team to a geomagnetic node in the Upper Amazon with an interphaser, the distinctive pyramidion of which jutted at an angle from her backpack. Though none of Team Phoenix had heard her explicitly instructed so, they had all just assumed she'd bounce back to the climate-controlled confines of Cerberus as soon as she dropped off her delivery. Then again, despite the brevity of their acquaintance with the gamine albino, the four men all understood she wouldn't exactly feel slavishly bound by instructions, no matter who issued them.

"You think I'm afraid?" She laughed, delightedly, like a child told an absurdity: that the world was round, or that the sun was farther than a hundred feet away. "I'm used to Indians. I helped you get through Sky Dog and his bunch."

Robison winced. "We'd kind of rather you not remind us," he said, "given how we kind of killed some of them before we found out we and they were really on the same side, more or less."

UPON BEING REVIVED from cold storage, the men of Team Phoenix had been directed by a holographic projection of their employer—supposedly recorded before his death shortly after the big nuke—to save the shattered America from the threat of enslavement by the barons and their allies in Cerberus redoubt. He claimed to have foreseen it all using his special predictive computer programs. Since his company had made him fabulously rich by being the number-one supplier of software to the darker agencies of the U.S. government, there had seemed nothing intrinsically implausible about it, much as it went against each man's strongly held notions of free will.

So they had made their way toward Cerberus redoubt with the single-minded determination of men with nothing to live for and nothing more to lose, men who had not known—because how could they have known?—what it truly meant to shed their time and everything familiar like a snake its skin. All had lost whatever family they had to various tragedies before being recruited by Bates. Now, chronically marooned, they had literally nothing to live for but the mission. And if they died trying, who was left to miss them?

Their path led them right through land claimed by Sky Dog and his Lakota band—a bunch known for giving warm welcome to trespassers. Domi, who by that time had fallen in with the team, and become friendly with them, tried unsuccessfully to dissuade them. Fanatically determined, the team had blasted its way right through the heart of the Lakota Nation and Kane and Grant before attaining their goal.

Only to learn that everything told them was a lie. The

people of Cerberus redoubt—including director Dr. Lakesh, painted by Gilgamesh Bates as arch menace and the man who would be king of America if not the world—were fighting to *end* the barons' ruthless dominion, not perpetuate it. And that Bates himself, far from dying of cancer in some bunker during skydark a few years after the war, was alive and lamentably well, a freezie himself.

In fact Gil Bates was the man with the plan for world domination. And the secret of control over the mat-trans network, held within Cerberus, was to be his key. Confronted with the brutal realization that they had been used, they swore to avenge themselves on Bates.

Except…they had no idea where to find him.

"WHAT MY ASSOCIATES are trying to say in their ingenuous tongue-tied way," Hays said, "since they're far less used to the company of beautiful women than I am, is that we wonder why you're choosing to stay with us on the ground when we face danger from the bioforms, as well as possibly unfriendly locals."

She shrugged. "Been in danger before, once or twice. Didn't kill me."

"There's always that first time," Reichert said.

"Different danger," Domi said. "Spicy."

Larry Robison blinked and pulled his head back on his powerful neck as something like an insect whirred past his face—to light on the bole of a tree at face level with a most noninsectile thunk.

"People didn't used to use blowguns this high up in the Amazon basin, did they?" he asked in a conversational tone, reaching out with big blunt fingers.

"Don't think so," said Joe Weaver, the team's expert on Latin America.

"They do now." Robison plucked a small dart with a splint of green leaf for a flight from the trunk. "I suspect we've found the locals. Or they've found us."

"Was wondering when you'd notice," Domi said.

Chapter 7

The hiss emitted by the creature like a flying fox grafted to a giant scorpion was clearly audible through the allegedly break-proof armaglass pane, resonant with harmonics of menace. Its black-tipped stinger struck the see-through synthetic with a dull clack.

The giant man with a great mane of reddish-black hair and dark reddish-purple skin drew back from the window in alarm. "Is it really wise, Gilgamesh, to release such horrors upon the world?"

"Don't talk about my creations like that!" the red-haired woman beside them exclaimed. "They are superior to you in every way."

His brow furrowed as he gazed mildly down upon her. She would have looked small next to a man of normal size. Beside him she looked like a child. "They're not intelligent. No more intelligent than dogs."

She smiled. "That is one of many ways in which they are superior," she said. "Untouched by the taint of rational thought."

A second man, his long ovine face dough-white, almost blue, behind his red beard in the fluorescent lights of the subterranean lab, raised a hand. He was spectrally thin and enormously tall. Yet the dark giant towered over him by a foot.

"I can see many happy hours of debate in the offing," he said mildly. "Might I suggest we defer the pleasure in the interests of tending to more urgent matters?"

The giant wore a tunic of heavy twill in dark blue-gray, with large brass buttons, over gray trousers with dark red stripes—the dress uniform Gilgamesh Bates had mandated for his bodyguards, of which the huge man was commander. His big square jaw worked in evident dissatisfaction but he didn't speak.

The woman smiled with sweet malice. She tended toward gauntness, with narrow, sunken-cheeked features and eyes like mad blue stars. Her hair was scarlet and hacked off any which way. She was a rock star's daughter who had become one of the leading bioengineers of the last years before the nukecaust.

"Besides, Enkidu," she told the wild-haired giant in a lilting English accent, "you've nothing to fear. The array of organisms I have created have been designed specifically as successors to the corrupt cancer cells, humans and the poor creatures of Earth they have tormented, twisted and tainted for so long. They will conquer the world for our master, and leave you nothing to do."

The man Gil Bates had christened Enkidu flared a nostril. A corner of the broad, full-lipped mouth opened to expose big, flawless white teeth. "You'll save the world by destroying it?"

He had been, improbably, among the world's leading contract assassins. Then he had repented. Unfortunately, perhaps, by that time Gil Bates had found him and placed him—with his unbreakable code of honor—irremediably in his debt.

"I'll save the world by destroying *man*."

Enkidu turned to his master, opening and closing his huge hands helplessly. "What is all this? Is this how you plan to save humanity from strife and misery?"

"It is a means to an end," Bates said imperturbably.

"What end? The end of humankind? Don't tell me you buy into her bullshit. She's as much a monster as any of her pet horrors."

Ishtar herself took no affront at the giant's words. She was tapping on the window and cooing to the winged, scorpion-tailed thing on the other side. Gilgamesh Bates extended a finger like a giant albino spider's leg and crooked it for his chief bodyguard to follow him out of the antechamber.

In the doorway Enkidu looked back over his shoulder. Ishtar had pressed herself up against the window and seemed to be writhing against it. One hand was pressed, fingers splayed, against the armaglass. The other disappeared somewhere around in front of her hips.

Shaking his head, Enkidu joined his master in the small office where Bates sat with his long legs folded, one knee over the other.

"Those who oppress this world hold the upper hand,

Enkidu," Bates said. "We are few. Too few, as you well know. Ishtar's creatures give us leverage."

"Which we can use precisely how? Listen to the crazy bitch. She intends to wipe the world clean and start over!"

"Ishtar is a woman as troubled as she is talented," Bates said. "As for how we may use what I might term the very solid artifacts of her delusional system—that is a strategy issue, and all I am free to say is that I am on it."

Enkidu frowned. "What about the oppressors, then?"

"The next move is up to them. I will respond appropriately. Or, as required, you will. I have every faith in you, Enkidu."

He rose and patted the giant on a muscle-clotted arm. "When will *you* learn to have faith in me, my friend? Have I not brought us all safely through two centuries of unparalleled disaster? I may not know all, but I certainly know best."

The big man hung his head. "I am sorry, Gil Bates," he said. "Sometimes I forget myself."

Bates smiled like a cheerful ghoul. "I have already forgotten, myself. Come, let's get some tea."

SMILING, SEAN REICHERT spoke a greeting in Spanish. The men who had stood up out of the underbrush, or swung around the boles of trees to level lances and shotguns at Team Phoenix, had light copper skins and were tall for South American Indians, although the tallest was still shorter than any of the North Americans.

But their features, not to mention the paint jobs, made unmistakably clear that was what they were. Most wore loincloths. Some had clean but ragged shirts. A few wore floppy hats, others turbans of bright cloth. They failed to respond.

"They might not speak Spanish," Joe Weaver said. "Back before the nukecaust lots of Indians in Latin America didn't. Or wouldn't."

"Where's Domi?" Larry Robison subvocalized over their team net.

"Seems to've ducked out," Hays said. "Smart girl." He addressed the people pointing guns at them. "Your move, people."

"Americans?" a female voice asked.

"You speak English?" Mike Hays asked in surprise.

"Yes." Slipping from the underbrush without making a sound, a woman stepped forward. She was clearly one with the rest: slim, copper skinned, dark, with heavy raven hair tied in a ponytail that hung well down her back. She was tall—like her exclusively masculine companions, taller than Larry Robison would've expected. She was also intensely pretty, in an exotic way. She wore an oversize man's olive-drab shirt, possibly a uniform part, khaki shorts, low-topped hiking boots and a straw hat that had probably once been white. "Are you *estupidos?* Why have you not put down your weapons?"

"We didn't want to do anything without instruction here," Robison said. "We'd like to avoid misunderstandings if possible."

"Put them down now," the woman said, "slowly. Do not misunderstand *that,* if you wish a chance to live."

"Given the choice between a chance to live and the alterative—" Reichert began.

"Belay the stand-up routine, troop," Hays growled, unslinging his chopped-and-channeled machine gun and stooping to ease it onto the spongy ground. "And just remember the old saw: comedy is hard, dying is easy."

The others likewise complied deliberately. The locals tracked their every move with their weapons.

"Do the Indians around here use blowguns?" Robison asked subvocally.

"They've had two hundred years to take it up if they didn't before," Weaver replied.

"Your packs and pistol belts, as well," the apparent leader commanded.

Team Phoenix did as told.

"Now back away," the woman said briskly. "Be very careful. My people have little reason to trust light-skinned strangers."

The team complied, then stood with hands vaguely in the air. Their captors didn't seem big on prisoner-control techniques, which had been au courant two centuries before and a hemisphere north, such as having them lace fingers behind heads or making them lie spread-eagle on their faces. Then again, with numbers, the drop and a pretty unanswerable edge in knowledge of the local terrain, the Indians may not have seen any point in bothering with anything more elaborate.

Talking among themselves in low gutturals, several of the Indians quickly swooped down and scooped up the discarded weapons and packs. They seemed surprised at the heft of the rucksacks, and how festooned they were with exotic weapons and even more exotic gear. They kept their faces impassive as carved idol heads. The team members—three with military special-ops experience, one with extensive local cultural knowledge—understood that like a lot of tribal groups around the world, these people were very likely unwilling to display emotion of any kind before strangers.

Mike Hays squinted up at the sky. The sun was almost at the zenith. "They don't seem to be clued into our communicators," he subvocalized. Both bone-conduction speakers and microphone were tiny and flesh-colored, as were the wires running from them down the backs of the men's necks and down to the actual comm units, secured in buttoned pockets. Even a cursory body search would turn them up, but their captors seemed disinclined to get too close to their outsized prisoners.

"Great," Reichert answered. "We got 'em surrounded."

The woman, who showed no sign herself of being armed, stepped up to stand before the four, gazing up at them with fists on hips. "Very well," she said. "Now, who are you and whom are you spying for?"

Robison flicked his dark eyes sideways to Mike Hays. The major hitched a tiny shrug.

"We aren't spies," the big ex-SEAL said. "We're on a biological expedition. Investigating what you might call an apparent outbreak of a plague."

"Biology." She parsed it into syllables as if tasting each one. "Nobody does science any more. It's something you read about in books. If you read and have books."

One of her men, muttering, came up to show her Hays's machine gun with the shortened barrel and the pistol foregrip attached to the gas tube. She frowned at it, reached out, just touched it, then she looked back at the team.

"Why so many guns, if you are biologists? Especially studying microbios?"

"We aren't biologists, ma'am," Robison said. He shifted his right hand to thumb away a trail of sweat trickling down the right side of his forehead and threatening to run into his eye. "And this plague isn't exactly microbes. At least, not all of them are—we're not exactly sure. Some of these organisms are pretty big. As large as a small dog, at least."

"You call these a disease?"

"We call them a plague," Mike Hays growled. "They come in various sizes, and they destroy everything in their path. There are even alien growths that crowd out the local plants."

She stared at him a moment, face as hard as fired clay. "Do you think I am a child, *norteamericano?*" she said. "Not even a child. A simple one. Even a child would laugh at such a story."

"You won't think it's all that funny," Weaver said, "when you meet these things."

"If we were going to tell you a lie to cover our real mission," Robison said, "wouldn't we come up with something a bit more plausible?"

Without changing expression, she spoke to her comrades, who had now pulled back a few yards but continued keeping well-armed watch on the intruders. This broke their hard faces into grins. Several answered.

"They say no," the woman said. "You might just be stupid."

"There's that," Larry Robison said.

"Do you mind my asking just who you are?" Hays asked.

"These are my people. We fight for our freedom against oppressors from the west—*criollos,* European-descended ones. We are Atshuara. Of the Shuara nation." She smiled. It was not an altogether pleasant expression. "You may have heard of us."

Almost as an afterthought, she added, "I am Consuelo."

"Well, Consuelo, we brought some evidence we can show you to try to change your mind," Hays said. He nodded toward their guarded packs. "It's all in there. If you give us a chance we might be able to help you. Might be better to go about it in a different setting, too."

The small guerrilla leader spoke to her people. Several of them discussed the issue briefly among themselves. They seemed disinterested. Robison wasn't sure whether that was a promising sign or not.

A decision apparently reached, Consuelo turned her fierce dark gaze on the captives. It hadn't changed. As far as Robison could tell, she always looked fierce. So there was no knowing if it was a bad sign or not.

"Very well," she said shortly. "You will come with us to our camp. It lies no great distance away."

She shrugged. "We can always kill you later."

"So what's with this 'Atshuara' stuff," Major Mike subvocalized about ten minutes later as they tramped through the forest. The terrain was hilly. Patches of dense brush interspersed with stands of tall trees. "Our charming hostess sounded as if we ought to recognize it."

"It did sound familiar, now that you mention it," Robison said. "Can't quite place it, though. Just on the tip of my tongue."

"I can tell you what it means," Weaver said. "The Spanish-speakers—the ones they call *criollos*—call them Jivaros."

Reichert stumbled slightly, caught himself. The guard walking behind him jabbed air with his lance and grinned menacingly at him, but didn't touch him.

"Holy shit," the young man said. "I've heard of them. But aren't they—?"

They topped a rise. In the little clear draw before them nestled a dozen small hootches, some with rude plank walls, others wattle-and-daub. Most had palm-thatch roofs.

From a palm tree at the right and higher end of the ville dangled half a dozen wrinkled objects the approximate size and shape of withered grapefruit.

"Headhunters," Joe Weaver said with what sounded like a certain satisfaction. "Good to see some of the old folkways still survive."

Chapter 8

The Latina stood in malodorous shadow with her back pressed to a warehouse wall altogether typical of the Cobaltville Tartarus Pits: chipped and nasty. She had a mass of black hair with a distinct undertone of copper, bright metallic, visible when the light struck it: a legacy of the "leather soldiers," Indian mercenaries brought north with their families by sixteenth-century Spanish colonizers to guard their remote territories from the likes of Kiowa, Comanche and Apache raiders. The leather soldiers were Tlaxcaltecan Indians of the Valley of Mexico, whose characteristic striking red-copper hair predated the Europeans' arrival.

The woman was tall and exceedingly well built, with dark eyes and cinnamon skin. She would have been strikingly beautiful but for a port-wine birthmark that covered the upper right quadrant of her face like a bizarre carnival mask. It drew the eye irresistibly.

A huge black man stood beside her with his arms folded across his broad chest. He wore faded khaki trousers and a vest with many pockets, big boots, a loose white linen blouse with long sleeves. A rag, once camou pattern and now itself faded to the hue of dust, was wrapped around his head. A long thick braid of black hair hung over one shoulder like a hawser. Goggles hid his eyes.

"This is a terrible idea," he said in a low growl. "An all-time worst."

"Which part?" The man peering around the end of the wall was an albino, with a big floppy hat to shield his chalk-cheeked, white-bearded face from the dangerously intense rays of the Rocky Mountain sun, and the collar of his flannel shirt was turned up to guard his pallid neck. His eyes were rubies. He sounded entirely cheerful. "Entering a pit full of pissed-off scorpions? Cobaltville's three all-time most-wanted fugitives returning to the scene of their many crimes? Or the mission that brought us here in the first place?"

"Yes," Grant said.

Kane the albino laughed a soft, wolf's laugh. "Think about this—the very unlikelihood of our coming back to Cobaltville at all, much less walking bolt upright through the main gates in the full light of day, is our best possible disguise."

"Classic point man logic," Grant sneered. "Ballsy yet stupid."

Kane shrugged. "I didn't hear your brilliant alternative plan, Mr. Experiments." He had picked up the name from a character in a late-twentieth-century short vid he had overheard Sean Reichert and Larry Robison discussing enthusiastically one afternoon in the Cerberus commissary. It was called *Science Bastard*. All their efforts to explain it to Kane simply confused him more. The name stuck in his head, though.

"Will you two quit striking attitudes and pipe down before someone hears us?" the Latina hissed ferociously.

Grant made a sound like a boulder rolling down a wooden chute.

"You sure this is the right place, Baptiste?" Kane asked. From out on the street wafted the sounds of a typical Tartarus morning: skirling off-key music, multiple babies crying, a woman's laughter with a hysterical edge, another woman screaming, angry voices, a sound like a blow. The smells of spice and decay and despair floated along with the sounds.

Brigid shot him a narrow-eyed glare. The chocolate-brown contacts might have hidden the laser-intense emerald-green of her eyes, but did nothing to lessen their death-beam impact. "I saw the maps," she said simply. As if that settled it.

It did: she had an eidetic memory. Working in concert with Sally Wright, who originated from Snakefish-ville's Historical Division, Brigid had turned up blueprints among the files looted by Lakesh over time from Cobaltville's own data storage. Among them she had found a means to infiltrate the all-important Administrative Monolith.

When they had escaped from Cobaltville several years before, Kane and Brigid in particular had availed themselves of an unauthorized connection between the

Pits and the bottom-level maintenance shops. It was no great stretch to presume that, in the wake of their escape, it had been found and neutralized. It was also no great stretch to suppose that, human nature being what it was, some alternate means had been found of effecting illicit traffic between those below and those above.

While Lakesh still maintained lines of information into the villes, he also stayed cagey about what they were. In any event his contacts were unlikely to provide information about officially unknown illicit access routes.

So the three were going to make a new one.

"Okay," Kane said. He slipped around to the rear of the warehouse. An alley about two yards across ran between it and the wall of the base of the monolith itself. A bunch of piled crates and sodden cardboard boxes clotted the alley.

"According to the architectural drawings," Brigid said, all business as usual, "the wall is especially thin here. On the other side is a storeroom, and beyond that a parking area for low-priority vehicles awaiting repair."

"You sure about that?" Kane asked. The glint in his eye betrayed that he was baiting her.

The glare in hers showed she knew that, but she answered anyway. "I am sure of the information contained in the database. Whatever changes have taken place recently, it seems unlikely any major structural alterations may be among them. As for what we may find on the other side, if you want certainty, Kane, all I have to offer is this—that one day we will all die."

He showed her a lopsided smile through his bleached beard. "And maybe it doesn't take even then," he said quietly.

She touched herself reflexively at her breastbone. In the mind-and-soul-wrenching throes of jump nightmares they had been shown visions of being *anam-charas,* soul-friends, and that their destinies were intertwined, through many past lives, and presumably future ones, as well.

"Let's get this over with," Grant rumbled. "Discipline's gone to hell in the ville, but somebody's going to stumble on us if we stand here all morning running our heads."

Still grumbling low in his throat, Grant shucked his shabby backpack, rooted around in it, came up with something that resembled part of an undersized folding chair: just two sticks of well-weathered wood, pinned together at the centers. He strode up to the concrete inner wall.

"This the place?" he asked.

Brigid nodded. She seemed distracted by something. "Yes," she said. "That's right."

Grant grunted. He opened the sticks into an X. Digging with a thumbnail, he brought up the end of a strip of tape along one side of both sticks, stained to match the sticks themselves, peeled it down. It revealed a sticky surface, by which he stuck the X onto the weak spot in the wall as indicated by Brigid. Finally, he took an initiator from a pocket of his vest, keyed it alive and stuck it to the junction of the X—which was cast of plastic explosive tinted to resemble wood.

Brigid stiffened. Then she grabbed Kane, who squatted beside her on his heels like an obedient servant, hauled him upright, slammed his back to the wall and pinned him there with an impassioned lip-lock.

CONSUELO'S FACE WAS hard as a carved wooden mask when she looked away from the projected images dancing on the lumpy mud-stucco wall of the darkened hut. "I don't believe it."

Sean Reichert made a disgusted sound. Mike Hays raised a hand to quell him. Out in the night the forest pulsed with insect sounds.

"Why not?" Joe Weaver asked in Spanish.

Consuelo turned her head quickly to look at him, her mouth like a trapdoor. She seemed to be personally offended that such a gringo-looking gringo should speak Spanish as well as he did. But she did respond.

"It is absurd," she said. "You show me monster movies and expect me to be scared."

"They scared hell out of *me,* lady," Hays said in English. "What can we do to convince you they're real?"

She shook her head, frowning in annoyance. "We are the Atshuara. We know all the creatures of the forest, all the plants. We have seen nothing like what you show."

"That's the point," Robison said. "What killed our friends was in effect an alien invasion."

"Aliens from outer space, perhaps?' Her smile was arch.

"Not necessarily. We suspect they're products of genetic manipulation, like the mutants that appeared after the big war."

"Those were products of radiation," Consuelo stated. "No powerful pockets of radiation remain this far upriver. There were never many. Thus I know there can be no mutations."

The team exchanged frustrated looks in the semidark. They had still not been body searched; each had any number of useful goodies hidden on his person. Breaking out of the hut with its single guard outside the door, even if he was armed with an AK-47, would have presented small difficulty even had they had been stripped buck-naked.

But neither their concealed toys nor all their lethal resourcefulness suggested a way they could escape through a landscape as utterly unknown to them as it was utterly familiar to their captors. For the moment they had nowhere to go. More to the point, they needed to talk to these people, to convince them of the awful danger they faced, not run away from them. So they would stay until a better alternative presented itself, or until their captors, who seemed mostly puzzled by them, decided to try something more draconian than mere enforced hospitality.

"Haven't you heard reports of unknown creatures and plant life?" Reichert asked in Spanish. Although Latino, he had not grown up speaking or understanding the language. He had received intensive training in it in Delta, and had fought in Panama and Colombia. "Haven't your people reported anything strange?"

"All the time," the woman said. "The woods are strange. My people are accustomed to viewing and speaking with spirits. But no strange animals or plants."

"What motive would we have for lying to you about this?" Larry Robison asked in English. His Spanish comprehension was better than his speech.

She put her hands on her hips and stared at them for a moment. In the yellow light of a hurricane lamp, with her hair unbound and gleaming, she looked almost like a pretty child, except for hard lines at her eyes and mouth. Outside a nighttime breeze dragged branches across the thatch roof of the hootch.

"Bearded white-skinned foreigners have always found reasons of their own to lie to our people," she said at length. "You might be emissaries of the one who claims to liberate us, at the points of guns."

"Who's that?" Robison asked. Major Mike scowled and tried to make *cool-it* gestures his teammate could see but their captor could not.

"If you truly do not know, perhaps you have fallen from the sky as you said. We know such things happened once. Perhaps they still do."

She frowned. "But I think perhaps I should listen to those of my people who say we should torture you until you speak the truth."

"Trouble with torture," Hays said casually, examining his smoldering cigar, "is that it doesn't get you the truth so much as what your subject thinks you want to hear."

"So I have heard," Consuelo said. "Since you seem truly not to know, I shall tell you. We fight the encroachment of the *criollos,* as I have said. The forces of the Republic of Marañón. The Liberation Army, they call themselves. But they are really conquerors."

"Are those their heads hung on that tree out there?" Reichert asked, eyes big in the gloom.

"Jesus!" Hays subvocalized. "Ixnay on the unkenshray eads-hay!"

"Why are you speaking pig Latin?" Weaver asked. "She can't hear us?"

"General principles."

Consuelo's eyes flashed. "Quit obsessing on the shrunken heads," she flared. "We're at war!"

Reichert held up his hands. "Sorry. Sorry. Culture shock. Forget I said anything."

She shook her head, still frowning. "Now I will sleep. In the morning perhaps you will either have come up with a more persuasive argument—or have decided to tell me the truth."

She turned and went out. A heavy wooden door was slammed shut and ostentatiously, or at least noisily, barred from outside.

"Tough house," Reichert said, slumping down on a swaybacked bench of rotting wood with his back to the wall.

"Why's she call herself 'Consuel*o,* anyway?" Major Mike demanded of no one in particular. "I don't know much Spanish, but the one thing I thought I did know was that women's names end in *a*."

"It's a noun," Joe Weaver said. He lay on his back on a reed mat spread on the trodden earthen floor with his head resting on a roll of cloth. "It means *consolation*."

"It's like *chupacabras*," Reichert said brightly.

"What is?" Hays demanded. "Consuelo? She's got a tough streak, but how the hell does that make her a *chupacabras*?"

"The word," the youngster said. "It has a feminine plural ending, but it's a masculine and singular to boot. It means, *one who sucks goats*. So *el chupacabras* is correct. Even though it sounds as if it shouldn't be."

Hays glared at him through the yellow dimness. "I worry about you sometimes. You just aren't *right*."

Two hours later the ringing rattle of gunfire hard nearby blasted them from sleep.

Chapter 9

Kane put his left arm to the warehouse wall and slipped his right behind Brigid's back. He kissed her back hard.

Her big faux-brown eyes went wide. She rolled them to her right, toward the other end of the warehouse from the monolith wall. His red eyes laughed back at her.

A pair of Mags strolled into view. They wore long black Mag coats of cloth-covered Kevlar over black field uniforms, the usual patrol garb, not the full-body polycarbonate hard-contact armor. They stopped and stared.

"Well, well," the shorter, wider one on the left said, "what do we got here?"

His partner had a long-bean head, all over pink splotched with orange freckles, button nose, long upper lip, slash mouth. His head was shaved. His hair would surely be red. He smiled a gap-toothed smile.

"She don't look too dirty, Malkorn," he said. "Let's put this taint in the dirt where he belongs and tear us off a piece for ourselves."

"That's just not a professional attitude to take, Wenderoth," the shorter Mag said. He had dark brown hair with a cowlick, a busted-up nose and hairy ears that stuck way out to the sides of his wide head. "So you got to go second."

Wenderoth laid a big hand furred all over the back with orange like an orangutan's on Kane's shoulder. "Peel yourself off the soft goods, Whitey. Stand easy and we don't bust you up too bad."

The chalk-colored face turned to his. The pale lips peeled back in a wild smile, mirrored in the madness of blood-colored eyes.

All the pink ran out the bottom of Wenderoth's long ugly face. "You're no Roamer," he gasped. "You're—"

The words died in a tearing sound and a gurgle as a ten-inch double-edged knife was suddenly punched through his throat from his left to his right, just behind his Adam's apple.

Approaching Brigid to claim his turn, Malkorn stopped as if his feet had been nailed to the planet. "You killed a Mag!" he exclaimed, more in uncomprehending awe than righteous rage. It was as if the natural order of the universe had been overturned.

"Naw," Kane said, ripping out his blade sideways in a gusher of red blood and letting the shave-headed Magistrate fall to strangle on it. "He was never a real Mag. He turned into just a scumbag shakedown artist. Now he's dead, and you're next, Malkorn, you pathetic maggot-dick."

"Kane?" Malkorn brought up his right arm to let his power holster slam his Sin Eater into his hand from its

concealment in his coat's voluminous tearaway sleeve. Brigid dropped to her side on the littered ground, hauled her skirt-covered knees up to her chin and kicked his legs sideways right out from under him.

As he fell he formed his hand into a half fist, initiating the power holster. The big handgun slammed free of his coat sleeve.

Kane's hand intercepted it before it reached its destination. "No guns," he said. "Noisy." He ripped the weapon free from the rig.

Spewing spittle and sounds of incoherent rage, Malkorn swarmed up Kane. He grabbed frantically for his Sin Eater. The machine pistol was a badge of more than manhood to any Mag. Along with the insignia of the Magistrate Division itself—crimson scales of justice against a nine-spoked wheel—it set its bearer apart from the rest of humanity, even the elite few specialists who lived in the Enclaves. The Sin Eater was the prime instrument for keeping the scum at bay—an important consideration here in the Tartarus Pits, where scum abounded.

Malkorn succeeded in knocking the weapon spinning down the alley toward the exposed monolith foundation. He head-butted Kane on the nose, causing red sparks to dance behind Kane's eyes. Then, tearing loose, he darted past his foe in single-minded pursuit of his side arm.

Grant came around the corner with his phony queue dangling down the left side of his chest. "What the hell's going on?" he demanded.

He saw the squat Magistrate scrambling toward him on all fours. Then his eye was caught by the Sin Eater spinning through the grit of the ground.

"No shooting," Brigid hissed.

Grant raised his right foot out before him and heel-kicked the weapon behind him. Malkorn uttered an incoherent groan of rage and lunged for the larger man. As he neared him he dived, trying to shoot for his legs and take him down.

But Grant had mastered the brutally blunt and practical Mag unarmed combative style long before he ever went off to study more esoteric arts at Shizuka's court. Anticipating the takedown, he stepped forward and brought up his left knee sharply. It caught the charging Mag as much in chest as chin, sparing him a broken neck, at least for the moment.

The impact slammed him mostly upright. Grant gave him a forward elbow slam to the side of the head. Malkorn rocked back on the heels of his black boots, stunned. Grant grabbed him and ran him face-first into the warehouse wall. Then he frog-marched him around the corner out of sight.

"What—?" Brigid started to ask.

Kane just shook his head, grinning an abstracted half grin. He leaned down with his big Magistrate knife to slash the unfortunate Wenderoth, who lay gurgling and twitching with his face masked in his own blood, across the side of the neck below the left ear. His carotid sprayed a fan of blood in rapidly diminishing pulses.

Grant nipped back briskly around the wall and set his back to it. He raised a bleached eyebrow at Grant.

"We caught a strike, that plucked ape Malkorn turned up when he did," Grant said, "for once."

There came from around the corner a sound like a car door slamming hard.

"He served both to muffle the noise and help tamp the force of the blast," Grant said. "Only decent damn thing he ever did in his life."

"And you say *I'm* a coldheart," Kane said.

Grant stooped to retrieve Malkorn's Sin Eater. He tossed the weapon to Brigid, who caught it one-handed as if she did that every day of her life.

"Here. Cover us while we check whether we broke through or not."

"You've come a long way from senior archivist," Kane said with wolfish approval.

She popped the magazine out to make sure it was charged. "And now," she said, expertly slamming the magazine home again with the heel of her hand, "I'm about to come full circle."

LARRY ROBISON STARTED awake and began to sit up from the leaf-pad bed their captors had provided. A hand clamped over his mouth stopped him. He glared around, hand going for a Cold Steel lockback folding knife carried in a small pocket on his right thigh.

From outside came shouts, the drumbeats of running

feet, the slam of a shot, followed by a snarl of full-auto fire.

"Easy," Mike Hays subvocalized softly in the darkness.

Chagrined that an older man—not to mention a jarhead—had responded more quickly than he had, Robison nodded to his boss to release him. Around him the others were moving in darkness alleviated only by greenish silver moonlight, cut with a jagged shadow cross, streaming in through a window of a raw plank wall of the hootch.

"Who do you reckon these dudes are?" Robison subvocalized as he joined his teammates taking quick stock of what the guerrillas had left them.

"Who knows?" Reichert said, inaudible to all but his companions. He was checking the load on a .40-caliber "baby" Glock 27 holdout pistol he kept secreted somewhere in his battle dress.

"Who cares?" Hays echoed, moving to put his back to the wall by the window. He had his own backup piece, a .380 Walther PPK, in hand.

"We might," Weaver said. His sneaky pistol was a palm-sized black Kel-Tec P-32. "Depends whether they're more likely to torture and kill uninvited guests than our current hosts are."

"Then Navy boy's job is to talk 'em out of it," Hays said grimly.

"Me?" Robison said.

"We're down here to convince the indigs to help us

assess and deal with the threat," the team leader said. He put his PPK away.

"What are you doing?" Robison asked.

"What are we gonna do?" Reichert asked.

"What we came down here for," Hays said, unwrapping a fresh cigar. "So put 'em back in your pants, boys. We await events before we take any action."

"Wait in here?" Robison asked.

"Unless you're eager to wander outside into the middle of a firefight in the dark between our captors and people we don't even know," Hays said, "yes."

"Speaking of firefights," Weaver said as a freshet of firing cracked off right outside the hut, "these walls won't stop many bullets."

A grind and bumping at the door. Robison looked to Hays. The heavyset leader stuck his cigar in his mouth.

"Stand easy," he growled. "But be ready to move."

The door was snatched open. A shadow figure stood there, diminutive and bandy-legged and pointing an AK-47, unmistakable despite the darkness, into the hootch. His posture showed he was tensing to shoot. Team Phoenix grabbed for their own reconcealed weapons, knowing there was no time.

A flicker of orange light and compound thunder. A shadow strobed across the floor of the hut. The guerrilla fell into it and lay still. The team saw a horse rearing up right outside the hootch. Then it was gone.

A collective breath was violently released from four sets of lungs. "That was almost a pretty damn sucky call on my part," Hays said, taking the smoke out of his mouth.

They crouched, then, low to reduce exposure to stray bullets. Robison felt a certain sick thrill, not at the danger—which was scarcely a novel element, if nothing to welcome or take lightly—but at the uncertainty. How to play this? With their backup weapons in their hands—which, in their highly trained hands, were far from inconsiderable, even matched against much more powerful weapons? Or as Major Mike wanted them to, barehanded, trusting in reflexes or maybe just Providence to keep them alive from one moment to the next as a battle raged right outside the hut's flimsy walls?

Reichert reminded them what had really been keeping them here all along. "It's not as if we've got any-place else to go just now."

Out in the black someone was screaming. Robison felt a drop of sweat run down his face and into his beard. They were fairly high up here, albeit not exactly in the Andes foothills, just in the high Amazon basin. It was cool at night.

It wasn't the temperature that made him sweat.

He glanced at the others, just visible in the light scatter of moonlight from the window. Hays, crouched like a badger, scowled furiously with his jaw clamped on his unlit cigar. Sean Reichert squatted, bouncing slightly on his heels, visibly struggling to contain his nervous energy. Only Joe Weaver looked impassive, sitting by the wall with his knees drawn up and his thick forearms

crossed over them, his craggy bearded face as immobile as a gold statue of the Buddha's behind the circular glasses.

The shooting faded away up the slope. From the
volume of firing Robison guessed Consuelo's people—whom he and the others had taken to thinking
of and referring to in their subvocalized conversa-
tions as guerrillas—had pulled out at the first sign of
attack. He took for granted that most of the gunfire
was simply caps being busted, for effect—mostly to
make the shooter seem valiant, or to reassure him—
and that few bullets strayed close to their intended targets if any. He'd experienced Third World firefights
before.

The gunfire thunder was replaced by voices shouting importantly to one another in Spanish. "Stand easy,"
Hays subvocalized to his teammates in a growl. "Just
be cool."

Reichert smiled a tight smile and nodded.

A shadow crossed the door. To no one's particular
surprise it was another figure incorporating an AK-47
silhouette. A scratch on the door frame, a flare of yellow light, and a bearded face stared into the hut in un-
derlit surprise.

"Hey," he shouted in Spanish, "they got gringos in
here!"

"Live ones?" a voice called back.

"*Sí.*"

"We'll soon take care of that." A bandy-legged man

in a beret and a bulky jungle-camouflage jacket stepped up beside the first man. He ostentatiously jacked the slide on a .45-caliber Colt Model 1911 handgun.

"We come in peace," Larry Hays said quickly in Spanish, holding empty palms toward him.

The *pistolero* was clean shaved and wore shades— despite the fact the string and penumbra of an eyepatch was clearly visible around the right lens. He grinned and raised the big handgun.

"Hold!" a new voice cried.

For a moment more the one-eyed man in the sunglasses held down on Larry Robison. Even in the darkness the fat bore of the .45 seemed an infinite tunnel into infinite blackness. I hope somebody's got a holdout on this dude....

With reluctance visible even in the crappy illumination, the gunman lowered his piece. He stepped back away from the doorway.

"Please come out," the newcomer's voice called in Spanish. "Slowly, so that my men do not become nervous."

The teammates looked at one another.

"Best offer I've heard all night," Reichert murmured. He tucked away his baby Glock, which he had been holding concealed behind his left hip as he squatted.

"Showtime," Major Mike said. He straightened and strolled out the door.

A tall man on a white horse awaited them. His long

sideburns framed a long face, and he had curly dark hair and lots of white teeth showing as he smiled.

"I am Simón the Liberator," he said in English. "Welcome, my friends!"

Chapter 10

"So far, so good," Kane muttered out the side of his mouth as they walked briskly down the Beta Level corridor.

"That's what worries me," Grant replied in a low rumble.

"Men are always looking for things to worry about," Brigid said. She looked cool, professional and in command, dressed once again in the crisp garments of a senior archivist. Like Kane she had hurriedly scrubbed off the skin tone from face, neck and arms in the stairwell, but her eyes were still brown and her hair the same brassy hue. They reckoned that her total appearance was different enough that leaving her with hair a red wildly different from her natural shade would scarcely increase her risk of exposure.

Besides, having two Magistrates, huge in gleaming black hard-contact armor and helmets, walking right behind her guaranteed no one looked too closely at her. Which was vital, since sooner or later an unfamiliar face would be spotted even if a familiar one wasn't. The presence of a pair of hard-contact Magistrates would certainly discourage anyone from indulging idle curiosity. Mags tended to think of themselves as the ones who asked all the questions. And when things failed to match their expectations they had some pretty brisk methods for getting reality to line up right in their eyes.

Of course there was always the risk a trained archivist's eye for detail would still pick up something that might unravel the whole scam, despite the tendency of everybody's eyes to slide away from Mags, especially faceless in full armor with slightly concave red visors on their helmets. It was just a risk they took. They had all been bashed about far too much by reality to imagine anything happened without risk.

Least of all penetrating the heart of an enemy stronghold—where they all had once, not too long ago, been very well-known indeed.

They moved through a seldom-traveled area within the great white monolith. Lakesh had provided them with counterfeit identichips that would grant them access to where they needed to go: to a special sensitive data-storage area whose workstations were not connected to any outside network, which was still the only real guarantee they couldn't be cracked and siphoned from without.

The one thing you could say, Kane reflected, was that they had worked so far.

"I'd always been taught it was women who were the worriers," he said from inside his helmet. Like Grant he had packed the whole-body armor suit into the ville, and the monolith, into a mock-shabby rucksack. The armor was bulky but not heavy, and the pieces could be nestled inside one another to reduce the space they took up. Fortunately, transportation was at a premium in the Outlands, and even when Roamers such as the three impersonated had access to wags the areas they were allowed to enter within the city were severely restricted. Traders from the Outlands staggering beneath the weight of overstuffed, monumentally heavy packs were a common sight in the Tartarus Pits.

"Another typical example of the male-chauvinist indoctrination you received growing up in the Magistrate Division," Brigid said crisply.

"Agreed," Kane said. "So I suppose your antimasculine bias is all natural? Or did they teach you that in little archivist day school?"

"By no means! I mean—what antimasculine bias?" Brigid had flushed scarlet to her hairline.

"Get a room," Grant growled. "This isn't the time or the place."

Brigid favored him with an extraferocious glare.

Kane stopped and swiveled his head to look up and down the corridor. "Grant's not the only one worrying," he said. "I can hardly believe this is going to work. Can't be this easy."

Brigid flared her nostrils and ran her chip past the sensor. The door opened.

Grant looked at Kane, who shrugged. "Okay, maybe it can be that easy."

A woman started to step forth from the secured-terminal chamber. She froze at sight of the sinister figures looming before her. "Oh, I'm sorry. Please, I didn't know you were here."

"Go about your business, Archivist," Brigid said crisply.

The woman, small, stooped and mousy, was of indeterminate age. All archivists Kane had ever seen looked middle-aged, to him anyway, except Baptiste. The archivist started to sidle past. Then she stopped and stared searchingly at the dark face of the taller woman in senior archivist garb. "Wait. You're not—"

She gasped. "Brigid! You're Brigid Baptiste, the renegade!" She turned and darted back inside the room.

"Alesia, wait—" Brigid cried.

Although the joints of his polycarbonate armor constricted his limbs, Kane glided into the room like a snake. His right hand rose to his ear and snapped forward. A flicker in air ended in a dull sound compounded of crunch and tear.

The fleeing Alesia slammed face-first into the wall angled to the one against which the secured console rested. She reached a pale hand, bones and tendons starting out from the skin, toward an alarm button on the wall. Kane straightened his arm toward her. His Sin Eater leaped from its holster and slammed into his hand, aimed at the back of her head, where she showed a slight bald spot.

Then a great flood of blood, dark red with pinkish

lung-froth to frost it, belched out of her mouth and slopped down her turned chin to smear the shoulder of her smock. She slid down, leaving a trail that glistened more black than red in the fluorescent inner light.

Brigid emitted a tiny choked gasp. "Alesia!" She rounded angrily on Kane. "Did you have to do that?"

Kane looked at her with eyes that would have been unreadable even had the scarcely translucent visor not hidden them from her.

"Yeah, he did," Grant husked. "Now let's get the hell inside and shut the door before somebody else stumbles onto us we have to kill more noisily."

The hard mouth smiled harshly beneath the lower rim of Kane's dished red visor. The Sin Eater snapped back into its forearm holster with a slight servo whine.

With a last scowl at him but no further sign of emotion Brigid swept forward and sat down at the terminal, putting on a pair of heavy-framed eyeglasses as she did. She did not glance at the body of her acquaintance, now cooling to ambient temperature. The things they had seen and done—and suffered—since fleeing Cobaltville together with Domi a few years before had hardened even Kane and Grant, who would've sworn beforehand that all softness had been crushed from them by their hard years as Mags. That much more had life in exile hardened Brigid—who, granted, had had farther to go. The fact was, though, that now she scarcely turned a hair at things that would have made her male companions blanch in their Magistrate days.

Grant and Kane shed their own packs—unusual, as well, but only a Mag would dare question another Mag. Kane pulled off a gauntlet and went to check the sad huddle of bloodstained clothes by the wall. The woman's neck was already clammy to the touch, stuck slightly to his fingertip, like chicken skin. He felt no pulse.

"Chilled sure," he said, straightening, with a shrug.

Brigid didn't so much as glance his way. Nonetheless he saw her tense, in the muscles of her neck and shoulders. I know her way too well. And vice versa.

"What?" he said. "You wouldn't want her to suffer, would you?"

"You're a bastard, Kane."

He shrugged. "And then some. But a *breathing* bastard."

"Very well," Brigid said. "I know what I need. I've found the references."

She swiveled the chair right and pointed to a locked cabinet of white-enameled metal. "In there. We don't have the access key for that."

"I do," Grant said. He removed his own heavy gauntlets and dug into the Mag-issue waist pouch he wore. He produced a small black stick of moldable plastic explosive. Mashing the explosive over the electronically keyed lock of the cabinet, he pressed a detonator into it.

"Fire in the hole." He stepped back. A moment, and then the charge cracked off. The door opened of its own accord.

"Thank you." Brigid knelt briefly, swung a hinged rack of CDs out, examined their serial numbers briefly, then stood with an iridescent plastic disk clasped between thumb and forefinger and went back to the workstation. "Now we see if what we want even exists."

"There's a cheerful thought," Kane said, "that we got all the way in here for nothing."

Brigid ignored him. Her fingers prodded the keys, paused, tapped more. The room was bare and tiny. Grant paced it. It took him about a step and a half each way with his long muscle-corded legs.

"You used to be the calm one," Kane pointed out.

"I used to belong in this goddamned armor with this goddamned badge on, too," Grant said. He shook his great head heavily.

"Who'd've ever thought it would happen? I was the ultimate Mag. Now all this shit gives me the creeps."

An alarm began to blare.

"I set it off," Brigid said exasperatedly. "There's a software watch on the information we're looking for that calls for help even if a user with baronial-class access tries to retrieve it—as I just did."

"I know that, Baptiste," Kane said. Then awareness shot through him like a blast of jolt. "Wait—does that mean you don't fucking *have* it?"

"Not at all," she said crisply. "It's all right here."

"Then we're not about to die for nothing?" Grant said.

"If you're trying to take up looking on the bright side," Kane said, "don't. You don't have a knack for it."

He raised his hand. His Sin Eater slammed into it. "Then again, I'm not exactly ready to die quite yet myself."

"Wait until the hard-contact ready squad gets here."

He looked to Brigid, who was standing up from the console. She had ejected the CD from the drive and was slipping it into the pocket of her smock.

"So that's it? No holograms? No rotating 3-D representations? Not even a trumpet fanfare."

"Saskatchewan," Brigid said. She was reaching inside her smock for something.

"Gesundheit," Kane said.

"That's our objective. The Totality Concept built an ultrasecret underground redoubt in Saskatchewan, in what was Canada. An area notorious for high levels of crop-circle activity, right before the nukecaust."

"Crop circles?" Grant asked. Kane shrugged.

From outside came shouts, followed by pounding on the door.

Grant's Sin Eater came out. "And now," he asked, "how do we get out of here?"

Chapter 11

"Ah, the guerrillas," Don Simón Romero, doing business as the Liberator, said in his deep plush voice and plangent accent. "You must understand, gentlemen, that I bear the Shuara tribesfolk no animus. But they represent retrogressive forces, the forces of reaction. For all their rhetoric, they are not objectively revolutionary."

They sat among thick green bushes exploding with yellow and blue and red-orange flowers and brief orphan arcs of balustrade of what looked like white stone and was probably concrete. They were in the garden of a great gleaming white plantation house outside a small ville on the river called Futuro. The morning was moderate, the breeze cool, the sky glorious. It might have been heaven, if not for the bugs.

Sean Reichert had his head turned away from their host and toward the others and was mouthing the word *animus?* Major Mike ignored him as he took his half-smoked cigar—a fresh one, pressed upon him by the ever gracious hand of their host himself—from his mouth.

"All respect, General Simón," he said, "we don't care."

Larry Robison, the team diplomat, screwed his big handsome squarish face up behind his black beard. But their host only smiled self-deprecatingly.

"Ah, no, my friend—no general I. But Major Hays," he said, leaning forward slightly, "whatever do you mean, you do not care?"

A servant, stiff in black tailcoat, his dark and distinctively non-Shuara Indian face looking like a dark carved stone inset in a crisp, immaculate white collar, stepped forward to refresh the major's silver goblet of chilled papaya juice. He looked as if he possessed the power neither of speech nor of laughter. Both he and his master, chatting gaily with his long lanky frame wrapped in a plum coat and dove-colored trousers, looked perfectly in place if the time had been the early nineteenth century.

"Your local politics are extremely interesting to you, as naturally they would be," Team Phoenix's leader said, leaning forward in his white-painted wicker chair. "But we can't afford to get distracted by them. We came down here on a mission of overriding importance, literally, for the whole world. And you and your people top the list of those threatened by—"

"By this curious outbreak of heretofore unknown species," Simón said, nodding vigorously. "Yes, yes."

"'Heretofore,'" Reichert subvocalized. "We're being entertained by the inventor of Scrabble."

"Knock off paraphrasing *The Last Boy Scout*," Robison responded, "before I throttle you." Reichert grinned and shot him the bird.

"Have we not managed to convince you, Excellency?" Robison asked aloud. He had not actually heard a rank attributed to Simón, nor did he give himself one—other than the Liberator—although he unquestionably held the title of Head Motherfucker in Charge. "We can show you further evidence if you desire—"

After Simón had at least lived up to his name in relation to Team Phoenix and the shack in which they had been sequestered by Consuelo's tribal guerrillas, the four outlanders had been bundled onto horses. They had not been bound, nor did the new set of captors search them, either. Simón's soldiers seemed to feel that if the Jivaros wanted to keep them captive, they had to be good guys.

And they were, well, white. Robison had served time in Latin America, as well as having been attached to the naval attaché's office in Quito, and he knew that at least up until right before the nukecaust, social standing and skin tone had a lot to do with each other. He observed that while by North American standards the Liberation Army troops were short and dark-skinned, they were by and large taller and at least somewhat lighter than the Shuara: not exactly what he would call *criollos,* which at least used to mean people of pure European descent. And they were much better dressed—and armed.

A quick cavalcade through dark forest and across fields, some fallow, some cultivated, brought them to what could only be a grand plantation house rising from the midst of fields of maize and beans, its tall walls glowing greenish-white in the brilliant moonlight. The four thought it had to be deserted. Yet they were given two rooms on the second floor, each in good repair with a pair of four-posters; so that a night that had begun with captivity and uncertainty ended in comfort and ease.

If not, necessarily, a lot less uncertainty.

Don Simón was shaking his head. He was a long, lean specimen with a long narrow head and face. His hair and long sideburns were somewhat curly, of a dark brown that showed red highlights to the morning sun. His deep-set eyes were hazel. He had a long straight nose and high, somewhat square cheekbones. His skin was olive, and not deeply tanned.

"Ah, but that will not be necessary, my friends," he said expansively. "I know that sometimes great and terrible things come into our world, inexplicable things. Even before this outbreak of which you speak our world was inhabited by horrific creatures such as the horned boa, which surely the hand of God never made. In sum, I am persuaded that the threat exists."

Hays looked around at his teammates. Larry Robison sat in a wicker chair at his side. Joe Weaver sat on a bench; Sean Reichert perched on one of the stone balustrades. A couple of the balusters by which his booted feet swung were pocked with unmistakable bullet holes, indicating that, of the sense of tranquil unreality they all got from the scene, the tranquility at least was transient. Larry thought it a useful reminder.

"It's a welcome change to be believed," Reichert

muttered. "That damned Consuelo wouldn't even believe her own eyes."

Their host turned a glittering gaze upon the youngest team member. "She is a stubborn woman," he said with a certainty that made Robison suspect he'd had more direct contact with her than as an opponent in the field. "She fights for what she believes is right—no matter if it is. But she has taken up the cause of bandits."

Hays nodded, frowning slightly. "Sure, Don Simón, but as I said—"

The Liberator held up a hand. It was a graceful hand, slim and long fingered. Robison's educated eye saw no calluses. It was not a hand accustomed to hard work.

"*Momentito,* Señor Major. Hear me out, please. You do not care about the ins and outs of our conflict because you cannot afford to care—it is of no importance to your mission. I hear and I applaud your dedication. But this which I have to say pertains directly to your mission and it is this—Consuelo and her Shuara stand in your way. I and my Liberation Army of the Republic of Marañón, on the other hand, stand ready to help you. Your course is clear. Join us in clearing this obstacle from our path, that we might shoulder to shoulder confront this otherworldly menace of which you speak!"

"Not exactly otherworldly—" Reichert started out.

"In fact we don't know where it originates," Hays said, fixing his subordinate with a blue gimlet eye. "And while we'd like to find out, that too's subsidiary to our goal of stopping it."

He put his cigar in his mouth and puffed furiously on it, hunched forward with elbows on the knees of his camou pants. "So you say this Consuelo woman is standing between us and our mission?"

Smiling, Simón spread his hands. "How else can it be, my friend? What did your experience teach you? She took you captive and would hear no explanations."

"He's got us there, Chief," Robison said.

Hays scowled a moment longer, then nodded. "All right. What's gotta be is what will be."

He looked up at Simón. ""How do we do this thing?"

Simón smiled till it seemed the upper half of his head might be in danger of toppling backward, as if hinged. He stood. "Gentlemen, we shall discuss the particulars of our joint operation to put an end to these bandit depredations once and for all. In the meantime—"

He clapped his hands. A number of his own men, wearing camouflage battle dress, trotted through the flower-overflowing shrubs laden heavily with—

"Our gear!" Reichert exclaimed.

And so it was: weapons, overstuffed rucks, web gear, the lot. The silent troops dumped their loads on the weed-grown flagstones and departed.

"It's great to have this back!" Reichert enthused as he checked the action on his AK-108 assault rifle, then buckled on his web gear with the special holster that carried his pistol-style H&K 40 mm grenade launcher. "I felt so naked."

"We coulda done without it," Hays growled. He couldn't help himself from hefting his machine gun affectionately, however. "But thanks, Your Excellency. This'll help us get the job done."

"Excellent." Simón bowed to his guests. "I must leave you now, gentlemen. We shall convene later to discuss our operation to eliminate the bandit menace, and clear the field for contesting this biological invasion."

He strode away quickly toward the manor house on long legs.

"Everything seems to be here," Joe Weaver's subvocalization sounded in his partners' skulls. "The Shuara are dog poor and up against it. Why didn't they take at least some of it?"

THE DOOR SLID OPEN. The Magistrates had taken a lot less time than Kane anticipated to override the security lock on the door.

A Mag plunged in, holding a Copperhead in both hands. He stopped dead, obviously not expecting to be confronted by a pair of Mags dressed, like him, head to foot in gleaming black polycarbonate armor.

Kane, on the other hand, saw exactly what he expected to see.

Back in the old preskydark action vids Domi loved to watch, people were always punching each other in the head. Magistrate Division unarmed-combat training emphasized that you never struck a bony part of a human body with a closed hand. Kane still remembered the weeks of agony of a broken hand after he, as an adolescent cadet, had been chosen to demonstrate to his classmates just why—although he had gotten the grim satisfaction of breaking his opponent's jaw, as well.

But that was an unprotected fist. Kane's hand now was encased in a gauntlet of exceedingly strong synthetic, complete with articulated joints for the fingers. The hard-contact helmets, meanwhile, left the wearer's mouth and lower jaw unprotected, in part for psychological effect, in part to reduce the risk of the breath fogging the inside of the visor.

Kane's hand was perfectly well protected against the impact that smashed the lower jaw of the first Mag in the door and drove his teeth like knives back through his tongue. He barely felt a thing. The Magistrate went down, gurgling and retching as blood torrented down his throat.

Less inclined to showmanship, Grant simply shot the Mag who had come in the door. He folded to the floor as if his hardsuit had abruptly become untenanted.

The man whose lower face Kane had smashed into white and bloody ruin grabbed his ankle. Kane kicked almost petulantly at the bubbling mass of his wrecked jaw, snapped his helmeted head back. The man's neck broke with a loud pop.

Kane scooped up the Copperhead that the first Mag had dropped to clutch at his face.

Playing point man himself for once, Grant had moved up to the door and stuck his great head out into the corridor for a look. A snarl of autofire responded instantly. He ducked back, cursing as a copper-jacketed slug glanced off the dome of his helmet and tumbled screaming down the hallway. "Fuck! That'll teach me to leave the sneaky-peeky shit to you, Kane."

Grant stuck his Sin Eater in his right hand and the other fallen Magistrate's Copperhead in his left around either side of the door and ripped off a burst toward both ends of the hall with each. He yanked them back quickly as a storm of return fire erupted from both directions.

"Dumb-asses," he remarked as hoarse shouts and a shuddering scream greeted the cross fire. In their excitement the Cobaltville enforcers were shooting one another. "Magistrate Division's gone all to hell."

He glanced at Kane. "What's the plan?"

"Kill all the bad guys. Get to the gateway. Blow this slag heap."

Outside the storm of firing had settled down. Smoke swirled, and men were shouting at one another, trying to sort the situation out. It sounded as if nobody was too eager to press home the attack.

"Does the expression, 'the devil is in the details' suggest anything to anybody?" Brigid asked acerbically. She was hunkered down by the cabinet Grant had blasted open clutching a big black 9 mm H&K USP in both hands.

Grant tipped his helmeted head to the side. "You're the point man."

"Give me all your grens," Kane said, slinging his scavenged Copperhead, "then grab the chair." He was grubbing in his pouch as he spoke.

Grant began pulling out microgrens. "This is another classic one-percenter, isn't it?"

Without looking up Kane tipped a black polycarbonate-encased finger off his visor in front of his brow.

"They sure seem to be coming around way more than one percent of the time."

"Think of it as entropy in action," Kane said.

Working fast but without haste Kane had armed several of the golf ball-size grenades and clamped them in his left hand with pressure on the safeties. Catching at least part of the plan, Grant armed some of his own and pressed them into his partner's right palm.

A black-helmeted head peered around the left-hand side of the door. Brigid thrust her arms out full length ahead of her and snapped off two quick shots. They cracked over Grant's right shoulder, narrowly missed the intruding head to ricochet off the far wall and go bouncing down the hall. The head ducked back abruptly.

Grant lifted his head and stared at Brigid, expression unreadable behind the dished red visor. Neither of the others needed to be able to see it to know the big man was scowling.

"You play it close to the bone, girl."

He slid to the wall to the left of the doorway. The Mag who had peeped in came in behind his Sin Eater. Grant grabbed the man's gun wrist, turned away from him and broke the man's elbow across his own armored shoulder. The man's hand went slack. The handblaster snapped back in its holster. Grant crushed the man's larynx with a brutal backhand chop and threw him back in the hall.

He moved rapidly and seized up the chair. "You first, left. Baptiste next. I bring up the rear."

"But—" Brigid began.

"Move yours," Kane said. *"Now."*

Brigid straightened and went to stand almost on tiptoe in anticipation behind Grant's broad back. Kane went to the door's right, crouched and flung his hands outward, left and right.

"Showtime," he said.

The latter half of the word was swallowed in the multiple crackling of nearly a dozen microgrens—frags and incens—going off. He caught up his recovered Copperhead with his left hand and his Sin Eater leaped into his right as fresh screaming started.

Grant was already in motion, dashing out the door and bulling left, trusting to his black plastic carapace to keep bullets out of his back—and Kane. Kane stepped back into the hall and pivoted right. As if they'd rehearsed the move all week, the unarmored Brigid sprang out between them.

Kane's end of the hall looked like hell's antechamber. Several overhead light strips had been knocked out, plunging the corridor into gloom. The walls were dotted like a planetarium ceiling with galaxies of tiny glows: flecks of white phosphorus burning at impossibly high temperatures, scattered forcefully by the incens. The frag-microgrens contained charges of powerfully brisant explosive. Their destructive radius was small, but within a yard or two their effect was ferocious.

One or several had gone off between the feet of one Mag, who sat with his back to the wall, staring dumbfounded at the red fountain gushing from where his right leg appeared to have been wrenched bodily off at the hip. The flood surged with every pulse of his panic-racing heart—but noticeably less each time.

Kane ignored him, as he ignored the Mag rolling on the floor shrieking and clutching his face, with tendrils of dense white smoke and blue flames jetting between his fingers as phosphorus fragments devoured the flesh and bone they had been driven deeply into.

Either brave or ignorant, three other Mags stood their ground the way he was facing despite the ghastly white-blue constellations glowing on their night-black armor. Kane felt the shock of multiple impacts transmitted through his armor as they blazed away at him full-auto. He put his head down to protect his vulnerable chin as much as possible.

The hard-contact suit's rigid structure distributed the impact energy, dissipating it. Despite padding, the armor stung at the contact points with his body. It was not perfect protection. The articulations at his joints were weaker, although Kevlar-backed, and given sufficient punishment even the tough polycarbonate shell would crack.

Kane held out his Sin Eater and started firing. He lashed his bursts at his enemies' guns. Not from any ancient vid-show notions of shooting the guns from the Magistrates' hands, but because their Sin Eater actions weren't armored—the weps themselves were their most vulnerable points.

Using the chair as a ram, Grant put his head down and charged the four Mags still on their feet down the hall to the left. Their armor might limit the effect of firearms. But it cut deeply into their agility. Naturally they were trained in close-combat in full hard-contact armor.

They just weren't as good at it as Grant was. He knocked them spinning and clattering in all directions. Then the fugitives were past, and running down a side passage toward the concealed entrance to what used to be Lakesh's private elevator.

Chapter 12

The man in the loincloth crouched on a jut of rock overlooking a small creek, a single-shot shotgun cradled in his ropy arms. A scrim of brush hid him from observation from the creek itself and its far side.

A slight rustle in the bush's leafy branches, a slight thump. The man rocked once on his bare heels and collapsed bonelessly onto the rock. The birds never even interrupted their noonday calls.

"Good shooting," Larry Robison heard Sean Reichert's voice say through his bone-conduction phones. "The way's clear."

Team Phoenix was returning from a reconnaissance into bandit territory. They had felt a certain amount of trepidation going in. For all the rhetoric the three military vets' respective services liked to spout about their boys being the best of the best, anywhere, anytime, all three had spent enough time on the ground in various Third World hellholes to know that the home team always had the advantage. Especially when the home team's lifestyle ran to hunting and gathering, which meant that each and every member had spent more or less his whole life getting to know every square inch of his territory—not to mention learning how to see things walking or crawling or resting peacefully upon it without being seen *by* them.

But the visitors enjoyed some advantages too. And not just the technotoys, nor the more systematic training, nor even the benefits of superior nutrition and medical care.

"I don't understand," Robison heard Weaver say as he moved cautiously into the open, holding his Saiga combat shotgun at the ready, preparing to cross the stream as Hays covered him with his MG. "These Shuara seem, well…."

"Lax?" Reichert filled in. "Just a bad case of overconfidence."

From somewhere to Robison's right a cloud of scarlet-and-white birds rose squawking into the air. Their cries weren't raucous enough to mask the clatter and thud of gunfire. It was hard to estimate distance from sound, especially in scrub like this. But by the birds the action was taking place between two and three hundred yards west of Team Phoenix's present positions.

"Don't forget to give a shout out to our Liberation Army friends for taking the heat off us," Hays said.

A sizable town lay down the river toward its confluence with the Amazon proper. It was called Santa Caridad, or Holy Charity. A characteristic that seemed notably lacking in this world centuries after the nuke-caust, the members of Team Phoenix had noticed.

Santa Caridad had been a provincial capital of something rejoicing in the name of the Kingdom of Marañón until a couple of years before, when a junta took over and proclaimed the ville the capital of the independent Republic of Marañón. The heavy lifting had been done by troops under Simón's command. The feat earned him the soubriquet "the Liberator"; his followers called him "Colonel," and he failed to discourage them in the teammates' hearing. He was, it would seem, the hard military arm of the ruling junta.

Larry Robison had picked up the facts in their past couple days' dealing with the Liberation Army soldiers and their undeniably charismatic, if eccentric, leader. But something didn't quite add up for him. Because Simón had his headquarters in Futuro, upriver from the capital. Of course, it might have simply been a handy forward base for operations against the Shuara, a federation of tribes who had been moving first into the Marañón basin and then down it for generations. But Robison wondered.

Despite Major Mike's formal disavowal of interest in local politics, Robison was learning what he could. Making explicit their intent to stay the hell out of local politics was necessary to keep from getting embroiled in them, to the mission's detriment. But understanding them could keep Team Phoenix alive.

Robison got over the creek by the simple expedient of jumping across, which was quieter than splashing through it. Then he went to a crouch in a shrub and covered with his full-auto 20-gauge as Major Mike followed him.

He let Hays pass by, moving along a path through knee-high grass, his chopped and channeled MAG-58 machine gun held at patrol position. Major Mike then dropped into a patch of scrub near a stand of young trees flexing with a breeze that had begun to quest down the steep-sided valley, dropping the bipod of his MG to cover his buddies' egress. Robison called to his remaining two teammates that it was time for them to come across, as well.

Sean Reichert came first, looking deceptively casual, positively rakish with his boonie hat at an angle on his head. Like Robison he'd let his hair grow out since discovering how they'd been lied to by their erstwhile employer, perhaps as a gesture of defiance against Gil Bates. Hays had said not word one about it, although he had remained high and tight like the deep-dyed Marine he was. They weren't in the military now, although each man still considered himself in service, even if none of them could articulate precisely to whom or what. What mattered most to Hays, although he would never say so directly, was the team itself. Being chronically marooned, two centuries out of their own time with no possibility of return—and each man had lacked other close ties even before being recruited—had forged a bond among them stronger even than that customarily created by shared danger and hardship. As long as each man held up his end, there were no issues. Formal military discipline had never been part of the structure.

Without glancing toward Robison, Reichert moved off to his right and went to ground to cover for the fourth member of the team, his partner for the day.

A moment later Joe Weaver appeared. He seemed to rise like Antaeus right out of the ground. He carried his hand-assembled Winchester 54 sniper rifle in .308 NATO in both hands. Slung over his shoulder with the light day-pack all of them were carrying was the weapon he'd used to take down the guerrilla sentry watching the crossing: a silenced DeLisle carbine, built by Weaver from an Isha-pore Mk IV Enfield with Mk III-style iron sights he had made and calibrated for .45 ACP ballistics plus a scope. The carbine's scope was off-the-shelf Leupold glass, good quality but not a piece of art like the big Unertl on his .308; the baseball-like trajectory of its handgun bul-let made shots beyond two hundred yards problematic. The quiet civilian master machinist could plunk an enemy in the head with the thing consistently inside 150 yards. As a skilled hunter of four-legged prey before he ever, in Bates's employ, turned his hand to the two-legged variety, he had stalking skills to match his three Special Forces vet comrades. He liked to get as close as he could to his target and leave as little as possible to chance.

Robison suspected he'd taken down the watcher on the creek from inside fifty yards. But he had no more heard the shot than the victim had. Firing from a locked-up bolt action, with an integral sound suppressor and a round designed and loaded for subsonic velocities, it was that rarity, a truly silent firearm.

Weaver walked past him, looking neither left nor right. Although he moved with the grace of perfectly controlled strength, there was about him the quality of a statue of stone or steel brought to life. Robison wondered that he didn't crunch when he walked, but he made no sound.

He had lost his wife and young daughter in a tragic accident a few months before being signed up by Bates's headhunters. Still, the Navy vet couldn't help wondering what had impelled Weaver to sign up for this desperate one-way mission. The world's slowest suicide mission? None of them was ever coming back alive....

Weaver marched off into the grass and vanished. "You can shift, now, Phone Man," his voice came into Robison's head, using Robison's call sign. In the SEALs his primary task had been communications, though like everybody in the teams he was cross-trained to serve any function at need. The Team Phoenix setup was the same.

"Roger that," he responded. As he rose the popping of gunfire died away.

"I told those boys not to go back the way they came," Hays's voice came over the net.

Moving hunched over his shotgun, past the small grove into which the team leader had vanished toward a deeper stand of woods, Robison smiled mirthlessly. He heard no one suggesting they go to the aid of Simón's ambushed soldiers. The patrol leader, a snotty lieutenant type, had refused Hays's offer to at least scout the route back to Simón's HQ in advance of his platoon.

"They didn't get wiped out, you don't think?" Reichert asked. He sounded worried.

"Don't worry, kid," Robison said. "We didn't sign for 'em."

"Ran out of ammo, more like," Hays said. "I think our little G brothers capped one or two and booked, leaving Simón's boys to panic-fire until they ran dry. With luck they even got 'em in a firefight with each other."

"Even with their better gear," Robison observed, picking a spot behind a fallen log to take his turn at overwatch, "it's not gonna be easy helping these guys beat down the locals."

"That's why we get paid the big bucks, Squid."

THE DOOR OF WHAT had been Lakesh's private elevator slid open with a hiss. The doorway seemed filled by a vast white wedge of back encased in a uniform jacket. Beneath were scarlet trousers and black boots to the knee, polished to laser brilliance.

Hissing in turn like a cat, the figure began to turn. His hair was dark blond and wavy. Even contorted into a snarl his features were injection-molded perfection.

Squashed into the rear of an elevator designed to carry two people, Brigid gasped. "Baronial guard!"

He was fast, inhumanly fast. Literally so: the baronial guards were genetically engineered to be as strong as they were quick, far beyond the human norm, and could absorb prodigious punishment.

But Kane, alerted by that sixth sense that made him the consummate point man, had launched himself in a forward dive before the door opened. Reflex made Grant follow his move without thinking.

Kane caught the spinning baronial guard around his wasp waist and slammed him forward to the polished marble floor. The guard arched his back to try to throw Kane off. Grant landed on his shoulders like a great panther, slamming that flawless face to the stone again.

Expressionless now, the guard performed a push-up, lifting Kane and Grant, armor and all, right up with him. But Grant wrapped his huge polycarbonate-sheathed arms around the narrow head and threw his weight to the side as Kane sprawled out his legs to try to stop the guard from rolling over with them.

Beautiful face immobile, the baronial guard thrashed furiously. He began arching his back high, then dropping his belly to the floor and bending backward. Barely clinging to his legs, Kane flopped like a hooked fish. A thin whistling squeal escaped the baronial guard's nostrils.

Grant got a boot on the floor and heaved with all his might. The baronial guard's neck snapped. His dying paroxysm flung Grant and Kane aside like dolls.

Shouts pealed down the hallway from their left. They were music: more guards.

"Baptiste!" Kane shouted from his sprawl against an oak-paneled wall. "Get to the mat-trans unit."

Her eyes snapped open, she nodded convulsively, then sprinted down the corridor with her Roamer skirts trailing behind her like drab, ragged pennons.

Both Grant and Kane still had scavenged Copperheads in addition to their own Sin Eaters. Both had reloaded on the short ride up from Bravo Level despite the contortions this entailed in a space that would have been overfilled by three riders as large as the two ex-Magistrates and Brigid were, to say nothing of the added bulk of two hard-contact suits. Now with Kane lying on his side and Grant on his belly, each thrust both weapons out to full arm's reach and blasted at a pair of oncoming guards.

It was like trying to hit the spot of light cast by a flashlight twitched around at random. The pair darted and dodged from side to side, shooting laser pistols as they ran. The beams cracked over Grant's and Kane's heads as ionized air fled their dazzling paths, and scorched brief smoking paths in the paneled walls. Fortunately both weapons were pulse lasers, so they could not simply be chopped down on the target like an ultra-long weightless blade, the way a continuous-beam wep might. And not even baronial guards could aim while running flat-out and dodging.

Both former Mags knew from experience the guards were extraordinarily hard to kill. For his part Kane didn't even try. He swept the Copperhead side to side at crotch level.

The nearer guard bloomed sudden deeper red on the

front of his trousers and fell sprawling on his face. He tried to get up, could not. A pair of strikes by high-velocity steel-jacketed 4.85 mm bullets had broken his pelvis. No matter how muscular a biped was, no matter how tough physically or mentally, or even adrenalized, he couldn't walk with a broken pelvis.

Even as the genetic construct Kane had blasted was finding this out, a grin still fixed on his perfect face and sweat standing out along the line of his wispy light brown hair, a bullet from Grant's purloined Copperhead caught the other in the right eye socket and took out the back of his head in a black-and-pink cloud of cranial contents. He went down in a flail of decontrolled limbs and rolled over several times on the slick floor before coming to a halt.

The injured guard, pulling himself doggedly forward on his elbows, tried to push his right hand, still holding a laser pistol, out before him to finish Kane. Kane put his wrists together, put his two weapons side by side, then sighted over the Sin Eater's perforated barrel shroud. He fired a quick pulse from both weapons simultaneously.

It was as if an invisible jackhammer had gone to work on the baronial guard's face. The unnatural meat sculpture imploded in ropy squirts of blood and sprays of bone chips and teeth.

Grant was on his feet, hauling Kane upright by the back of the web belt of synthetic he wore cinched over his polycarbonate hard shell. "No time to play around, pretty boy," the big man snarled. "Reinforcements are on the way."

Shouts from out of sight down the corridor confirmed his words. Kane turned and matched his longer-legged partner stride for stride toward Brigid, who was waiting at the mat-trans unit.

"Get us back to Cerberus, Baptiste!" Kane shouted.

She looked up. Along the way she had shed her brown contacts. Her eyes were once more her own piercing green.

"We're not going to Cerberus, Kane," she said.

And then Grant and Kane were almost on top of her, and shouts and shots were pealing out from down the hall to their left. Staring at Baptiste's grim-set lovely face, Kane opened his mouth to yell, *"What the fuck?"*

Then he fell headlong into those bottomless seas, her eyes. And a spectral hand reached inside him and yanked his soul inside out.

Chapter 13

"Are we sure this is a good idea?"

Three members of Team Phoenix busied themselves under a sheet of camouflage-pattern nylon, at a forward base in the bush. The sky was pale green above the Andes to the west. The early nighttime sounds trilled, throbbed and occasionally screeched around them, punctuated now and then by shouts of the Liberation Army troops bivouacked nearby. The air was cool and dry tonight; they were up in a sharp and twining if not particularly high system of ridges above the Marañón. The team's primary weapons lay disassembled on a Mylar drop cloth on the grassy ground for cleaning.

"Nope," said Mike Hays. "Which idea do you mean, Joe?"

The team armorer and all-around utility man sat cross-legged by the dropcloth cleaning the disassembled sound suppressor built into his homegrown DeLisle with a toothbrush and some solvent. He was wearing an olive-drab T-shirt and his bulky camou trousers.

"Taking part in Simón's private war against Consuelo's people."

"Do we have a choice?" Reichert asked. He squatted nearby, reassembling his AK.

"There's always a choice, son," Weaver said.

"We agreed," Hays said huskily. "We all agreed."

Tonight was the night of the big push: Team Phoenix had slept the day away, and they were now gearing up to go deep. At midnight they'd sneak out, swinging wide around the Jivaro camp they'd spent the past few days scoping out, to a spot where a stream cut a ridge-line in the guerrillas' rear. Just before dawn the bulk of Simón's Liberation Army, infantry and horse cavalry—a staple of the modern world, the team had learned since awakening—would drive down on the rebel cantonment. Consuelo's plucky little *indigenas* would shoot and scoot, leaving a few men to pop caps and make much noise while the rest ran for safety.

Dead into the killzone of the Claymore ambush and fire-sack Team Phoenix would have waiting for them.

If all went well—yet plans seldom survived first contact with the enemy. And none of the team had abundant faith in Simón's self-imagined heroes, who like a lot of Third World armed formations were long on swagger and short on skills. The "bandits," as Simón inevitably referred to Consuelo's people, were far better at what they did. But unless events just got way more FUBAR than even several decades' brutal accreted experience predicted, the Indians would be slaughtered. Their morale would never survive the level of losses they were due for, even if most of their fighters did. The days of the defiant Shuara nation would be done, at least this far from their home range up north in what had been Ecuador.

"I agreed," Weaver stated, threading washers back onto the carbine's barrel one by painstaking one. "Now I'm thinking more clearly."

"We are cutting it kind of close to where our friends back in the world say the bugs are," Reichert said. They were in satellite-linked communication with Cerberus. Following Kane's and Grant's quiet but fervent advice, they kept it sporadic. Being allies did not mean submitting to Lakesh's abundant love of micromanagement.

Hays took his cigar stub out of his mouth. It was unlit; he was too canny a bush-crawler to send out fragrant smoke signals to pinpoint their position. Nor was he about to head out to snoop and poop with hair and clothes stinking of tobacco.

"There's no world anymore," he said hoarsely. "Our world's been dead two hundred years. There's no recall from this one, kid. No rotation home. Don't ever forget that. That way lies madness."

Normally Larry Robison would have made a smart-ass remark here to break the sudden heavy pall of silence that descended inside the shelter, so thick the forest sounds barely seemed to penetrate. But he was standing watch outside, concealed and keeping silent—not even subvocalizing. Getting in tune with the discipline needed for a combat patrol deep in what was literally Indian territory. They were on the outskirts of the Liberation Army cantonment, so they could slip out when the time came without alerting any more of their allied forces than necessary, by preference none at all. This close to the enemy's stamping grounds they looked to their own security.

It wasn't as if they didn't trust their allies. They didn't. No "as if" about it.

"I'm not a big fan of Simón," Weaver said. "I don't feel too good about helping his thugs lean on the local Indians. I don't think they've got their interests at heart."

Hays sighed. He sat on a folding stool, leaning forward, looking like a big old badger. "I don't like to play the civilian card here. But maybe it's time. I don't doubt the Indians are getting the short end, here—again. I'm just as damned sure as you are they're getting screwed, blued and tattooed. But there's larger issues here. There's a little thing called 'world survival' that might just be at stake here. Stacked up against that, the indigs lose, no matter how just their cause or even what a little cutie Consuelo is. We got a mission.

"So we are going to nut up and screw, and blue *and* tattoo with the worst of them, and save a fucking ungrateful ball of confusion that will continue on its merry way, doing its best to kill us. End of story."

Weaver's brow set slightly. Reichert started looking uneasily between him and the team leader. That slight change of expression was the equivalent of another man's screaming fury.

"I finish what I start, too, Major," Weaver said. "It's

not the injustice I'm concerned about. Just as you say, it's not the first time these people have gotten shafted, and I take for granted it's not going to be the last, no matter what we do or do not do. But I don't trust Simón. Latin American history's too full of glory boys on horseback. They're not a very reliable breed."

"What choice do we have?" Reichert asked plaintively. "It's not as if Consuelo'd help us."

"She did take us prisoner, if that little tidbit slipped your mind," Hays said.

"It didn't," Weaver said. "But she didn't have us body searched, and she's clearly smart enough to think of it. And even when Simón's bunch chased them away she left our gear for us. *All* of it. I'll let you career military men tell me how often dirt-poor Gs do that."

That elicited uneasy silence and flickering eyes. The answer was *never.*

"Don't forget the one dude tried to whack us," Sean said.

"He was probably acting on his own," Hays admitted. "But maybe they just had to book too quickly to snag our stuff."

Weaver shook his close-cropped head. "Two centuries ago their ancestors were too poor to leave treasure troves like those behind, no matter what. These people are pitting bows and arrows and blowguns against rifles and machine guns. Even though they know how to use the primitive weapons to maximal advantage, do you really think they'd choose to rely on them? And it's not just weapons. Even if they couldn't figure out how to work some of our equipment, this is a part of the world where even a used tin can is salvaged—and used."

Hays shrugged. They'd seen as much in the ville where they'd first been held. His brilliant blue eyes were watchful. This was as many words as he could remember hearing the man, ex-lawyer or not, string together since first meeting him what was still less than three subjective years before.

"You're right," Reichert acknowledged. It was with evident relief. He had a tendency to hero-worship the few-spoken armorer, and it clearly pained him to disagree with him. And it still did. His young, slightly plump face tightened as he said, "But there's still Consuelo. She just flat blew us off."

"Mebbe that's because you didn't know how to talk to her," a voice said in English. A familiar voice.

A female voice. Lilting and more than somewhat slightly taunting.

"Domi?" Sean said.

"Knock, knock." A slight figure appeared in the entrance to the tent, dressed in khaki shorts, boots and a dirt-brown shirt. She was as pale as a sandwich bag of moonlight, as always.

"What the fuck, over?" Hays demanded. His cigar, which he'd stuck back in his face, fell to the ground.

Larry Robison loomed up behind her. "I have no idea how she got past me," he said. "No excuses."

"I snuck past you, soldier boy," she said cheerfully, half turning to stroke his bearded cheek. "No big."

"But I'm trained for this," Robison said aggrievedly.

Domi's laugh was musical, and only gently mocking. "You trained. I'm *born*. Outlands bred and raised."

Helplessly, Robison shook his big head.

"So what's the big word from Cerberus?" Hays asked. "How're our opposite numbers doing?"

As he spoke, Domi's eye had fallen on something. Her right hand had darted like a pallid falcon and snatched something off the doorjamb. She popped the wall lizard she had just snagged into her mouth, bit off its gaudy red-and-green head as if it were a candy bar and chewed.

The team members' eyes got big. They'd all eaten some fairly skanky things, the three military vets during their special-operations training, and Weaver with the others in training for their current gig. But never as casually as the beautiful little gamine albino—not to mention her *relish*.

"Don't look at me," Reichert muttered. "That 'Snake-Eater' nickname's mostly just PR."

"Dunno," Domi said, and swallowed. "Nobody's heard from them for days now."

"YOU IN SOME TROUBLE, girl," a voice said. "Ready to admit it to yourself?"

Slowly, stiffly, Consuelo turned on the folding wood-and-canvas chair on which she sat writing at a crate desk. She was no longer alone in the hootch high up in the forested hills above the Río Marañón. She could still hear the night's soft trills and susurrations, and closer by, the voices of her men chatting unconcernedly around their small, virtually smokeless, hard-to-see fires.

The intruder was a small woman with impossibly white skin. Her hair was short and silver-white. Her eyes were the color of fresh-spilled blood. The Shuara war leader recognized her as the fifth member of the party of intruders they had surprised down in the river valley several days before, the one who slipped away. *First,* she mentally amended—and cursed herself again for not ordering them killed rather than letting them fall into Simón the Betrayer's hands.

Yet even then she had doubted. And doubt, she knew, was a worse betrayer than even Simón Romero.

"Keep it low," the newcomer advised. "Anybody else hears us and comes poking in, things'll just get real complicated in a hurry.

Consuelo was a tad taller than the woman who had invaded her hut HQ. Though she carried little extraneous body fat Consuelo was thicker in the waist, more muscular, as well as wider across the shoulders. She was really quite sturdily built.

"So you're the one they call the Ghost Girl."

The intruder shrugged artlessly. "Probably. I can't usually understand what they're saying."

Clear but unstated was the fact that she was in the habit of eavesdropping, unseen, on Consuelo's fighters.

"Name's Domi."

Consuelo felt a flare of fury at this paper-white bitch. "You're albino. Albinos are weak. I bet I could take you."

Domi laughed. Her teeth were very white in her red mouth. "Mebbe you get a surprise, too. No matter! Think with your brain, not with the dick you don't got. I wanted you chilled, you be room-temperature right now, even if I weak as newborn runt puma kitten."

The guerrilla woman nodded. "Very well. You make your point. You took me by surprise. You could have killed me. You don't want me dead. What *do* you want?"

"For me to talk," Domi said, "and for you to listen."

"Why should I? You killed my men."

Domi shrugged. "Wouldn't listen to reason. Had to be big-big strong-strong. So I had to chill or get chilled. Question now is, you smarter than them? Way you act, you sure think you are. Now show it. Or is it just book-learning, not real smarts?"

Consuelo sucked in a deep breath. That cut deep. She nodded convulsively as she exhaled. "Speak, then."

"You know now those big gringo boys weren't just blowing smoke up your pretty little ass, yes?"

Consuelo scowled. "Why should I believe them? English-speaking white men telling big stories—when did it ever profit people like me to listen to things like that?"

"Save excuses for yourself. Wrong's wrong. Chilled's chilled. Except—" she nodded her head meaningfully "—when it ain't."

Though the night was warm for the altitude and time

of year, and next to stuffy from the heat and slight smutty smoke of the lantern, Consuelo shivered.

"You know what I talk about," Domi said. "Too well you do."

Consuelo squeezed shut her eyes and felt tears forced outward over the lids. Worse things than the ghost woman had begun to kill her men. Worse than the *criollo* invaders, even.

Internally cursing herself for weakness, she said, "But what can I *do?*"

"The only thing—get right with Team Phoenix. Help them fight the evil. Or let them help you. Same as they wanted to do up front."

"But I can't! It's too late. They've joined Simón. Already they hunt my people on his behalf. Like animals! They—"

"Whoa. Whoa. Stay on track here. Get too wound up grieving, you'll just get more grieving to do. Then you get dead."

She put her hands on her hips, surprisingly full for the slimness of her frame. "I know those boys. They're smart, but then they're not smart. Men are like stallions—if they not cut, they tend to get ideas stuck in their heads. This case, they see you as an obstacle to something they gotta do. Something they'll die before they let go of—and you know now it is something they got to do, or your people are history, and maybe all people everywhere."

"I know! I know that! And I *know* I made myself an

obstacle. I thought it was right… Yes, I know, too late for excuses. But for all I can see it's just too late now. I can't talk to them. There's no way to get a message to them, and if I could, they wouldn't listen to me…."

"Mebbe not," Domi said. "But they listen to me."

Consuelo frowned. "But they're surrounded by Simón's troops! How would you get to them?"

Domi's laugh was like a wolf's: silent, mouth open, head bobbing. "Listen at you! Your people can't catch me, and these their woods! What makes you think Simón's band of bozos can touch me?"

Chapter 14

It wasn't like being eviscerated—Kane had never been gutted alive, but he knew it wouldn't feel like this.

Quite.

But this might've been worse. It was as if every molecule, every atom of his being had been mapped onto a three-dimensional representation in outline on a computer screen, then somebody had stuck the cursor randomly into the middle of it, clicked to grab and then just yanked the whole structure inside out.

Then stretched it out to infinity.

What it felt like was…beyond pain. At some point, he knew from horrible experience, the circuits overloaded; they either tripped and you went out, or you just got numb. The torturer's art, he knew too well, wasn't in causing pain; any idiot could do that. Nor was it keeping the victim alive. It was keeping the subject conscious, and keeping the subject from getting used to the pain.

But Kane could not black out. Nor could he block out the sensation, the way you could the nerve's messages to the brain. Because this pain wasn't felt by the nerves, nor registered by his brain. He didn't even know if he had nerves or a brain any longer. This was pain in the depths of him: stone soul torture.

For some unbearable interval the cosmic racking continued. Kane longed for a voice with which to scream. He was denied even that.

Galaxies burned like cancers within his distended being.

Images began to assail him: lives, agonies, losses, disappointments. Only some of them his.

Or were they? Or were they all his? Had he really been…so many?

To the anguish, the physical torture of his nonphysical being, was added the torment of an infinite sense of loss. And now he burned to weep, with eyes he did not have.

The only shelter, the only possible respite was madness.

But there was that within him that refused to give in. That much, at least, remained within his power. Grimly he hung on to sanity. And endured.

HE BECAME AWARE of pain. But this was new, not the agony of being racked upon galaxies and seared with supernovae. Just plain old-fashioned ache that throbbed to the beat of a blood-and-muscle heart.

He became aware of something else: jump nausea more acute than anything he could remember. As if the realization was a trigger to his abused stomach, he turned his head aside and puked. The liquid noises echoed in his ears.

Over the sound of his own retching Kane heard

Grant's voice muttering to himself, "I hate this shit. I *hate* this shit. I really *fucking* hate this—"

From another quarter came the sound of sobbing, muffled but heartbroken.

"Well," he croaked when he was done, "at least I don't have to sing 'I Ain't Got No Body' any more."

"If I still gotta put up with your weird humor after all that, Kane," came a familiar deep-bass growl, "then we're in Hell. By definition."

Kane tried to open his eyes. To his surprise he discovered they already were. Wiping his mouth with the back of his gauntlet—foul clots on pristine black, but it'd rinse—he rolled away from the reeking pile of spew. The effort drained him, so he just lay a moment, like a beetle half expired on its back.

"We are not in Hell," came Brigid's voice. It had its customary crispness and had lost not a quantum of its usual supercilious tone, even if it did come on the tail end of a sniffle. Kane hated her fervently for her ability to recover so quickly from the extraordinarily brutal jump trauma. Or for being able to fake it so well.

He remembered, then, some of the experiences he had relived, in jagged flashes like light through claw-tears in a curtain, and felt an odd hot-fluid flush of shame flow through him. He already knew from experience, of which they had spoken little more than to confirm its simple irrefutable reality, that frequently he and she shared jump visions.

"If it isn't Hell," Grant said, and even that hard man's

voice sounded strained in the impenetrable blackness, "it's close enough for baronial work."

"How close an approximation of Hell it is remains to be ascertained," Brigid said coolly. "We have in fact arrived at Base Abaddon, beneath the prairie of what was once known as Saskatchewan."

"I'd say Baptiste just made something like a joke," Kane said, "except I'm on cognitive-dissonance overload watch as it is. Why the hell is it so dark in here?"

In response a beam of white glare stabbed out from somewhere to his left. Although it came nowhere near to shining directly in his eye, he winced as his head gave a silent internal clang of pain like a struck bell.

"I apologize," Brigid said. Her face, surrounded by a cloud-mass of shadowy escaped hair, floated like ectoplasm in the black above the source of the beam, a small flashlight. "I should have warned you to shield your eyes before I turned on my flashlight. It is dark because we are in a facility deep underground with no access to natural illumination, and the lights are off."

"Kane," Grant said. The big man was sitting up with his helmet off, rubbing the back of his close-cropped head. "If jump trauma's scrambled your brains for you, better scoop 'em back up and pour 'em back in your skull in a hell of a hurry. I got a bad feeling about this place."

"I got a bad feeling about just about any place, these days," Kane said. "Worse since the damn barons morphed into ancient gods warmed over. But this place has the virtue that nobody's shooting at us right now."

He struggled into a sitting position. It seemed to take all the strength of his arms to hold him there. His head felt like a rotten melon precariously balanced on his shoulders, at any moment liable to topple and smash itself to chunks and pulp on the hard surface, undoubtedly concrete, beneath him. He was none too sure he wouldn't welcome the process.

"So what's the bad news, Baptiste? Why is this place worse than any other?"

"Crap, Kane," Grant said. "I never been a big believer in the power of positive thinking. But you're taking things a little much to the other extreme."

"It's just logical," Kane insisted. He had taken off his own helmet now. The air currents flowing, faintly but perceptibly, across his face, were cool and sterile, which beat most of the alternatives he could call to his still-addled mind. "We have our own special entropy, a knack—or mebbe predestination—for moving from bad to worse."

"Redoubt Abaddon was an ultrasecret Totality Project center for biological research," Brigid said.

"Thought they had plenty labs for that kind of thing," Grant said.

"For their experiments on humans, hybrids and animals, yes."

"This is something else," Kane said slowly.

"Nanotechnological research. Extremely compartmented. Very high level need-to-know secrecy."

Kane found the water bottle in a pouch on his web gear, pulled it out, popped the lid, rinsed his mouth with brackish water and spat. "You found all that out at Cobaltville?"

Brigid nodded.

"So this is the place we were looking for," Grant said, rapping the floor gently, with muted clacks of his gauntlets.

"Indeed, it would appear so," Brigid said, standing up with slight but unmistakable effort.

"Tell me again why we had to go through all that hooraw to find this place," Kane said, trying to emulate her and opting to wait a little longer, at least until his internal organs got themselves sorted a little better back into place.

"Because apparently the forces the Totality Concept tapped into with their experimentation frightened even them," Baptist said. "So they halted all experiments, shut the facility and hid mention of it, even from their own successors. They could not, however, bring themselves to expunge all record of the base or its existence. Not even dread of the possible destruction of themselves and their world could overcome their obsession with the past, it seems."

"Uhh." Kane rolled over, put his hands on the concrete, then made himself spring upright in one heave. He swayed only slightly.

"The so-called gray goo," Grant said, climbing to his feet less precipitously but showing no further effects of jump. "Which we've come to take out into the world ourselves. What's wrong with this picture?"

"Lakesh believes that, if we find true self-replicating assemblers here, he can modify them to attack only organisms bearing the characteristic genotype of the Invader species," Brigid said edgily. Although she had her own issues with Lakesh she still felt some kind of obligation to defend her ex-mentor.

"If we only had samples of alien-bug tissues," Kane said.

"That's Team Phoenix's mission in South America," Brigid said with a toss of her hair. "We must rely on them to do their jobs."

"That I don't have a problem with," Grant said. "But Lakesh and this end-the-world bug, and Lakesh's slight little predisposition to outsmarting himself—"

"Look on the bright side," Kane said. "If it just comes down to a choice of which thing eats us all, maybe the nanomonsters hurt less than the full-sized ones."

"We should be moving," Brigid said. "We don't know how long it will take to locate what we're looking for, whether it's an actual culture or instructions for creating the assembler."

"Lotta things we don't know," Grant grumbled.

"Which way do we go?" Kane said, leaning down gingerly to recover his helmet.

"I suppose it doesn't much matter," Brigid said. "In the time they had before we jumped, Cerberus was unable to discover any layouts of the base. We appear to be on our own."

Kane shook his head and grinned ruefully. "This just keeps getting better and better."

"Stop whining," Brigid said. "The base is abandoned. At the least we have small fear of being discovered—"

The words cut off as the sound of sharp, hard claws rasping on concrete reached their ears.

Many, many sharp claws.

"WAIT!" THE GUARD SPUTTERED in Spanish, "you can't go in—"

"Too late," Sean Reichert told him. "We already have."

Inside the large pavilion-like tent Simón the Liberator sat grandly in a wooden chair with his knees spread wide and his trousers pooled about his ankles, getting head from a kneeling black-haired woman who appeared to be wearing nothing but a camou-pattern blouse. His legs were extremely pale and hairy.

His eyes bulged from his narrow handsome face in fury. "What is the meaning of this?"

The woman leaped to her feet. The blouse hung open in front. Shadowed round masses did interesting things as she wiped her mouth with the back of her hand. She favored the four men who had barged into the comandante's quarters with a smoky gaze.

"Plenty of time for victory celebrations," Major Mike announced, "after we've won some victories. We need to talk, Your Excellency. Now."

"Begging Your Excellency's leave for the interruption," Robison said.

Major Mike took his cigar stub deliberately from his mouth. "What he said," he added.

Simón stared from one face to the next, eyes still bugging with emotions now less readily identifiable. There was no sign of mockery or amusement from the interlopers, just business. The Liberator hauled up his drawers, lifted his skinny butt enough to scoot them under and up, got about securing them again.

"Go, Alicia," he said to the woman in Spanish. "We will speak of this later."

What seemed to Larry a look of concern flashed across her face. She was almost as lightskinned as Simón, in contrast to her jet hair. Her eyes were large, dark, slightly almond…

Whoa, big fella, he told himself quickly. Let go of that right now.

The woman disappeared out the back of the pavilion without bothering to do up her shirt. She wasn't wearing anything beneath it, Robison could not help noting.

"Not that we, ah, actually *saw* anything, Your Excellency," Reichert said. "That is— Ow."

Robison had just elbowed him sharply in the ribs. Reichert gave him a reproachful look.

The Liberator had recovered a modicum of his used-car-salesman composure with his trousers. "Gentlemen," he said, just a trifle huskily, "I take for granted you can have only the most urgent business with me, or—"

He let it hang. Robison got the distinct impression he had the impulse, born of habit, to add a bloodthirsty threat or even two. If he did, he kept it in check. Perhaps the presence of four big seasoned killers bristling with weapons had a calming effect. At least on those impulses.

"You take right, sir," Hays said brusquely. "We got something we think you should see."

Simón arched a brow. "Something?"

Hays grinned. "Yeah. Something. For your eyes only. If you know what I mean."

His tone was frankly lascivious. "Yes," Simón said slowly. "I think I do."

He opened his mouth to summon guards. "Uh-uh," Hays said, waving an admonitory finger. "Not unless you feel like sharing with the enlisted men, Excellency."

"Hmm," Simón said thoughtfully.

"Hmm indeed," Hays said.

"WHY COULDN'T IT BE simple this time?" Reichert groused under his breath. He had the point, moving through the dark underbrush uphill, into deeper woods. The moon had risen. The wan light was broken into shards by branches and leaves.

"It's never that simple, kid," Hays responded over the team net.

At the top of the rise stood a dense growth of trees, their bases obscured by thick underbrush. Trotting at Simón's side was a short man with bow legs and a barrel chest, wearing a beret. He wore dark sunglasses despite the hour, and a patch over his right eye. His name was de la Sombra. He was Simón's chief lieutenant. He was also the man whom the Liberator had dissuaded from shooting Team Phoenix the night they were freed from the guerrillas.

Robison wasn't sure if he had contrived to invite himself, or been asked, but Simón insisted he tag along. De la Sombra seldom strayed far from his boss, and as seldom passed up opportunities to give the team the evil eye. Generally he had kept clear of them in the few days since the *norteamericanos* had cast their lot with the Liberation Army; he had the air of someone who only thus could restrain his impulse to destroy them one and all.

Robison had seen this make and model before. The problem with it was that it wasn't predictably all show and no go. Sooner or later a braggart like this felt a wall touch his back and felt he had to deliver on his bluster and bravado. Which made him dangerously unpredictable.

"I hope Bozo the Clone here doesn't fly off and cause us to have, you know, issues," Reichert subvocalized, as if reading Robison's mind.

Major Mike let himself chuckle in his throat, where only his buddies could hear. "I dunno," he said. "I kinda hope he does act out."

After Reichert came Major Mike, his machine gun cradled in his arms, then Simón walking with long-legged strides and de la Sombra trotting at his side. In the act of swiveling his head side to side, as he did constantly, Larry Robison, who came right after, noticed Joe Weaver slip sideways and vanish into brush.

At the top of the hill Reichert stopped beside a break

in the brush. He beckoned the Liberator with a sweep of his hand. "After you, Your Excellency," he said. "I think you'll find what's beyond very…stimulating."

De la Sombra couldn't restrain himself cackling and digging his taller master in the ribs with an elbow. Simón looked a bit grim at that, but smiled at his lackey and stilted forward, through the gap like an open gate. De la Sombra crowded close behind.

Beyond the opening was a clearing perhaps ten yards across, densely hemmed in by undergrowth and trees. Sitting on the far side in the light of a kerosene lantern, upon ground bare but for a litter of leaf mulch, was Consuelo, the bandit chieftainness, with her head down and her hands behind her back.

Chapter 15

Kane dropped to the floor on his belly with a thud and a clatter of his polycarbonate armor, trying to ignore the way his brain felt as if it was doing the same within his skull. He had lost hold of his stolen Copperhead. But he got out his Nighthawk microlight, and his Sin Eater slammed obediently into his hand with reassuring authority of impact.

The beam stabbed out. Its white glare illuminated horror.

Horror on a hundred legs: a giant millipede, its segmented body as high at its multiple shoulders as a good-size dog, was scurrying toward them, its claws tatting out a sinuous staccato on the concrete floor.

Its face was like a human's, but stylized to the point of inhumanly refined and perfect beauty. But in the glare of Kane's microflash it showed an unhealthy pallor, as of a corpse dead long enough for decomposition to become apparent. The skin had an unpleasant look: not soft, exactly, but doughy, spongy, as if a finger press might leave a lasting depression. The eyes were huge, the irises lavender. The lips were black and smiled a tight, pinched little smile, as if at some private joke the apekin wouldn't understand.

Kane's nostrils filled with the brain-cramping reek of a week-old grave uncovered. Clamping his mouth against a squirt of sour, thin vomit, he gave the face a triburst, dead center. Three bullet holes appeared, startling black in that mime-mask face, two on the right side of that thin nose, one in the left cheek. They looked more like pores suddenly gaping unnaturally wide than entry wounds. As Kane watched the edges of the holes seem to suck together. The wounds closed like sphincters. The dead skin of the face seemed coarser than an instant before, but showed no sign of damage.

Neither did the horror, which continued to mince forward on a hundred tiny hard feet. "Bullets don't do shit to it!" shouted Grant. "What do we do now?"

Run away would have been Kane's usual reflex response, delivered with no conscious thought and acted upon with scarcely more. Yet he tried—and found he couldn't rise.

He was able to pop the spent magazine from the well of his Sin Eater, slam home a fresh one and jack back the bolt handle to recock the piece. Then he took it in both hands and aimed right between those lavender eyes.

The black lips smiled and kept expanding. As the expression opened in a huge grin, huge teeth revealed, a jagged jumble, akin more to a shark's teeth than human. Wider and wider the mouth opened, until the jaws themselves seemed to detach, the horrible teeth pivoting outward, reaching for Kane's face like talons.

He triggered another triburst. A single ragged hole appeared between those violet eyes. As the gunshot yammer echoed in his ears, Kane grew vaguely aware of someone shouting his name somewhere. It might have well been echoing out from the terrible jump nightmares. He couldn't respond to the voice, could scarcely track it. His whole being had focused down to a tunnel centered on that hideous face.

Great black pincers rose clacking above the awful head to either side, apparently projecting from the forwardmost segment of the millipede body as the beautiful, hideous face laughed through monstrous teeth. The lobed hole where Kane's bullets had gone sealed itself. The teeth and pincers reached out for Kane's face....

An impact slammed him in the tailbone. White sparks exploded behind his eyes as pain shot up his spine. His eyes spasmed involuntarily shut.

When he opened them the horror was gone. By the throbbing silence he could tell Grant had stopped shooting, as well.

"Where is it?" he demanded. "Where'd it go?" He felt shame at the way tears leaked from his eyes, although the coldly dispassionate core of his mind knew it was a physiological response to the powerful blow he'd received to his coccyx.

"Nowhere," Brigid said, her voice as tight as a hanging rope. "It was all in our minds to begin with."

With a scraping of abused polycarbonate on concrete Kane rolled onto his side and twisted his head to look at her. She stood above him, a shadowy form in the light from his microflash.

"Why the hell'd you kick me in the ass like that? It hurt."

"That was the point, Kane," Grant said. "She did the same to me."

"Breaking the spasm," Brigid said. "Distracting your mind—breaking its concentration upon the illusion—made it go away."

Kane started to shoot back some kind of retort. He settled for gingerly sitting up, grumbling inarticulately low in his throat. You couldn't argue with results.

Any more than you could argue with Brigid Baptiste.

"What I want to know," Grant rumbled, "is why you figured it out so quick and we didn't."

"Hypotestosteronism," she said.

"Say what?" Grant demanded.

"She's jacking with us," Kane said, climbing to his feet again. He felt as if he'd fallen down all the flights of stairs in Cobaltville from Alpha to Epsilon. Couple times. He didn't want to stay prone any longer, though. Aside from the position's relative immobility, he was none too happy with how it smelled down there. "There's no such word. She just means we got too much testosterone in *our* systems."

"There is too such a word," Brigid insisted. "I just coined it, according to accepted patterns of usage. However, for a rare occasion Kane has put his mind to use. While you men were busy fighting the phantom, my reaction was to shut my eyes. And I found I could still see the monster quite clearly. So I realized it was an illusion—and it went away."

"You couldn't have just told us?" Kane said.

"Stop whining!"

"She's got a point, Kane," Grant said without apparent joy. "She had to get our attention somehow."

"I tried shouting," Brigid said. "Really."

"Uh-huh." Kane eyed her suspiciously. His tailbone still hurt. He hoped she hadn't cracked it. "Well, we better get a move on before something a bit more substantial than that hoodoo happens along." He shook his head, trying to shake the last vestiges of the terrible image from his mind.

"Right," Grant said. "Which direction?"

"Baptiste didn't get any blueprints," Kane said, "so one way's probably as good as any other."

He paused, considering. "From the slight echo effect I'd say we're in some kind of pretty big chamber or room." He swept his microlight around and quickly saw his surmise was correct. They stood about a third of the way from the end of a space that had to have been nearly a hundred yards long by half that wide, and a little toward one side. The arched ceiling was perhaps eight to ten yards overhead. The room itself appeared utterly empty except for what seemed to be little drifts of dust and amorphous trash scattered sparsely on the floor. A second-story metal-frame catwalk ran along the perimeter of the great chamber.

"Reckon we're underground?" Grant asked, craning to look up with his own microlight. It illuminated light fixtures above.

"Feels like it," Kane said. "That sort of cavern chill. Obviously the ventilation works, though, even if the lights don't."

"Perhaps they're just switched off," Brigid suggested.

Kane shrugged. "Could be. More to the point, we're looking for this evil superbug Lakesh is all hot and bothered to make his pet."

Grant pointed an arm toward a door in the long wall nearest them. "Through there."

Kane cocked his head. "And how do you know that, big man?"

"Don't. What I do know is, what we're looking for isn't in here."

SIMÓN SWELLED VISIBLY. "You have brought me a most remarkable prisoner, my friends," he said low in his throat.

Consuelo rose. She shook back the long black hair that shrouded her face and held up her hands to show the absence of fetters. "No prisoner," she said. "I came of my own accord...cousin."

"*¡Engañada!*" de la Sombra hollered. With commendable alacrity he whipped his big hogleg .45 auto-pistol out of his ostentatious shoulder holster hung in the sweat patch beneath his left armpit. He had no trouble fiddling with the thumb safety lever. Like any self-respecting Third World *pistolero,* he didn't have the safety engaged in the first place.

Standing nearest him was Larry Robison. With a simple slide-step Robison was at his side as the gunman shoved the pistol to his arm's extension. Illogically, he aimed it toward Consuelo, the only person in view other than Simón himself who wasn't showing any weapons. Still gripping his own autoloading shotgun by the pistol grip, Robison reached out, wrapped the top of his big square left hand over the .45's square receiver. He dropped his pinky finger down between cocked hammer and firing pin, so that strain as de la Sombra might on the trigger, the piece could not fire. Then Robison twisted the handgun back toward him.

De la Sombra's gun hand was not hinged to go with it. The blaster came loose. The *pistolero* wheeled and knotted himself all up as if to spring upon the ex-SEAL, who topped him by a head. But he found himself staring down the Holland-tunnel-sized business end of his own weapon.

He contented himself with sucking on the knuckle of his pistol hand, cruelly scraped by the trigger guard, while snarling around it, "You will die a long time for this, gringo!"

"Since I'm a charitable hombre, I'll take that to mean, a long time from now," Robison said, smiling big through his beard.

Simón finally found his voice. "You evil bastard!" he growled as if past a half-taut noose.

Robison shrugged. "Good, bad, I'm the guy with the gun."

"Ash," Reichert promptly said. "*Army of Darkness.* Right on."

He and the ex-SEAL bumped fists while all three of the locals stared in utter incomprehension.

"Don't worry," Domi said, emerging from the screen of black brush behind Consuelo munching on a papaya. "They're always like this."

Simón had quickly recovered his composure. "What is the meaning of this?" he asked in tones more of calm concern than the sputtering outrage he had exhibited seconds ago. "Why do you betray my trust, my friends?"

"We don't," Major Mike said. "We don't betray our own trust, either. We're here to do a job—implicit in which is saving all your unreasonable asses."

"But *her*—" Simón had to pause a beat, as if his throat had filled with venom "—*she* stands in your way. In *our* way!"

"No longer, Simón," Consuelo said. They seemed to be on a regular first-name basis—leading Robison to wonder if the woman's calling him "cousin" was more than just a figure of speech. "As we know now—when it may be too late!"

Simón was starting to look less cocksure. Confident for the moment that his little buddy de la Sombra accepted that he was outgunned, Robison flipped up the thumb safety with his left forefinger and lowered his borrowed .45. For serious social work he still had the Saiga, after all.

"What makes you say that?" the Liberator asked querulously. "What might be too late?"

"Everything," Consuelo said, sounding annoyed and making a little semicircle with her hand. Then she turned and said something in the native language into the darkness over her shoulder.

Simón's handsome olive face lost a couple shades, which made him an interesting chartreuse. De la Sombra, on the other hand, purpled up and a vein throbbed so mightily on his forehead right below his Che beret that Robison was afraid he'd stroke on the spot. Although, he thought, perhaps *afraid* isn't the right word....

"Before you go popping off about betrayal again," he said, pointedly but affably, "remember, if we wanted you dead, you would be already."

"So shut it, Buttercup," Hays said, gesturing at de la Sombra with the unlit cigar stub clasped between his first two fingers. "Look, listen and learn."

Four of Consuelo's Atshuara tribesmen shouldered through the opening with a crunch and rattle of brush. They carried a fifth man with them.

He was dead and naked. His body was covered all over with holes the size of the empty eye sockets gaping in his head. His mouth was open in an eternal scream of ultimate agony.

Chapter 16

"What do we do now, Baptiste," Kane said, "wander the halls until we either turn up something promising or we all grow long white beards?"

"If you have a better plan, by all means, share it with us, Kane."

They had come into a high, broad corridor, still unlit. It was familiar, in its way. The walls were the unadorned vanadium-steel walls of a standard redoubt, echoing, uncompromising, glinting in sinister ripples when the lights played across them. The trio had as yet found no way to turn on any illumination, although apparently intact fixtures were visible overhead. Nor had they found a way into most of the rooms they passed along the way. Most were shut tight. They knew from experience that it would take heavier demolitions than any they carried. Redoubts were built to withstand danger within as well as without.

They had passed a few rooms whose doors yawned open. These were utterly empty, devoid even of debris larger than little piles of dust blown in by the still-functioning HVAC system.

"How far've we come?" Grant asked. "Any idea, Baptiste?"

"I have an eidetic memory, not a mental tape measure," Brigid said. "But I would guess no more than one-half of one kilometer."

"Seems a lot longer than that," Grant said. They had already been down a multitude of curving corridors and across junctions, placed according to no discernible scheme or rationale. "Poking around dark places never really creeped me out before. But this place—the walls just seem to suck in the light. It's like, if you leaned up against one too long, it'd suck the life right out of you."

"You must be affected, to wax all poetic like that," Kane said.

"Yeah. This darkness is getting to me."

"And then again," Kane said, "there *are* the monsters."

Even as he spoke he shone his light directly forward down the corridor to illuminate what looked like a cone of pulsating pinkish flesh and purple membranes, topped by a cluster of waving, fleshy green tendrils. Halting, he closed his eyes: sure enough, the vision persisted. He concentrated on making it go away. It did, and when he opened his eyes the way ahead was clear.

"It's not them so much," Grant said as they began advancing once more. "That one wasn't so bad, anyway—not like those decomposing green babies."

"Or the animated skeletons," Brigid said.

"Naw," said Grant, "the skeletons didn't do much for me, either. What does bug me is, what's causing them?"

Kane flashed his light up toward the grille of an air vent. "Spores or gas of some kind, something hallucinogenic?"

"Then why don't the visions persist?" Brigid asked. Although Kane and Grant each had a Copperhead in hand, she had holstered her side arm; she didn't want any accidental discharges if some sudden apparition induced a startle reflex in her.

Kane shrugged. "It's got weak after all these years? Maybe it was a defense that got triggered a century or two back, and this is just, say, the dregs getting to us. Leftovers."

"Then how come all these hoodoos have baron faces?" Grant asked.

"That cone thing didn't."

"Yes, it did, Kane." Brigid sounded haunted. "At the top. All those tentacles were sprouting from its mouth. It was as if a baron's face had been stretched across the apex. Or smeared."

"Whoa," Kane said. "Glad I missed that detail. So you think somebody's sending us nasty visions, is that what you're getting it?"

"It's what my gut tells me," Grant rumbled.

"That's just hunger growling. *I'm* the point man here—I'm the one who has gut feelings. You're the cold, rational one, remember."

"While it is hypothesizing in the absence of many facts," Brigid said, "some kind of psychic projection could account for what we have been experiencing."

"Would we be able to shake 'em off so easily?" Kane asked. They were walking through the space apparently occupied by the ten-foot cone a moment before. It seemed to him the air temperature dropped perceptibly, and a dank smell came to his nostrils.

He shook his head. Imagination, he told himself. Better clamp down hard. If it gets out of control it'll finish off what that jump started....

"I cannot claim sufficient familiarity with psi phenomena to harbor any kind of opinion as to that," Brigid said.

"Could it be some kind of machine, tuned to mess with our brain waves?" Grant asked. "Mebbe it's run down...."

"Could be," said Kane. "I don't know any more about psychic stuff than Baptiste. Way less, if you want my guess. But what I do know—"

He paused to lean forward and flash his Nighthawk gingerly left and right along a crossing corridor. He saw no more than they had seen in every corridor they had traversed: the blank faces of sealed alloy doors, staring at one another across empty passages.

"—is that we need to find some kind of service elevators or stairwells. Maybe a central core. This level's big as all outdoors. If this place has a lot of levels, and we tramp all over all of them, when we come out the prairie'll be ass-deep in those damned things from South America."

"There's a cheerful thought," Grant said. "No matter how bad things get, Kane, you can always make them feel worse."

"It's a gift," he said. "What's this?"

The ceiling of the left-hand corridor, he had failed to noticed before, was crusted with what appeared to be black coconut-sized nodes. As his light beam brushed one of these, it slowly extended batlike wings, then dropped from the ceiling to flutter in his direction. As it did, those around it stirred and began to do likewise, as if disturbed by its activity.

Each, Kane saw, indeed resembled a largish bat in size and proportion. But instead of a head, each possessed another miniature baronial-class hybrid's face staring in all its inhuman perfection from the center of its torso.

"Damn, now these things are just nasty," Kane said. "But I'm not even going to bother wishing them away. It's not like they can do anything—ow!"

The first flyer to awaken darted for his face. He felt impact on his left cheek and then a savage sting. As the headless baron-bat fluttered away, he slapped a hand to his face.

When he lowered it, the fingertips glistened with blood in the light of his flash.

The corridor filled with demonic laughter.

SIMÓN TURNED AWAY and puked. Larry Robison didn't feel so good himself.

"This is what remains of a man named Juanito," Consuelo said in tones so bitter they were alkaline. "Not that his name would matter to you, Simón—you have never thought the Shuara human enough to deserve names!"

"It is not that, Consuelo," he said, half offended and all pedantic. "It is that they resist necessary progress—"

"Enough," Hays said loudly. "I got no stomach for dialectics at the best of times. We have an emergency, here, people. So, save the world now. Debate politics later."

Both Consuelo and Simón turned to stare at him as if amazed he would even suggest such a thing. Robison cleared his throat discreetly.

"What happened to Juanito, Consuelo?"

She glanced down at the horrifically violated body, then hurriedly turned away. "He was out hunting in the woods with his brothers when he realized animals of every size were rushing past him in blind panic, as if fleeing fire. Yet they knew there was no fire—they would have smelled it on the wind. So they went to investigate what might be frightening the beasts."

"Pretty ballsy," Reichert murmured.

"It was no mere curiosity, nor yet *machismo,*" she said fiercely. "It was concern for others. They feared that whatever was scaring the animals might prove a threat to the people of the forest, the Atshuara. And they were right!

"Suddenly they came to an area where the vegetation had withered and died. Beyond that point they could see that what they knew had been forest—a dense stand of ancient trees—was gone, and in its place a profusion of all kinds of strange blue-colored plants they had never seen before. This scared them and they started to withdraw. Too late!

"*Monsters* poured out of the strange brush and swarmed over them. Juanito's brother Pablito was ripped screaming to shreds before the others' eyes, by creatures that slithered and hopped and flew."

She paused to draw a shuddering breath. Her eyes were turned downward. Her hair hung unbound, framing her porcelain-doll-fine face.

"A cloud of flying creatures enveloped Juanito. He screamed like a man afire. The eldest, Diego, was able to quickly strike flame into a handful of dry moss and use it as a torch to drive the monsters back, although he burned his hand terribly in the process. There was not enough fire to keep them off for long, and he was himself bitten and stung repeatedly, but he was able to get to Juanito and bear him away, still shrieking."

"So fire scares 'em, anyway," Reichert said. "That's good news."

"Fire scares everything," Weaver said. "We're not out of the woods yet." The younger man looked stung at having been corrected by the older man, although Weaver had spoken with nothing but his standard gruff good humor. Kid's still a hero-worshiper, Robison thought.

It might have amused his former fellow Delta operators that he felt that way about an old guy, and a life-long civilian to boot. But then, Larry reflected, they don't know Joe.

"When Diego came into camp," Consuelo went on, "stumbling from his burden and sobbing with fatigue, Juanito had subsided into a strange lethargy. His eyes were wide open—they were still intact then—but showed no response, even when a torch was held near to them.

"Diego gasped out the story. Then he went into convulsions. His limbs began to darken and swell. He vomited—dark and lumpy, as if he had swallowed much coagulated blood. His features seemed to blister, great blackish pustules that burst to ooze more blackened, clotted blood. Soon he died. But not soon enough."

"Hematotoxin," Reichert said.

"Say what?" Hays demanded.

"Blood agent. Hemolytic—busts red blood cells. Makes them explode. Like rattlesnake venom. Or certain war gases."

Hays looked at him a moment longer. Reichert had received the most intensive medic training of the group when he joined Special Forces, before he was tapped for the Combat Assistance Group. "Swell," the major said, and put his cigar back in his mouth.

"But he didn't show any of those symptoms," Robison said, gesturing to the present corpse. "Juanito, I mean."

"Ah, no," the woman said. "His fate was much worse."

Without a gun barrel up his snoot de la Sombra had gotten some of his swagger back. "Señor," he said to

Simón, "must we concern ourselves with what befalls these Jivaro animals? Although such tales are amusing to hear, they have nothing to do with us."

Consuelo's eyes blazed up like black fires. For a moment Robison feared she might launch herself at the one-eyed man's throat. He was still debating internally whether he'd try to stop her when Simón held up a long and elegant, but no longer near so languid, hand.

"No," he said. "Be patient, de la Sombra, my friend. Our friends from *el Norte* have reason—this does concern us."

He nodded to Consuelo. "I apologize for my man's outburst," he said. "Please proceed."

She looked at him a moment longer, hard, as if suspecting his civility more than his enmity. "Juanito lived the night and most of the rest of the day in that state. Like a coma, but with eyes wide open. Then in the late afternoon he began to scream."

She had to draw a deep breath before she could continue. Robison realized he was leaning forward on the balls of his feet with the intensity of his concentration on what she was saying. He sensed the others doing likewise.

"He began to thrash uncontrollably," Consuelo said, her voice soft to the edge of audibility. "Four men tried to hold him down. He threw them off. Six men tried, then eight. Our men are not large, as you know, but they are strong. And Juanito, as you can see, is no large man, either.

"Then we saw to our horror that his skin was bubbling. It was like watching water boil—bubbles growing, jostling one another.

"Then one burst, and a tiny winged thing crawled out. Like a wasp, but it had ears, and a muzzle like an animal. The size of my thumb, perhaps. Another emerged, then another.

"The men holding Juanito down jumped back in terror. He was no longer thrashing. Instead he emitted a terrible keening, rolling from side to side as if his agony was too great to allow him to move his limbs or even to scream.

"The little monsters emerged from all over him. One split his tongue—he bit the creature in two in his mindless contortion. Finally, one of our hunters had the presence of mind to shoot him in the temple and end his agony."

"What about the larvae, the little creatures?" Hays asked. "What happened to them?"

"They moved slowly at first. Their wings were wet with Juanito's blood and body fluids—they could not fly for a minute or two. We beat them with leafy branches from the brush. Some managed to take off. One of our women, remembering how we deal with wasps and bees, got a mostly green branch to burn. Its smoke seemed to stun the horrors. They dropped to the ground, where we crushed them with our sandaled feet and stones and clubs."

"There's news we can use," Hays said. "Smoke stuns them."

"When they're young, anyway," Robison said.

"It's something," Reichert said. His brown, dark-lashed eyes were huge. Given the nightmare the relative youngster had lived through in Mogadishu, when still an adolescent, the fact he still had the capacity to feel horror said something for his resilience, Robison thought.

Simón was nodding judiciously. Even de la Sombra looked green around the gills at Consuelo's account; he seemed deflated.

"A fascinating story," the Liberator said, "and a most sobering one. Which proves beyond doubt the need for a strong hand in dealing with this crisis."

He looked at the others and straightened. "Now, my friends, I am afraid the time is up for you. I was not so ingenuous as our *yanqui* friends presumed. My men have even now surrounded this grove. You now have a choice—surrender or die, *all* of you."

Chapter 17

Kane was not so overwhelmed with pain and surprise that he neglected to hold his Copperhead up one-handed and pump a burst into the bat-winged thing with a baron's face. It blew out like a balloon full of ink.

The corridor filled with flapping wings from waist height up, all driving furiously for Kane's face. One bounced right off the visor of his helmet. Its eyes stared into his, wide and placid. Then it opened its fanged mouth and added its squeaky voice to the cacophony of mad laughter, which Kane now realized was mostly in his mind.

Thunder enveloped Kane as Grant practically laid the muzzles of his blasters to either side of Kane's helmet and triggered bursts into the seething mass of flying things. Yellow muzzle-flash lightning seemed to wash out Kane's vision from both sides. Had he been relying on the helmet's low-light vision capabilities they might have overloaded, and at the least would have blanked most of his field of view filtering out the flashes. Had he not had on the visored helmet, the flames and fragments of unburned propellant, hot drops of lubricant and tiny bits of metal shaved from the bullet jackets ejected at high speed from the weapons' muzzles would have endangered his eyes.

The bullet sprays tore into the swirling cloud of bat-horrors like scythes. Yet even as a dozen or more of the small monsters were ripped to pieces, the laughter continued in Kane's head, undiminished by the gunfire roar.

"Enough!" he shouted. He couldn't hear his own voice. But Grant heard him somehow, or else sensed it was time to let Kane beat a strategic withdrawal. The storm of light and noise and high-speed metal cut off. Kane sensed Grant moving back and to the side to clear his retreat.

Hurriedly he took advantage of it. He fired a last tri-burst from the Sin Eater now in his gloved right fist as he jumped back around into the corridor down which they'd approached the T-junction. A flapping monster followed, fluttering wildly and erratically on a broken wing. He smashed it against the vanadium wall with the back of his armored fist. It squeaked piteously as it burst in a spurt of dark juices.

The laughter within Kane's head ended. The chittering and shrill laughter of the flying creatures pursued him.

"Baptiste!" Kane bellowed. "Get back! These things'll rip you apart like a school of airborne piranhas if they get at you!"

"Piranhas actually pose small threat to humans," she said primly, but she backed off quickly.

"Two hundred years ago they didn't," Grant muttered. He was digging in his belt pouch. "Who knows what they're like now? Mebbe they fly, too."

He held up a huge fist. "Suck a deep breath down, hold it and jump back," he commanded.

The mental laughter had cut off when Kane pulled back out of the corridor. Now it began again, more wild and unhinged than before, yet slightly musical, and he realized with a start that it sounded like the amplified laughter of a child. As if they had paused to rally, the flying creatures came swarming around the corner in a rush, a floor-to-ceiling wave of black wings and staring pallid faces.

Grant flung his right hand out before him. A half-dozen big plastic marbles bounced on the synthetic black runner on the floor in front of the advancing swarm.

Nothing visibly happened. Grant pulsed out three quick tribursts, left to right across himself, deliberately aiming the first and last so that the steel-jacketed bullets sparked off the vanadium-steel walls and ricocheted with damned-soul moaning through the swarm, in case the creatures were able to respond to his movements to stay out of his line of fire. The tumbling ricochets followed erratic courses, utterly unpredictable as they ripped like miniature circular saws through the winged mass.

It was enough to cause the swarm's forward motion to tumble into a chaos of random swoops and dartings as the creatures bashed into one another in their frantic attempts to escape the gunfire. Kane added a couple of bursts from his own Sin Eater for good measure. It's pissing in the ocean, he thought grimly. There's still a good hundred of the fuckers.

But the little monsters had begun acting very strangely. Some of them began to flutter about, aimless as butterflies on a summer afternoon. Others smashed themselves repeatedly against walls, ceiling, even the floor. Still others fell on one another, rending with the long sharp fangs in their slightly muzzled faces and their sharp outsized talons.

"What was that?" Kane demanded, holding his Sin Eater up but withholding fire for the moment.

"Luci gas microgrens," Grant said with satisfaction. "Figured with their hyper metabolisms, the stuff'd work triple quick on the little bastards."

"Ace," Kane said approvingly. "How persistent is this stuff, anyway?"

"It retains potency for less than a minute after being exposed to oxygen," Brigid said. "The effects last far longer, half an hour or more, depending on concentration and individual susceptibility."

"Right," Kane said. "I knew that." He had little experience with hallucinogenic gas, but the characteristics made sense if it was intended to be used to disorient subjects so that they could be safely overwhelmed with a quick rush. Gas masks were fine, but why let the stuff hang around once it had done its job?

He waited a minute and a half by his wrist-chron and moved forward gingerly into the roil of tumbling, squalling shapes. He swatted one or two down with his hand, thought better of it, reversed the Copperhead and swung it like a baseball bat, knocking the already delirious bat creatures senseless to the floor.

"We'll police up after you, Kane," Grant said. "Just make sure you beat 'em all down before they snap out of it."

The mental laughter had ceased again. Kane had an impression of sullen disappointment.

"Whatever was guiding those things," Brigid said, "appears now to be sulking." She had accompanied Grant and was helping him stamp the fallen creatures to death with the ragged Roamer boots she wore as part of her disguise.

"You felt it, too?" Kane asked, glancing back at her.

"We all did, Kane," Grant said. "Careful there—"

Kane ducked back as one of the bat things, quicker to recover or more resistant to the drugged gas, swooped to his face. He chopped sideways with his reversed assault rifle. The creature broke with a squeak and fell twitching to the floor.

"What *are* those things?" Grant demanded in disgust, as he gave an extravicious heel grind to the last.

"Is there any question?" Baptiste asked. "They're biofacts. Constructs."

"Why did the Totality Concept create them?" Grant asked. Brigid shook her head.

Kane peered cautiously around the corner. His light enhancers showed no further signs of life; neither did passive IR reveal any characteristic blobs of active exothermic metabolism, just smears of dull glow fading on the walls and floor as the bat creatures' shared blood cooled toward ambience.

"That's a lick on me," he said, drawing back. "Should've used infrared sooner—that'd help sort out the difference between hallucinations and real threats."

He gestured down the corridor. "Let's go."

Brigid stood her ground. "What's the matter, here, Baptiste? As you yourself keep reminding us, we're on the clock here."

"Indeed," she said, nodding didactically. "And that means we cannot afford to wander at random."

"We don't have the information to do anything *but*," Grant said.

Kane held up a finger. "Mebbe we do."

"Explain," Grant said.

Kane gestured at the tiny ruptured and broken carcasses. "This is the first solid opposition we've run into inside this hellhole. Now, mebbe these things all nested down here by accident—"

"Droppings cover the floor," Brigid said, running her own flash down the corridor to reveal dark smears and shapeless mounds. "They have nested here for quite a while."

Kane shrugged. "No difference. Mebbe they like nuances of the scenery only bats—can see. The point is, they're either here for reasons of their own—in effect at random, because they gotta be somewhere, philosophically speaking—or they're here for a purpose."

"As in to guard," Grant said.

"Bull's-eye. I grant it's almost invisible, but it's the only intel we got. You got anything better to offer, Baptiste? Because I know my idea sucks, and, believe it, I'm dying to hear a better one."

"You are correct. We must act in a virtual informational vacuum, so we can't afford to ignore anything that might be a clue. Lead on—"

She went rigid and flung out an arm to point over Kane's right shoulder. "There, Kane! My God—*a little girl!*"

DELIBERATELY Major Mike Hays took out a lighter and puffed his stogie butt to cherry life. Simón's eyes bulged out of his long sallow face.

"We got a third option," the team leader said easily. His two mates ostentatiously pointed their long arms at the heads of de la Sombra and Simón.

Major Mike raised his left hand and shot the Liberator the bird.

Simón stiffened. "If you think to take us hostage, dismiss it from your mind, gringo," he said briskly. "My men will storm the hilltop regardless. Either de la Sombra and I survive, or we will give our lives for the *struggle,* as we vowed to do long since. In either case, your best course is to pray they do not take you alive!"

"You don't get it, do you, asshole?" Hays said, grinning hugely beneath his silver mustache. His blue eyes were big bright lamps of evil mirth. "Nobody's surrounding this fucking hill. Except three of your troopies sporting a third eye each, courtesy of Joe Weaver."

"But I heard no shooting—"

"The DeLisle carbine in action," Reichert murmured blissfully. "Silent but deadly."

"The rest ran off when they saw their buds go down," Hays said, and emitted a blue gout of smoke. "Saved their lives. Never saw such a bunch of clubfooted retards in the bush in my life. And that's saying something."

Simón's face had gone a shade of white that all but rivaled Domi's. "If you're bluffing—"

Domi laughed delightedly. "Don't you get it yet? Or are you too fused out to see these boys don't have to bluff?"

"My people will take this arrogant *criollo* and his pet torturer off your hands," Consuelo said grimly. "We know how to deal with their kind. Many are the debts we owe them. The Shuara are not by nature cruel, but—"

"Jesus Christ!" Reichert burst out. "Don't any of you people get it? What is the air like on your planet?"

He turned, and as he did so the muzzle of his AK-108 swung to cover Consuelo and her men. They went ashen under their leather complexions. Unlike most people in the postskydark world—as well as the world before the big nuke, for that matter—most explicitly including Simón's and Consuelo's blastermen, Team Phoenix paid scrupulous attention to where their blasters were pointing. Their own loose gun-handling ways notwithstanding, the tribesmen knew a threat when they saw it.

"Listen up, and listen close," Reichert said, looking fierce. "We got a global emergency here. So here is the plan—you are going to put your differences aside and join each other and us to fight this thing. If when the smoke clears, you want to leap all back at each other's throat, that's no skin off our ass. But if you think you are going to keep playing out your petty rivalries while the survival of all humanity is at stake here, you are putting yourself in our way. And if you do, we'll blow you down—" he snapped fingers before his now-stern young face "—like *that*. Like you were a tree in our road. *¿Comprenden ustedes?* Or is anybody all eager to start putting theories of the afterlife to the test?"

Consuelo and her four *compadres* stared at Simón and his chief lackey. Then she sighed, and the tension visibly flowed out of her shoulders and lovely face.

"They have reason," she said. "If we do not put our petty differences aside, these *monsters* will settle them for us. I can pledge only my own wholehearted cooperation, but that I do pledge, and I will undertake to persuade my people to agree."

She looked down at the violated body of Juanito, screaming with a hundred silent mouths between the two hostile camps. It cost her visible effort to do so. "They already realize we have no choice."

Larry Robison and Major Mike looked to Simón;

Sean Reichert was still covering the Shuara contingent, just in case some of the possible lack of unanimity Consuelo adverted to set in suddenly.

The Liberator bowed. "The force of our friends' arguments surpasses even that of their firepower," he said through a most genuine-appearing smile. "A gentleman of reason can but agree, and pledge his cooperation. And, unlike our lovely associate, I can pledge the agreement of my men, indeed the agreement and wholehearted support of the Republic of Marañón."

Reichert growled at the continued backbiting. The major waved him off.

"One more thing," Hays said, and there was no humor in his voice or eyes. "Right here, right now, we're all going to swear to work together on this. I don't care how—swear on God, or Marx or the people or the ancestors or whatever higher power you believe in. But I suggest you also swear on your *own asses,* because if you try to go back on this, that's what it costs you."

Chapter 18

If it wasn't ecstasy the thin, beautiful biophysicist was moaning in as Gilgamesh Bates, pumping into her from behind on the burgundy satin sheets of his immense waterbed of command, she was doing a good job of faking it.

Never overburdened with body fat, the woman who answered to no name but Ishtar had lost a substantial amount of weight in the past few months. Now she was almost emaciated, the prominence of hips and ribs and joints putting Bates unpleasantly in mind of anorexics from their own lost time.

However, although smaller than before, her breasts, tipped with aureoles of a pink so deep and intense as almost to be purple—now peaked and rigid with passion— were still distinctive and pleasingly shaped when Gil Bates let his big spidery hands ride up inside the bloodred baby-doll nightie he had insisted she wear tonight. And perhaps because of her fanatical, almost penitential, devotion to working out in the hidden fortress's exercise rooms, especially riding the stationary bicycle, her ass was deliciously round with muscle despite the dearth of adipose.

As his excitement increased, so did the pace of his strokes. So did the red-haired woman's; her motions grew more frenzied with each stroke. He reached over her hip, around and down to feel her slick warmth.

He didn't try to stimulate her in any way with his hand, but just kept it there, exulting in the feel of her excitement as he fucked her harder. She began to groan and drive backward, using her hands to impale herself more deeply on his rigid cock.

The door to the bedroom whispered open. A giant figure, clad in dark blue-gray tunic, gray trousers and high black boots came in.

"Master," the giant Enkidu said. "You summoned me—"

He stopped, eyes bulging at the spectacle on the bed.

Both participants ignored him. Enkidu stammered an apology and turned to go. Bates looked up at him.

"No," he said. "Wait."

The huge man's bootleather complexion went redder and darker. He stood by the door, shifting his great hands from the sides of his thighs to the front, crossing and uncrossing his arms, as if he didn't know what to do with them.

The microbiologist screamed aloud as Bates grabbed her rump with both hands and drove himself as deeply into her as he could. As he exploded in orgasm, she went wild, thrashing, moaning, then giving voice to a series of brief explosive yips as she came, as well.

For a time they lay like that, exhausted. He fondled

her ass idly, not as a gesture of affection—which she would have rejected—but for the pleasure of touching her pale, almost blue-white skin, which was very satiny.

The giant cleared his throat.

Bates favored his chief bodyguard with a lazy grin. The billionaire, who fancied himself an infallible judge of human character, understood that Enkidu felt what he was being subjected to was violation. It added to his enjoyment—his sense of power.

Which was his greatest delight, what he lived for.

An outsider might have suspected Bates was playing with fire: humiliating his own personal sec boss, a man of superhuman stature and strength to match, and a former professional assassin into the bargain. But Bates knew his man, so he was convinced. Enkidu was cursed with a sense of honor—and of guilt. These weaknesses Bates knew to perfection how to use against him, and insure he was thereby controlled.

Bates pulled himself to a seated position against a pile of pillows at the head of the bed. He tossed the maroon top sheet over the lower part of him, not to spare Enkidu's sensibilities, but because the draft of the ventilation system was beginning to cause his sweat-dampened extremities to chill.

He reached for a controller beside the bed and clicked it. The wall opposite changed from a view of dense triple-canopy rain forest into a satellite eye view of the upper Amazon basin.

"I wanted all of us—myself, my chief scientist, my chief strategist—to review the situation. At this point it appears that the spread of the Successor ecosystem is living up to dear Ishtar's projections."

She snuggled up against him. Her red nightie was still up around her gaunt ribs.

On the screen the infestation was perceptible as a roughly oval blotch of a somewhat different shade— bluer and darker than surrounding vegetation. Bates pressed more buttons, and a scale appeared. The bio-invasion was already fifty miles by about sixty at its greatest extent. It was beginning to encroach upon the upper reaches of what would become the Amazon.

Bates clicked again. Thermal satellite imaging appeared. The invading life-forms stood out in bright relief. They had higher metabolic rates than the forms they were supplanting, so radiated more heat.

"Our biofacts are now advancing at a pace of five miles a day. This means that the ecosystem in the area first colonized has stabilized, and begun sending new soldier and messenger forms forth to join those spawned within areas most recently overtaken. For a time we can expect that rate to remain constant—which will, however, indicate ever increasing activity, since of course the total area subjected each day will increase."

Enkidu's big square face was grim. "What does this mean, Gilgamesh?"

Bates laughed and pressed more buttons. The brighter area began to expand quickly as the computer added projected growth to the display. In a short time the whole upper Amazon was glowing the yellow-white of the infestation. Then the whole of the basin; the plague crossed the Andes and began to march both north and south along the Pacific. The image widened to show the relentless march of the infestation, until all South America glowed with it, and the lethal brightness began to creep up Central America toward the north.

"In due time Ishtar will release long-range messenger forms to spread the joy to other continents," Bates remarked. The biologist practically purred beside him.

"Five miles a day is not so fast," Enkidu said, sounding half relieved.

"Even so, enough to encompass all of the South American landmass within a few short years," Bates said. "But the process is projected, indeed designed, to speed up after a conquest zone of a certain size has stabilized into the Successor environment. We can expect to see the continent subjugated within two years, the world within five."

The security chief had gone ashen. "More to the point," Bates said, "we will within a matter of weeks reach a point of no return, at which time the Successor ecosystem will have proved itself capable of overcoming all natural resistance, and after which no power on Earth will be able to stop it. Except, of course, us."

"And we won't do that, will we?" Ishtar asked low in her throat, half sulky, half thrilled.

Bates tipped his head to the side. "Not unless we receive what we want."

"What *I* want," Ishtar said, "is to see the last of humankind destroyed. Only you and I, my love, so that we may die together, knowing we have carried out Gaia's will."

"Yes, of course," Bates said, raising a forefinger out of the woman's view to forestall an objection from Enkidu, who had clouded up with outrage again.

"Nothing can stop my darlings now," the woman said blissfully.

"Perhaps," Enkidu said bluntly.

Bates raised an eyebrow at him. "What? What the hell does that mean?"

"Our contacts in the outside world indicate that certain elements of the population along the Marañón have begun to join together and organize a resistance to the spread of your hellish plague."

He made no effort to keep a note of triumph from his voice. He had insisted upon employing human agents on the ground outside Bates's hidden fortress despite his employer's objections. He also insisted there was a security risk implicit in moving operators in and out of the facility to make contact with the agents on the ground. The spies *could* communicate by radio, but they needed to be recruited in person, and required a certain amount of maintenance—usually a euphemism for *payment*—in gold, meds and weapons, the common currencies of the day.

The risk was real enough, Enkidu agreed. And there was likewise risk in deploying the aircraft Bates used to augment his overhead surveillance by satellite. Even communication with the satellites Bates used to spy on the world, not just the immediate environs of his base, made the secret facility subject to detection. Bates used milliamp maser microbursts to control and receive information from his spy sats, intrinsically very difficult to detect. But not, as Enkidu liked to point out, impossible.

But neither satellites nor overflights had told Gilgamesh Bates what his spymaster just had. Nor could they.

Let the bastard gloat, Bates thought, tight behind the smile of his mouth. I'll just get the pleasure of reminding him who holds the whip hand, sometime soon at my leisure.

Then he thought more on *what* Enkidu had just told him. And he laughed aloud.

"Let them try!" he crowed. "Blowpipes, bullets, bulldozers if they have them! What can they do to our gene-engineered minions?"

Ishtar favored Enkidu with a lazy lavender look, half-lidded and more smoky than would have pleased Bates had the mogul seen it. "My creations will defeat them, whatever they try."

"Perhaps," Enkidu said grimly. "But I refuse to underestimate either human ingenuity or human stubbornness."

KANE SPUN JUST IN TIME to see her: a child, no more than seven or eight, dressed in a black pinafore and black stockings, duck down a side passage at the corridor's far end with blond pigtails flying. At the same time he thought he heard a snatch of giggling.

"What the hell," Grant said, "would a little girl be doing in a hellhole like this?"

"Mebbe she's another illusion," Kane said. "I'll scope her with passive IR next time and we'll see."

"The facility might still be manned," Brigid said. "Possibly there exists a colony of descendants from the original personnel, who may or may not understand or be able to carry out any of the establishment's functions. But one thing is certain—we can't just let a little girl wander the corridors, now that we know there are physical dangers, as well as psychic ones."

"Not our job," Grant growled. "Lotta little girls'll die if we don't get this plague stopped. All of them, everywhere."

"Ah, but she's the only possible source of information we've run into," Kane reminded him, "unless you think we should've tried to keep one of those baron-bat things alive to question."

A shudder ran through Grant's huge frame. It was his only response. It was more than enough.

"Unless, of course," Kane said, "she's the one *responsible* for the hallucinations."

"Kane!" Brigid exclaimed, outraged. "She's a little girl."

As if in response another peal of girlish giggling came echoing down the corridors. It sounded not at all like the laughter that had filled their heads moments before.

"Yeah," Kane said. "Guess we'll just have to catch her and see."

Without looking to see if the others were following he headed off down the corridor.

Chapter 19

The wild pigs were surely not natural creatures themselves. Not originally, at any rate.

The pack alpha boar had to be two yards high at the peak of its back. The ruff of bristles appeared to be the only concession to hair except a tuft at the end of its tail. Its sides were armored in hide resembling that of a rhinoceros. Its face seemed to be plated with slabs of exposed bone, and the yellow curved tusks that jutted from it were the length of a big man's forearm. The boar's whistling squeals of rage as it fought suggested a stuck steam valve.

The sows, down to half a dozen or so in just a matter of heartbeats, were smaller, sleeker and less overtly armored. They were fast and strong, though. Between them and the boar they had racked up an impressive total of torn and trampled Invader dead in under a minute of being flushed from the brush.

"Whoa," Sean Reichert murmured as the big boar spun as if pivoting on a pole down its middle, like a merry-go-round animal. It hooked its big ugly head, and a land-borne creature that looked like a cross between a rabid fox and a black-and-yellow scorpion went flying, trailing green loops of guts through the air. A swarm of smaller Invaders with outsized heads began ripping the thrashing monster to pieces before it was even struck down six yards away.

"No such thing as sisterhood in this brave new world," Joe Weaver's voice remarked.

Lying up under cover of brush atop a low bluff across a stream from the drama, Reichert watched transfixed through his binoculars. It was a bad idea to get caught in the glass in Indian territory—even if the Indians were the good guys, as now. Anything at all could sneak up and put the bite on you.

Seeing the kind of things available to do the biting, he fervently hoped his two Shuara escorts didn't themselves get so caught up in spectating that they let the horrors catch them out. The invading bioforms hadn't crossed the stream yet as far as anybody knew—the salient or tentacle that had caught out the wild-pig pack was the Invaders' lead element in this area.

Reichert hoped that Weaver, his partner for the day trip, was getting some good telephoto shots with one of their digital cameras. The earthbound fox-scorpion beasts were new, although they seemed mainly to be a larger version of the flying-fox creatures with a couple extra pairs of legs in lieu of leathery wings.

The pigs were giving a hell of an account for themselves, he had to admit. They were fast, strong and mean, and while the females' tusks weren't as imposing as the male's, they knew how to use them. But they seemed to favor sharp hooves and bodyweight—Reichert ballparked them at between two and four hundred pounds each, with Big Daddy at least half a ton of muscle and malice—to kick their bigger foes and smash their smaller ones into orange-and-green jam.

But they were losing, and not slowly. The big foxscorpions had fully functional fanged jaws in their canid head as well as scythelike pincers on the ends of their forward pair of arthropod legs, which could, with a lucky shot, take a leg off one of the sows. They had fully functional stingers like their flying cousins. The littler creatures, with heads like bleached dog skulls twice too big for their furry six-legged bodies, tended to grab a faceful of any pig they got in reach of and hang on, bleeding and weakening their victim with jaws that stayed clamped even if the bodies they had been attached to were battered to pieces by a pig's frantic gyrations.

Though after the video they'd seen from the first Cerberus expedition, and the instructive fate of Juanito, the Team Phoenix operations were well aware that although the Invaders seemed partial to large warmblooded hosts to sting their parasitic spawn into, they obviously weren't averse to just hacking down and devouring large mammals. But here the big boar's own armor prevented the jaws and claws of the monsters from inflicting any substantive injury, although its hide streamed with blood from various small gashes. But a flying fox had landed on the boar's back, gripping and stinging repeatedly with its almost prehensile-seeming tail, until an especially shrill squeal indicated the toxin-bearing organic needle had gone home.

The winged monster's triumph was short-lived, as was the creature itself. The boar launched its giant bulk in a half backflip, landing on its back with its full weight on top of its tormentor. The flying fox-thing burst like a bag of well-rotted hamburger.

But it had won. When the boar rolled over onto its belly and tried to rise, its hind legs didn't cooperate. It raised its barrel chest off the ground, grunting and snarling defiance. But the boar's hindquarters dragged uselessly as the paralytic venom took effect.

The other horrors instantly backed off. The sows were all dead and being devoured, so lustily Reichert could hear the crunching and rending from three hundred yards away. The wind was blowing from the scene of the action into the humans' faces, thus helping them stay hidden by keeping their scent away from the Invaders. Scuttling fox-scorpions surrounded the boar, menacing it with their pincers and shrill barks that were almost canine. Something about the tone put the hairs on the back of Reichert's neck on end even in a way the brutality of the scene did not.

"I bet the other monsters can smell the fact that the big boar's been stung," Joe Weaver's voice said in Reichert's skull. Weaver had his own hide somewhere within fifty yards of Reichert, likewise surveilling this stretch of stream. "They're leaving him alive for a host."

Even as he spoke, several flying-fox bioforms came flapping from the overcast sky, skimming the tops of a grove of trees already stripped of leaves and bark by herbivorous Invader forms and beginning to show the blue-green scales of early-stage colonizing organisms rising from their bases. These descended on the boar, hovering just above it, jabbing with their stingers. The boar spun as best it could with only its forelegs, but had all its limbs been functional it would have been overmatched by the multiple aerial assault. The boar's breathing became labored and punctuated by shrill screams as a series of stingers sank home to pump in more paralytic poison and withdraw.

The boar's orbiting had its great bony face turned right toward Reichert, who felt a strange urge to look away so he wouldn't have to meet the doomed beast's eyes.... An ax-blow report of a powerful rifle cracked off from somewhere to Reichert's left.

A beat, and then Reichert thought he saw dust puff from between the boar's small pig eyes. The creature's anguished squeals cut off midbreath, and it fell onto its side with no more than a twitch.

"Whoa," Reichert said again. He thought he did a creditable impression, even though to his mind Keanu would always be more Ted than Neo. "Great shot, Joe."

"Just a little intragenotype courtesy," Weaver said.

Analysis of dead Invaders had demonstrated that although they resembled unearthly composites of various earthly organisms, in fact they shared no common genes with any terrestrial organism whatever. It had ignited quite the debate between those who thought they were made by Terrans and those who wondered if they were the product of some sort of truly alien attempt at seeding the planet with new life-forms via comets or meteorites.

"Time to tell our friends that if we're going to try this experiment, we'd better get on it right now," Weaver said. "The bad things will come across the creek to play with us in a very few minutes now."

Reichert swallowed hard before replying, "Roger that." He was more than brave—one thing Bates had made clear from the outset, two centuries and six-billion-odd lifetimes ago, was that to make the cut for his proposed team of supersoldiers-cum-nation-builders, you had to have proved possession of Jupiter-size balls of chilled titanium beyond even a shadow of doubt. That made it easier for the ex-military members to overcome their prejudice against civilians playing commando and accept Weaver, among other things. Reichert had been through Hell more than once, eyes open and fighting every step—even if he still had nightmares, as well as physical scars to show for it. But *these* things made being captured alive by Somali warlords or Afghan hillmen look like a party. Being a living hatchery for baby monsters—he shivered.

He used a handset walkie-talkie to call the contingent of Simón's men hidden a few hundred yards upstream to his right. The Liberation Army possessed few radios; Lakesh had with ill grace opened the Cerberus armory to the extent of setting up at least a small commo net for the anti-Invader resistance.

Somewhat to Reichert's surprise the Liberation Army squaddies answered right back, even using the correct call signs; he would have given even money they'd book as soon as he had left their sight. But not all Simón's troops were numb-nuts, even though those predominated. Any more than Simón, jerk and self-inflated buffoon balloon that he was, was a total incompetent. And it had begun to sink in that they were fighting for little things like homes, families and their own personal asses here. This was an enemy that no amount of bribery, betrayal, or simple evasion could get around.

The Invaders, Reichert reflected while waiting for the Liberation Army soldiers to call back that they were ready, were like a cross between *The Terminator* and "Leiningen versus the Ants." Except they'd eat the Terminator for lunch—at least the organic, Arnie parts of him—and probably hoover up soldier ants for hors d'oeuvres. He personally would pay to see a grudge match between an ant swarm and the Invaders—especially since report had it that soldier ants now grew to palm size some places not very far away. Not that there was any question of the final outcome. But he had a hankering to see some of the Invaders get eaten alive for a change, rather than doing all the munching themselves.

"How's it coming?" Weaver's voice said in his skull, his voice calm. "Our little animal friends are getting mighty close."

So they were. Reichert's handset squawked for attention. He almost fumbled it getting it to his ear.

"We are ready, Señor Rico," the Liberation Army team radioed. The ex-Ranger and Delta operator had picked that as his call sign for use with the indigs: "rico" as in *rico suave,* and also Johnny Rico, the bug-fighting young Filipino in Heinlein's classic novel *Starship Troopers,* not to mention the movie made out of it, which Reichert secretly loved even as he knew how wretched it was.

"Make it so," he said. "Rock'n'roll."

He looked keenly at the stream through his glasses. The horrors were right on the bank. Was that a faint pearlescent sheen on the gently undulating surface of the water?

A wall of orange flame erupted from the water, a good four yards high. Over the sudden surf-roar of the fire rose a chorus of screams of fear, fury and pain.

"WHAT'S THE MATTER with you adults?" the little girl taunted from the head of the stairs. "Are you all out of shape? Can't catch Mary, nyah, nyah!"

It was their fourth flight of stairs in half an hour, with long maze runs in between, and not a break in sight. The little girl had a sprinter's legs and a marathoner's wind. Even Grant's tongue was hanging out.

"Can't I just wing her," he wheezed. "Please?"

Brigid glared. "I'm surprised you'd even joke about such a thing, Grant! She's a little girl!"

Grant matched Brigid glare for glare. "Who said I was joking?"

Kane extended a hand, palm up, to indicate benign intent. "Please, Mary," he said. "Won't you just talk to us? Answer a few questions."

She frowned, as if he were a bit dim. "It's a game, silly," she said. "I only talk to you if you win."

"And to win we've got to—"

"Catch me!" She spun and vanished out the door of the landing overhead.

Kane sighed. "I'm with Grant," he said. "Next time she shows I'm busting one—"

"Kane!"

He shut it. He had been kidding. Mostly. He knew that no matter how great the urgency of the situation, or the stakes, if he deliberately injured the child he risked permanent rupture with Baptiste. And somehow he couldn't face that.

Wearily he started up the stairs.

He thought he heard Grant's joints creak as the big man goaded himself into motion by sheer force of will. They were all running on empty here.

"How can this little girl keep outrunning us?" Grant demanded, straining up the stairs in Kane's wake.

"She's carrying twenty pounds less body armor than you or I," Kane said, "and a lot less body weight than any of us."

"Are you saying I'm fat?" Brigid demanded.

"I'm saying she's a yard tall and skinny. How's that?"

"How do we know she's real?" Grant said.

"Because she has a heat signature in our visors," Kane reminded him. "Mirages don't."

"Still don't know how she keeps up this pace."

"Aside from youth?" Kane reached the top. Like the other landings they'd encountered in Abaddon, it was all but disturbingly normal. A metal platform with a metal door opening off it. He peered through the small window that was crisscrossed by metal mesh.

Another corridor. Dimly lit and blank. This time, though, there was something different: about ten yards along, a second doorway with rounded corners stood open. Beyond it the flooring changed to some kind of perforated metal plating. The walls were metal ridged and seemed to have unidentifiable mechanisms lining them.

"Now we may be getting somewhere," Kane said as his partners joined him. "Cover me."

As Grant braced himself to cover and Brigid, unarmored, took up position where she would be masked by the door itself, Kane opened the entryway and stepped inside with Copperhead presented. Nothing happened, any more than it had when they went through all the other doorways they'd been through in this damned hole in the ground.

Kane sidled forward, weapon ready. They had encountered neither hallucination nor actual monsters since the bats with barons' faces. He was far from lulled into complacency. His tautly wound senses heard the soft scrape of Grant's boots and Brigid's careful footfalls as loud as shouts.

A third door at the curious chamber's far end opened. Mary stepped back toward the trio and stood with hands clasped primly behind her back, watching them.

Kane pointed his Copperhead toward the ceiling. "Come on, Mary," he said, gesturing with his left hand. "Come talk to us."

Golden curls bobbing, she solemnly shook her head.

"You'll be more convincingly friendly if you put your visor up, Kane," Brigid said.

"Oh. Yeah." He did so, then knelt so as not to loom so threateningly. "Come on, honey. You know we're…not going to hurt you."

He had almost said, "If we wanted to kill you, we would've blasted you already." Once upon a time, he would have. He wasn't sure if it was progress, but it was change.

Brigid elbowed past Grant and moved past Kane to kneel. "Come here, please, Mary," she said, holding out empty hands. "My name is Brigid. I'd like to talk to you."

"Then come here," Mary said.

"Very well." The woman started to rise.

Kane stopped her with a hand on her shoulder. She turned a puzzled expression down on him. "What?"

"Not sure," he said. "Just—don't."

Brigid looked exasperated. But she straightened, shook back hair just beginning to show paler red roots. "You've led us on a long chase, Mary. It's your turn to come to us."

"Yeah," Kane said. "Have pity on us old folks."

Again the head shake. "Please," the little girl said. She did that little-girl thing, leaning slightly forward and dipping at the knees for emphasis. Kane had seen it happen in Outlands villes in which, while mostly squalid and poor, the people led more normal lives than the cloistered inhabitants of the Enclaves.

"I'm sorry, Mary," Brigid said, smiling and shaking her head. "It's your turn to come to us now. Show us we can trust you."

Suddenly the little girl stuck out her tongue. "Can't catch me!" She turned and bolted down the corridor.

"Damn!" Kane exclaimed. He ran after her. Brigid paced him, and he heard Grant pounding behind.

Several steps past the second door Brigid stopped dead on the perforated-plate floor. Kane moved to go past her. She flung out an arm to stop him.

"Kane," she said, "she's not real!"

Kane stared at her blankly. "What? Who?"

"Mary. She's another projection."

Mulishly Kane shook his head. "Can't be. She shows on infrare—"

Something grabbed his shoulder. He was yanked backward off balance. He saw Grant pivoting and driving with his legs as the big man hurled him bodily backward out the door they'd just entered through. As Kane sat down hard and went skidding backward on his slick-armored behind, Grant hurled Brigid after him. Then he plunged for the portal himself.

A door slammed across from the side, pinning him against the jamb.

Behind him the passageway filled with brilliant yellow flame.

Chapter 20

"They're coming!"

At the Atshuara cry, hastily repeated in Spanish and Spanish-flavored English along the west bank of the Río Pastaza, Larry Robison fought a reflex tightening of his shoulders as he stood in the fighting trench behind a sandbag rampart. Relaxed awareness, he reminded himself. Anyway, this is a piece of cake. You've done this a thousand times before.

Only he hadn't.

Never against an enemy like this: literally inhuman, capable of inflicting fates quite unimaginable to the most skilled or tradition-steeped of human torturers. His skin felt as if it seethed with a million creeping insects at just the thought. And the images that flashed behind his dark eyes—

Or maybe, he thought, it was just flashbacks from the previous night.

Of course, there was nothing like spending the night having visions of otherworldly beings to prepare you for a day fighting actual monsters.

He could see them across the river, seething along

the bank like an animated carpet. The Pastaza flowed perhaps forty yards wide here, a brown expanse stretching away to the right with trees crowding close on either side. The Marañón joined it a few hundred yards to the left of Robison's position, securing that flank. At dawn there had been flats over across the river, fifty yards wide and grown with thick silvery-green grass, and then a mud beach, to match some broad mud-bars in the stream itself. Now most of the grass and shrubbery had been consumed. Behind the Invader horde rustling and stirring a scrim of grass as they mowed down the last of it, the husks of the trees were scabbing over with blue-green infestations.

They don't like water, Robison told himself, for the minor but real reassurance it gave. The horrors had yet to cross the Marañón; widened to a hundred yards more after freeing itself from the confines of a series of knife-cut gorges not many klicks upstream, so far as scouts and satellites could tell. But no one doubted that the Invaders would find some way to cross a water barrier too big to wade across. Sooner rather than later.

Indeed, none of them doubted the horrors would find a way to cross any water barrier at all, in time. Such, as, say, the Pacific and Atlantic oceans. It was another reason to make a stand here. Mainly for what could be learned: nobody, even Simón at his most grandiose, believed the scratch forces could turn back the monsters with their current paltry knowledge and skimpier means.

But maybe we can hold, the ex-SEAL thought with grim satisfaction. Long enough to learn how to really fight the fuckers, at least.

"How's it hangin'?" came the familiar rasp of Major Mike's voice. The team leader was approaching along the trench from the north, with a couple of the crowd of Atshuara who had attached themselves to the team trotting right behind. The indigs seemed to think of themselves as bodyguards for their new brothers from *el Norte;* they believed, largely because Consuelo had told them, that the gringos were military specialists uniquely qualified to figure out the best means of fighting the menace that had already driven thousands of Shuara from their homes and devoured hundreds more—or worse.

Team Phoenix mostly used the self-appointed bodyguards as runners, since walkie-talkies still lay thin on the ground and the Shuara weren't keen on them anyway. Major Mike's current pair wore red face paint and feathered turbans, and clacking vests with overlapping shingles of thick bark hung from ropes over their shoulders: poor man's armor.

That was one of the lessons their scouting had taught, specifically the demise of the wild-pig pack witnessed by Reichert and Weaver: armor helped. As did water.

And so did fire. "Everything in place upstream?"

Hays nodded. He had his usual cigar stub stuck unlit in his mouth and his modified FN-MAG gripped by the rear pistol grip in his right hand, the rest of its weight being supported by a long sling around his neck. Robison felt a reflex twinge and thought of warning him about the risks of lip cancer. The next breath he almost laughed aloud at how absurd that was, and wondered what unearthed it.

"Affirmative," Hays said. "Got a barge upstream, well clear of any place the swarm's liable to be hitting the river. Today, anyway."

The two main contingents were split, for obvious reasons—like water and sodium. Shuara held the line to Robison's right. Makeshift camps packed with hundreds of their refugee kinfolk lay among the forested hills several klicks east. More poured across the river, well north of here, every hour, and more had escaped north back into the traditional Shuara lands of what had been northern Peru's and Ecuador's Oriente region in advance of the monster swarm. In all events the Invaders' main axis of advance seemed now to lie along the Marañón: right into the defenders' faces.

Reichert was up among the new blood brothers, keeping close to Consuelo. She seemed most comfortable around him out of all the team, and no one thought it was just because he was, and looked to be, the group's only Latino.

Weaver was perched in a tree with his big sniper's rifle several hundred yards closer to Marañón, amid the Liberation Army contingent. His official assignment was to pick off targets of opportunity, and especially to keep an eye open for anything resembling directors or officers among the invading mass. Nobody knew or had any reason to believe that some of the horrors weren't intelligent and in tactical command, as it were—although Robison shared the opinion of his teammates that, whatever their origin, the creatures exhibited standard swarm behavior.

Of course Weaver's real task, as much as anything, was to keep an eye on the Liberation Army. Hays didn't trust them and their painfully fragile bravado, and especially he did not trust their glib if charismatic commander, Simón. Having surveyed the northern half of the defensives, Hays was headed to his battle station in the southern sector, where he could stiffen the defenders' spines a little and hopefully keep Simón's mind right.

Hays's escorts suddenly began talking to one another in excited voices. At the same instant from the right came an eerie, wordless, drawn-out cry, instantly echoed off to the north. It was the Shuara war cry, spooky and sinister and enough to lift Robison's nape hairs even under the circumstances.

The guards pointed across the water wending its lazy way under the morning sun. The last of the grass was down. The Invaders stood revealed.

They streamed across the narrow mud beach. Hays had a radio handset to his ear and was barking orders to the barge crew upstream, having instructed Reichert to make sure they did what they were supposed to. Robison once again checked that he had a 20-gauge shell, brass and yellow plastic, locked up in the breech of his full-auto-capable Saiga. Major Mike's pals pointed their own shotguns, both single-shot break-open models.

The smaller life-forms, the hand-sized scourers with the dog-skull heads and smaller, more insectlike ones, as well, stopped and jittered nervously when they came to the water. The bigger ones, the scorpion-foxes, stopped and milled briefly.

Gunfire cracked out, mostly from Robison's left. Some of the Invaders fell or began thrashing in pain, quickly to be overrun and devoured by their fellow bioforms. Simón's men had longer-range weapons than the Indians, for the most part, and there was no reason not to start punishing the creatures at a distance. The defenders didn't have enough ammo to shoot all the bastards anyway, so being stingy with it didn't make much sense. Hays didn't want anybody dying with full mags.

Himself included. He was unlimbering his machine gun from its sling as he headed down the trench at a jogging trot, into the Liberation Army positions.

"Barge crew say they've got the barrels in the water," Reichert reported.

"Roger that," Hays called back, puffing slightly as he trotted. "Let's hope I didn't cut it too close."

Some of the scorpion-foxes, after orbiting in small circles for a few moments, plunged into the water and began to dog-paddle across the river. Bullets splashed among them. To Robison's left he saw bigger splashes shoot up like milk-chocolate geysers, followed heart-beats later by the ax-crack of grenade explosions. Machine guns began to rake the water and the mudflat, and small mortars began to crack off on the far shore.

The defenders cheered as little monsters and parts of the bigger ones were tossed in the air by explosions. Robison cheered with the rest. But he knew mere MGs and mortars were not going to turn this attack—not if they had ten times as many of them.

"Here comes the monster air force," Joe Weaver reported laconically.

What seemed a dark haze had appeared in the air over the far side of the Pastaza. It quickly resolved into dozens of flying objects. Then hundreds, each the size of a small-to-medium dog. Reichert's breath caught in his throat, although he didn't neglect to feel a moment's thankfulness to a deity more than half forgotten that the horrors hadn't manifested in truly insect-sized aerial forms. Yet.

Wasps were ever so much harder targets than flying foxes.

With a whir and crackling of wide leathery wings, the front of the alien-flesh tsunami swept over the river. Few of the flyers strayed below three yards: they didn't seem fonder of the water than their ground-bound comrades.

Now the Shuara shooters came into their own. As Consuelo had explained to them that first night, they never used poison blowgun darts against humans. There was little point in using the needlelike but very low-velocity projectiles against men *without* curare. Their traditional weapons of war were Third World bush favorites: the lance and the shotgun.

They had a mess of scatterguns, too; any warrior worth his salt carried one, as well as a razor-honed machete and a wood lance with a good iron head. Some of them were flintlocks, black-powder burners. But surprisingly few—despite vigorous embargo of Marañón river traffic by the republic downstream, fresh shells reached them in abundance.

Team armorer Joe Weaver had examined these with a professional eye and pronounced them recent manufacture: heavy paper, waxed to keep out moisture, set in formed brass bases and filled with black powder, wadding and lead shot, then crimped shut. They would have looked familiar to any shotgunner of the latter half of the nineteenth century. Someone—a lot of someones, by the markings and differing details of the shells—was cranking those bad boys out even now.

Robison lined up his sights on a snarling black-and-red-brown visage making a beeline toward him and fired. The face shattered amid a blossom with thin liquid petals as the whole firing line erupted with noise and smoke.

Most of the noise came from the left. Throwing what fire discipline they had to the wind, as Team Phoenix had known they would, even Simón's rifle-armed men were blazing away at the sting-tailed flyers.

As the swarm bore down upon him, Robison fired his 20-round drum mag dry in what seemed like seconds, clawing apart at least a dozen of the shrieking, fang-faced monstrosities. His subconscious ticked off the shots; he dropped the empty drum and was pulling another from an outsized pouch of his chest pack without his ever squeezing the trigger to be answered by resounding nothing.

Noise surrounded him: shotgun blasts, screams and squeals as the flying swarm arrived among the defenders. He slammed home the magazine and jacked the action. Just in time—wings filled his whole field of view. A creature had its fang-cornered mouth open, a red shout before his eyes, scarlet eyes wild with what seemed glee. His head filled with a strange stink, tinged with decay of earthly flesh, but mostly unlike anything he had every smelled before. A heavy segmented tail swung up and forward to drive a curved yellow stinger into his flesh.

He pulled the trigger three times. The horror burst like a blood piñata. Reeking gore spattered his forehead, nose and bearded cheek.

Right beside his left boot one Shuara lay sprawled gracelessly, staring up at the sky. Maybe he was dead, maybe just paralyzed—no time to check. Another clutched screaming at a flyer that had glommed onto the front of his skull, its wings buffeting the man's head and hands, battling his attempts to dislodge it. Its stinger clacked ineffectually against the wood-plank breast-plate hung from his neck.

Robison was preoccupied by more flying-fox-scorpion crosses homing in on him. As he fired into them, he saw a flicker and heard a squall of rage. Another Shuara had, with a machete, sliced a wing off the beast belaboring his partner. A second stroke split the thing's rib cage in two from the side. It fell. The rescued man dropped to his knees clutching a face streaming blood from the being's claws.

Robison was unsure how many of the creatures he killed, firing into a descending cloud as fast as the action would cycle. He could hardly have missed even without a scattergun. All he knew was, however many he destroyed, it wasn't close to enough.

The man at his side dropped hands from his bloody face, grabbed a spear thrust into the dirt beside him and hopped right up again to do battle. These Atshuara were the real deal, smart, tough and mean.

An impact staggered Robison, knocking off his ballistic-fabric boonie hat. The scorpion-tailed foxbats were light for their size, as any flyer would be—even alien ones, unless they were powered by miniature fusion batteries, instead of metabolisms. But they still weighed as much as a hefty chicken. He felt a secondary impact on the steel-and-ceramic trauma plate covering the middle of his torso as the creature that had just latched on to his arms and shotgun jabbed furiously for his vitals with its stinger.

He let go with his left hand and reached behind him. His hand closed around reassuring hardness, warm in the morning sun. A length of native hardwood a bit over a yard long and maybe an inch through came out of the mud where he'd stuck it vertically, in emulation of his Atshuara pals' spears.

The Shuara had laughed when their new best gringo buddies all solemnly possessed themselves of similar implements. How could a mere stick be taken seriously, next to a good machete or spear? But a humble instrument of that approximate size and shape was known to the Japanese as *hanjo* and to Americans as a good old-fashioned ax handle. In either case it was the most underestimated close-combat weapon on Earth, the length and heft of a good broadsword—and if the Japanese experience could be trusted, in some cases even deadlier.

Now Robison jabbed the winged thing in its furry and apparently soft gut, just as it snapped for his nose. Saliva struck his cheek right below his left eye; the skin tingled, he hoped in revulsion, rather than from venom. The gut poke forced the air from the monster and made it let go his shotgun. Before it could recover Robison had cocked the stick and whipped it down viciously, snapping the thing's wing and staving in a goodly number of ribs.

For a moment he was clear. Without looking, he put a booted heel on the broken creature flapping and thrashing against his shins and ground the rest of its life. Then he switched hands to give himself the best power and control over his staff.

All around him men were locked in frenzied battle

with small but horrifically dangerous monsters. He smashed the spine of a horror clinging to a man's back, then bashed in the face of one flying at him. A fox-scorpion reared up off the sandbag berm before him, dripping water, its rank fur smelling even worse wet. He blew it apart with the Saiga.

But that was the bad news: the swimming monsters had started to make it across despite being flailed with gunfire. The problem was the same as with the flyers: the things just didn't seem to have a *retreat* button anywhere.

"Mechanic," he called to Weaver, "we need to bring the fire—now!"

Chapter 21

"Grant!" Brigid screamed.

Grant groaned with effort as he tried to press open the door enough to free himself. But despite his enormous strength he couldn't keep it from tightening inexorably on his polycarbonate carapace. In a matter of moments it would fail and his rib cage would be crushed.

And even now a crematory blazed at his back.

Kane and Brigid ran to him. Brigid grabbed an arm and tried to pull him free. More familiar with hard-contact body armor, Kane began to fumble with the connectors that held his partner's breastplate and backpiece together.

It wasn't working. Sweat streamed from beneath Grant's visor, dripped from his broad chin to form droplets on the armpiece of Kane's black armor, which reflected highlights of yellow fire. Kane could feel the heat stream past his partner on his own exposed lower face. He made himself take shallow breaths, lest he draw in flame and chill himself on the spot.

Brigid shouldered him away. As big and strong as she was, and taken by surprise as he was, she did so easily. He slammed against the wall.

By the time he got out an outraged "Hey," Brigid's fingers, unencumbered with plastic armor, had undone the snaps on Grant's cuirass. Catching on belatedly, Kane unfastened the web belt cinched around Grant's cuirass. Then he helped her grab his partner and yank with one boot braced against the doorjamb.

Grant popped free of the armor. He, Kane and Brigid all went down in a heap. Behind him the door compressed the backplate, which was softening rapidly in the heat, as yellow tentacles of flame flicked over and above it. Shiny black drops of plastic fell from the armor piece, bursting into smoky blue flame before they hit the floor.

Grant rolled off Brigid, sat up. With a strangled sound he tore off the helmet and flung it away. The back of it had deformed and bleached in the heat, and was smoking. He began to rip at the fastenings of his thigh armor.

Kane pulled himself to a sitting position and checked Brigid. She was dazed from having all the breath exploded out of her by Grant landing on her, but seemed intact. A jape about finally having a man on top of her tickled the tip of Kane's tongue. He found the thought caused anger to spike through him, and chose not to go there, even for alleged humor.

She sat up and gave him a smoky green look. He had the hot-flash sense that she had seen his thoughts. But she didn't take it any further, either.

"I'm fine," she contented herself with saying.

"Grant?" Kane asked, turning to his partner.

"Water." Grant's utility belt had been ripped free and

lay huddled against a wall like a stunned snake. His pack was gone with his backplate.

Which had melted away, allowing the piston-driven steel door to slam closed. All that remained was a trickle of melted plastic, and that burned with a blue flame.

The door itself glowed cherry-red in the gloom.

The big man had gotten the rest of the armor suit off. The backpieces of his leg armor were still softened from the heat, to judge by the way they had slumped lying on the floor. Kane fetched a water bottle and handed it to his friend.

Grant uncapped it and poured a stream over his head and down his neck and back. The rough clothes he'd worn beneath the polycarbonate suit, part of his original Roamer disguise, were actually browned on the back in spots from the heat.

"How'd you know she was a fake?" Kane demanded, turning on Brigid. It came out almost an accusation. "She showed up on my passive IR."

"If she, or whatever causes the hallucinations, can cause our eyes to see normal-light images of them, why can't it make us imagine we see heat signatures in a visor, too?"

"Shit." Kane bounced an armored fist off a wall. "So you figured that out?"

"Just now," she said, gingerly picking herself up, as if still not quite sure all her parts would come with her.

"Then what—?"

"I don't know, Kane. I just had a sense we were

heading into danger. Deadly and immediate danger. It made me stop and concentrate, and that broke the spell."

"How about you, Grant?" Kane asked, turning. "You up to traveling?"

Grant stood upright now, rubbing the back of his neck. "Got less to carry now than I did."

Then he lowered and shook his head and muttered, "I am definitely getting too old for this shit."

"Where do we go, Kane?" Brigid demanded. Her eyes were bright and her cheeks glowed with spots of fever pink. "We're running low on time. Cut off from outside the way we are, we could already be too late."

"Can't say about that," Kane said. He raised his right forearm. His Sin Eater slammed into his fist. He popped the magazine to make sure it was fully stoked.

"But I do know where we're going." He slammed the mag home again.

"Your sixth sense?" Brigid asked, with apparent seriousness.

Kane shrugged and made the wep go away. "Mebbe. But I just figure it this way—she was leading us up. So the way we want to go is down."

A SURPRISING AMOUNT of trade plied the far-upper Amazon basin—surprising, anyway, to Team Phoenix, all of whose experience of a postnuke world had hitherto come in North America. South America had, as all four team members knew firsthand, been nowhere near as prosperous as the north, and its overall technology level had been lower. But parts, anyway, had sprung back quicker—without the Mags to hammer it down again.

Even this far, almost to the reach of the Marañón's navigability, little steam-powered stern-wheelers made semiregular visits. Like most of the Shuara's shotgun shells, these seemed to be strictly homegrown. They burned wood, turned water into steam in a boiler, drove a piston that in turn cranked the big stern wheel. It wasn't complicated, was certainly not rocket science.

In his classic *Life After Doomsday*—one of a tiny handful of nonfiction speculative works on nuclear holocaust and its aftermath that was actually worth reading—North American survivalist author Bruce Clayton had theorized that, even in the case of the most destructive possible war, human technology would fall to about the level of the American Civil War: black powder and steam. So Team Phoenix had been taught during its training, and so, on the basis of a better than merely good grasp of modern technology, its members believed.

There were various parties extracting petroleum from the earth in South America, too, and engaged in refining it at varying levels of efficiency and sophistication. There were no roads in the area, so that the only vehicles available were found almost exclusively in and around cities like the capital of the republic. There was plenty of river traffic, mostly in the form of dugout canoes, though some outboard motors were still in service. But with gasoline horribly expensive, albeit available, why use it when wood was plentiful and steam worked fine?

Nonetheless Team Phoenix had managed to acquire a few precious barrels of gasoline and kerosene. For once without complaint Simón had broken open his secret stores to provide for the defense, although Team Phoenix suspected he still held out on them. He had even, via courier, managed to wangle a few more barrels out of Marañón City, although Simón's uncle, President Rodrigo Vásquez, still seemed to suspect this was all some scam concocted by his nephew.

But there weren't enough petroleum distillates for serious use. Fortunately there was a lively local industry in extracting palm oil. It was laughably crude fuel, all told.

But it would burn.

And it would float.

So in the past few days the little stern-wheeler steam packets had delivered to the defenders several hundred casks of palm oil. At an arranged signal the crews on the barges upstream on the Pastaza had begun pouring opened casks into the current, as well as lustily busting them open and booting them overboard. They threw in a little of their precious gasoline and kerosene for good measure.

At Robison's cry, Reichert fired a flare into the river. A dragon belch of yellow flame rolled down the Pastaza.

Robison had momentarily gotten clear of flying horrors by slashing wildly with his stick. Now he saw fox-scorpions trotting toward him across the ten yards of exposed mud on this side of the river. He blasted them with his shotgun.

The tribal warriors around him were being overwhelmed by the flyers. Just in his peripheral vision he caught the impression that half the men in his field of view were down, paralyzed or dead. A fresh wave of flying monsters rushed at him, grinning and yelping triumphantly.

And the wave of orange flame washed over them.

A horrid cacophony of yipping shrieks arose as the monsters swimming the river burned. The monsters on the mudflat shrank away from the fire like dogs with tails between their legs. They seemed frightened and nonplussed to find a wall of flame behind them. Even the flying creatures seemed demoralized as some of their brethren came crashing wildly among them, smoking or trailing flames.

"Let's get them!" Robison roared. Seasoned Third World hand though he was, he shouted it in English, which not a man in earshot of him understood. But the meaning, accompanied by an overhead sweep of his stick, was universal. Cheering, the Shuara rallied.

The disorganized flyers still over the trench were blasted apart in midair by shotguns or knocked down with wooden staffs and beaten to death on the ground. Then men were leaping out of the trench to charge the scorpion-foxes dithering between them and the flames, which were lower now, but roaring enthusiastically.

Their lances outreached stinger-tipped tails; they quickly slaughtered the creatures on the mud.

Reloading again, Robison looked left and right. As far as he could see, men were doing the same thing: taking the fight to scattered monsters trapped on the east bank.

"That's it," a voice said in his skull. "They're pulling back from the west bank. The fire's stopped them."

"IT'S NOT POSSIBLE!" Ishtar screamed. "These savages cannot have stopped my children! It just is not possible."

A pair of security guards in their gray-blue tunics and gray trousers exchanged nervous looks at the shrieking display by the slight scientist, who was clad in blue jeans and a turquoise T-shirt beneath a green lab coat. Enkidu stood impassive with his hands clasped behind his massive back.

Ishtar was never one of our politically correct Green environmental enthusiasts, Bates reflected. As usual he wore one of his cream-colored jumpsuits. She thinks downtrodden indigenous people are cancer cells like all the rest.

"It is true," Enkidu said stolidly. "Our overflights have confirmed what my spies report. The local population has established defensive lines at the confluence of the Marañón and the Pastaza. There is even a shantytown of sorts that has sprung up around a little village recently abandoned because of the fighting between

Río Marañón and the Shuara tribes. It's called Esper-anza."

Bates laughed out loud, a sound as much akin to sneezing as to laughter. "'Hope.' Well, they've little of that."

Ishtar had dug her nails, which were none too long, into her own face so deeply that her left cheek bled un-noticed. Then again, she frequently did things that drew her own blood, as if by accident. "Do you mean to tell me," she screeched at Enkidu, doing a creditable im-pression, their employer thought, of one of the noted local howler monkeys, "that the soldiers have joined forces with the headhunters?"

Enkidu nodded. "Simón Romero's forces fought be-side the Shuara in successfully repelling your monsters."

"But they've been battling each other for possession of the region for years," Bates said. "How can they fight together now?"

Enkidu shrugged like a mountain losing a few climb-ers. "Romero is nephew of President Vásquez." The names and Spanish words gave him no problem; he spoke eleven languages well, including French, Ger-man, Russian and Urdu in addition to Spanish, and could get by in numerous others. "The self-appointed chieftain of the indigenous resistance is President Vásquez's ille-gitimate daughter. They were raised together—surely it isn't so surprising they might come to terms."

"But they hate each other!" Ishtar screamed, foam flying from her purplish lips.

"Survival makes odd bedfellows," Bates said with a shrug. "These are lying in our way. The question is, how do we remove them? And more immediately, how were they able to halt the irresistible advance of Ishtar's creations?"

"The defenders set the river on fire," Enkidu said. "They had also established excellent defensive positions, including machine guns with overlapping fields of fire—rather more professionalism than we've seen from either faction hitherto, Gilgamesh. They managed to inflict enough casualties on the monsters to invoke some degree of survival response in them. Now the beasts fear the river, and only mill on the shore. They've taken to eating one another for sustenance."

He was unable to restrain a broad grin as he imparted the last. Knowing what an enormous capacity for self-control the man possessed, Bates was surprised. It was possible Enkidu wasn't trying very hard.

"But they're not supposed to *have* a survival instinct!" Ishtar screeched. She followed it with a wordless soprano wail and began to beat herself in the face with clenched fists. "It's my fault! I failed! I tried to make them selfless, completely selfless! But the evil of selfishness appeared in them anyway!"

She dropped to her knees and commenced alternately belaboring herself and gouging at her face with her thumbs. Even Enkidu raised a brow in alarm. She appeared bent on doing herself serious hurt.

Bates strode toward her on his long thin legs. He

grabbed her hank of magenta hair, hauled her head back and slapped her with savage emphasis that left a squashed-spider imprint of his great hand on her cheek in red. She stopped howling and mauling herself and stared at him with eyes that had little human in them.

"Focus, Ishtar," he commanded. "You must tell me—can you defeat this unexpectedly strong resistance? Tell me you can, surely you must be able to. Tell me. Then you can punish yourself all you want. I may even exact some punishment of my own later."

She drew in a deep shuddery breath. Then her expression changed. She smiled—and Enkidu drew back in horror at the nature of that smile.

"Yes," she hissed. "I have other creatures they have yet to see." A wild peal of laughter ripped from her. "I was saving them for when my darlings got nearer to so-called civilization! But I'll use them now, yes, I will! And these savages will die screaming the way they deserve!"

And she laughed, a shrill vibrato that rose and rose and went on and on without her seemingly needing to draw breath. At last Bates looked up at Enkidu and nodded meaningfully.

The giant in turn gestured to his two sec men. They came forward. One drew a hypospray from a belt holster and pressed it to her neck. She subsided instantly, her final mad laugh trailing away into a hiss accompanied by a ropy strand of drool. Her head lolled to the side. The security men caught her.

"Take Dr. Ishtar to her office," Bates instructed. "She'll feel more…at ease there when she comes back to herself."

"If she can ever be said to come back to herself."

Bates shrugged. "The world's a big, bad place, Enkidu—to change it forever for the good, one must employ the means at hand, no matter how flawed."

He patted one of his sec chief's oak-limb forearms, as one might reassure a horse or dog. "That's why, reluctantly, I am forced to use such stringent methods as Ishtar's little nightmares-made-flesh. One cannot make an omelet without breaking eggs, after all."

Enkidu's eyes were half-lidded. Bates cocked his head suddenly to one side. "You've something else to say to me, don't you, you scamp? Out with it!"

Enkidu smiled grimly. "My spies also send me word that may explain the sudden upturn in the effectiveness of the local forces."

"Spill! Damn you, don't hold out on me, or I'll—"

"You know you have no need to threaten me, Gilgamesh," Enkidu said mildly in his fluid basement bass. "I was merely waiting to tell you until I had confirmation. This has just been obtained through monitoring the Liberation Army's radio traffic. Their communications discipline is deplorable. They have few radios, but they seem to try to make up the deficiency by sheer volume of chatter—"

"Out with it, damn you!"

"The resistance is being organized and led by your

own Team Phoenix. They appeared suddenly in the eastern fringes of Shuara territory less than two weeks ago. It would appear Dr. Lakesh jumped them from Cerberus redoubt in to deal with Ishtar's plague of demons."

It was Gilgamesh Bates's turn to put back his head and howl like a stuck steam whistle.

Chapter 22

A circus of horrors beset the trio from Cerberus as they made their way down into the depths of Abaddon redoubt.

Creatures sprang at them. Creatures twined up the metal railings of the endless stairway, leaping at them. Creatures flew at them, or dropped from the ceiling on them, or rushed out of doors on landings at them.

Brigid had schooled herself now to discriminate quickly between the real and the illusory. All it took was a brief concentration of will. She advised the two men as to which was which.

If it was an illusion, like the horde of rats that spilled down on them in a torrent from a landing above, not squeaking but laughing tiny maniacal laughter out of miniature baron faces, they ignored it and drove on.

If it was real, like the giant fleshy-lobed plant that suddenly burst open the door on a landing two levels below the landing they had arrived at and spit venom at them from a baron's face—so real it scored the front of Kane's armor, hissing, and stinking—they blasted it. Once or twice when she was slow making a call, or when a true physical threat approached from an unexpected quarter, Brigid shot it herself.

A pantherish creature dropped onto Kane's back from a turn of the endless stairway, slamming him into the railing. His carapace saved him from cracked ribs. Reflexes and balance saved him from toppling over as the beast squalled and kicked at his short ribs with powerful strokes of its massively muscled hind legs.

It was a big beast, at least one hundred pounds, greenish-black and glabrous, with a line of spines down its back. It had the same face as all the other nightmares. Its features, of Danaan-like perfection, were distorted by a savage snarl.

With one hand and a heave of his back muscles Grant tore the beast from his partner's back. With his own bellow of rage he flung it bodily against the far wall, then blasted it with his Sin Eater before it toppled into the depths.

Brigid helped Kane back to his feet. His only comment was a weary, wary shake of the head and a tip of a forefinger off his visor to Grant.

Not until they reached the bottom level—or at least the lower extremity of the stairway—did Brigid stop, frown in concentration and then say firmly, "She is here. It's not a projection this time," she warned.

"Makes sense," Kane said to Grant, leaning against the wall for something resembling a brief rest. "You have a deep dark secret, bury it deep."

He expected to have to blast through the door. It was

unlocked. At first glance the corridor looked innocuous: sealed doors to either side. Kane led off cautiously, Copperhead at the ready.

Twenty yards down, a metal door blocked the way. Kane paused with his back against it. Grant and Brigid stood watching him expectantly.

He reached back and turned the handle. Yanking the door open, he spun through.

A great voice belled in his head, "You have found me. I'm sorry."

Another large chamber opened out before him. Here illumination spilled from the ceiling, dim and greenish-yellow; he had no need to activate the infrared filters in his visors. It shone upon a matrix of squat steel vats. Some had metal covers. In others an unidentifiable liquid bubbled. It was slightly sheened with polychromatic reflections, as if oily.

"Why?" He almost jumped at Brigid's question from behind. The word pealed like a bell, and echoed off the high ceiling. "Why are you sorry, Mary?"

"You have to die because you found me." The voice had a distinct little-girl sound again. Or quality—it was all in the mind, Kane quickly realized.

"What's different about that?" Grant growled. "She's been trying to kill us for hours."

"Why, Mary?" Brigid asked.

"I won't say. If you go away now you'll be okay. I won't try to stop you."

"That's nice of you, Mary. But we can't do that."

Nothing.

With a gurgling sound something began climbing out of an open vat five yards to the left and about seven in. Kane spun that way, rifle raised. A mass of tentacles was emerging, writhing, shedding the oily-looking fluid.

He saw a small splash toss up a thin tendril of liquid from the uneasy surface. He heard a plop. Then the vat erupted, spewing a gout of murky liquid and unidentifiable organic-looking chunks ceilingward. It fell back with a splash, leaving a pool of fluid with bits of meat in it, half-submerged and flaccid.

Kane looked over his shoulder at Grant. His partner shrugged.

"We'd better move briskly," Kane said, "in case more of these things wake up."

As if in response a sealed vat clanged open. Then another and another, in an anvil chorus with a counterpoint of slogging splashes.

"Run?" Brigid suggested.

"Good idea." A clear aisle lay ahead of them. Kane raced down it. There must be hundreds of these damned vats in here, he thought. If they all give birth at once—

"Kane," Brigid called from behind him.

"Just run!" Grant yelled.

They did. Kane just pelted all-out for the door, trusting his peripheral vision to tell him if something horrific was making a play for him. Something did: dark tentacles and murky, unclean-looking translucent blobs reached for him from vats and reared up from the floors, which were now awash in mystery fluids. Transferring his Copperhead to his left hand and popping his Sin Eater into his right, he crossed his arms and began to fire full-auto to both sides simultaneously, placing his fire so that the bullet streams would pass above the presumably hard metal vats and not coming zinging back at him and his friends as ricochets.

"Stay close!" he shouted, not daring to look back.

"We are!" Brigid yelled back, almost in his ear. He heard microgrens cracking.

He hit the far door expecting to bounce. Instead the pressure bar opened it straightaway. He actually stumbled going through from meeting such nonresistance.

Grant and Brigid tumbled through after him. "What's back there?" Kane gasped. He shoved up his visor. His Sin Eater was holstered, his Copperhead hung by its sling, and he was bent over with hands on thighs sucking at air.

"Don't ask," Grant said. "Just shut the damned door and drive on."

"Roger that."

The new area was another corridor, though this time the doors featured frosted windows. Meager illumination drizzled down from overhead fixtures, yellow and dispiriting.

As they advanced, they were overcome by a sense of terror. Yet they had faced terror before. They kept walking.

The dark chamber was heavy with the smells of green growth and mildew and flesh and overlying all, the rich reek of organic decay. The smells of chemicals, nutrient and cleaning. The smells of metal, of walls and floors and mechanism. Also present were the odors of burned propellant and oxidized lubricants, of ruptured guts and blood, as creatures made to attack the trio, and died pierced or blown apart by microgrenades.

Fear assailed them. Dread rose around them up so thick it threatened to clog their throats, to transmute at any moment into shrieking panic that would never end short of madness or death.

Loneliness suffused them. A sense of emptiness worse than all their lives' nightmares of abandonment and desolation at once. It was as if each were doomed to spend an eternity in ultimate aloneness, without even the hope of contact with another human being.

As they walked on, small soft things scuttled toward them along the floor and even the walls. They squeaked from their tiny perfect faces as they died of bullet or boot or fist. In the end they fled and would approach no more.

They came to a sealed vault. "This is the place," Brigid said in hushed tones.

Kane and Grant stood flanking, weapons at the ready. Grant had stripped off his Roamer shirt and stood with his great wedge of chest encased in a black undershirt, soaked through with sweat beneath arms and over belly. He had torn a strip from his cast-off shirt to tie around his head to keep the sweat from his eyes. For though it was chilly in the depths of Abaddon, each of them streamed with sweat, of exertion and fear and passions in conflict that bent them this way and that—but never broke them.

From her perfect memory Brigid tapped out a sequence on the pad placed at shoulder height beside the great door. The door began to slide aside with a hiss of equalizing atmospheres as the gasket seal broke and a subtle creaking of a mechanism long disused.

The way was blocked. A living web had woven itself across the entryway within, as of pallid vines with blood for sap. The great veins wrapped around the tendrils pulsed both blue and red, as with blood both venous and arterial.

A hundred baron heads confronted them on stalks, each palm sized, each laughing and hissing with forked adder tongues lolling beneath fangs like curved needles. "Come to us!" they sang. "Come! Feel our kiss, and die!"

Their voices, though tiny, were like their faces: inhuman in their purity and beauty of tone.

So were their screams as they burned in the heat of Grant's incendiary microgrens. Then it was as if not blood flowed through their veins, but gasoline.

When the roar and billowing orange glow of the fire died away, sometime after the shrieks of anguish, and only withered, blackened stumps tipped in embers barred the way, Kane batted the way clear with his left gauntlet and the barrel of his Copperhead and stepped cautiously through.

Another door confronted him. It apparently opened into a cylindrical chamber five yards across, a few yards less than the circumference of the room that contained it. Armaglass windows to either side showed another chamber within that, whose walls were sheened with condensation. Even through his armor Kane could feel desperate chill from that next door cooling the sweat on his face and body.

A rustling to his left. He spun, Sin Eater slapping his hand, as a vast tubular shape as wide as the passage itself rushed upon him, a jaw as tooth-ringed as a great white's gaping wider than he was tall.

Before his stunned mind could react the great worm swallowed him whole. Blackness engulfed him.

Chapter 23

The short woman wrapped in the red dress sang words to Sean Reichert that he didn't understand. "She says, dance with me," said an Atshuara warrior who stood nearby swigging from a gourd of the native beer. Reichert had been told he didn't want to know how it was made, and believed it. In all events it was probably spiked with firewater, high-octane distilled liquor brought up the Marañón on a paddle-wheel steamer for the celebration.

Also, he suspected, in hopes of getting the pesky locals thoroughly habituated to drinks of far higher alcoholic content than they'd ever encountered before. A drunk Jivaro was a good Jivaro, the authorities downstream in Santa Caridad probably reckoned.

The shantytown that had sprung up behind the Pastaza defensive lines pulsed with celebration. Music creaked and tootled and pounded, from guitars and flutes and drums, some improvised—some in fact no more than handy posts or logs, clacked against with sticks. Torches flared from every hootch, threatening the flimsy board construction and especially the hastily thatched roofs. In between bonfires celebrants danced, while drunken Liberation Army soldiers stoked them ever higher and challenged one another to leap through them. One of their number, drunker than the rest, misjudged his trajectory badly and fell smack into a blaze. His body squashed the flames and sent them squirting out to the side, blue and yellow, and almost doused the fire. He was totally befuddled when his mates dragged him out with the seat of his camou trousers smoking.

Another soldier dropped a bottle from his lips and slung a clear scythe of its contents into the fire. The flames instantly flashed back up with a *whoomp*.

"Whoa," Reichert murmured to himself. "Glad Major Mike told us to lay off the sauce."

He hadn't told them not to succumb to some of the other temptations, though. The native woman danced nearer. She had a vivid yellow flower in her hair. She was tall even for an Atshuara woman, and light-skinned. She had a very pleasing face, oval with many laughter lines, and black eyes that shone. She also had nipples that aggressively pushed out the pliant material over them, he couldn't help noticing.

She danced her body close to his and then she smiled. Her teeth were dead black, so completely so that only the red gleam of firelight off a tooth or two showed that she was presenting him with anything but a rank of raw untenanted gums. It was the product of a local herb used, ironically, to prevent tooth decay.

Such hearts-and-mind training as he'd had came to

his rescue. Smiling all over his handsome young face he said, "Tell her I'd love to, but duty calls," in Spanish to the tribesman who had first translated her invitation for him. Without waiting for an answer he turned and strode away.

He had no particular destination in mind at the moment. The mushroom village Esperanza was surprisingly extensive, covering several hectares. It had numerous people to house: troops, laborers, the inevitable camp followers, although pursuant to the urgings of Mike Hays, Simón had tried to mitigate the latter's numbers. To Simón's credit, Reichert grudgingly allowed the Liberator may've actually had the idea himself. He was a strutting self-important sack of shit, in Team Phoenix's joint estimation, but he wasn't *just* a clown. He had some real ability, was razor-edged shrewd—and altogether unscrupulous.

The little makeshift ville also had to feature warehouses—even if they were only poles supporting light frameworks below interlaced palm-frond roofs—to hold stacks of supplies and *matériel*. Since the recent victory at the Pastaza, the demand for supplies for downriver had been great. Team Phoenix had driven its indigenous allies—and of course themselves—without mercy, improving their positions and defenses for the next Invader push everybody knew was coming. Men and women and even children had slaved at hacking back vegetation. A pair of bulldozers, lordly D-9 cats, had been hauled up the river on log rafts by the tireless little steamers and went blatting and farting to work knocking down trees and leveling a killzone for thirty yards back from the original line of resistance.

Felled trees were used for ramparts and breastworks and to shore up the new trenches. Fields of fire were mapped out and sites prepared for the machine guns of Simón's Liberation Army contingent. Mortars were emplaced and presighted. Landlines—God knew how old the wire was, but it seemed to work still—were run along the trenches for telephone communication among the defending forces, as well as back to the mortar pits and even to observation posts perched in trees.

Through it all there was no sign of activity from the enemy. The tall trees looming beyond the Pastaza's far bank, stripped of leaves and bark by various Invader bioforms, did take on encrustations of blue-green organisms—scale, mold, who knew what—and were then twined from the ground up by venous growths of Invader vegetation, which then put forth their own unnatural fronds to suck down the sun's rays. But of the monstrous animal forms whose swarms had been driven back, leaving thousands of corpses to bloat and rot and stink in the sun, there was no sign. They had drawn back from river's edge like a human army rendered cautious by defeat.

Team Phoenix was not deluded. The creatures would be back. It was all the harder, laboring in the heat and humidity of the river valley, knowing all the while that this was in the end futile. No matter what they did here, the Invader menace would find a way to overwhelm them in the end. Whether with some new horror that hadn't yet been inflicted on them, or overwhelming them by sheer biomass, the outcome would be the same—and equally inevitable.

Nonetheless there was a certain desperate edge to the gaiety in Esperanza tonight, the first Hays had allowed his team off from the frenetic drudgery of improving the defenses. People drank a little too hard, danced a little too wildly, laughed too shrilly and way too much. They *knew,* even if their anointed leader thought to kept the bad news from them, that they were all doomed, every soul, with merely agonizing but rapid death one of the sunnier alternatives that awaited them.

Watch it, *mijo,* Reichert told himself, then winced: his mother, though Anglo, used to call him that, a contraction of *mi hijo,* meaning, *"my son."* His mother gone to dust in some place and manner he would never ever know—his mother who, like a few billion other souls, was forgotten by all that lived. All but him.

And that's not a much better line of thought, he chided himself, eluding the drunken embrace of a settler woman, big and brassy and smelling like a flock of goats that had been involved in a nasty distillery accident. She spit curses after him in Spanish that he affected not to understand as he walked on pursued by the harsh-voiced laughter of her male companions.

For a while he kept his head on a swivel like a wary old tomcat, for fear one of them might back up on him and decide to avenge the honor of his *campesina* with a dagger in the back. They weren't Liberation Army soldiers and didn't look like they'd seen a whole load of hard labor of late, either, which suggested they were scavengers come to look for what pickings might be found. But apparently Team Phoenix's rep had spread; no one followed him. Which saved him some sweat and them some bleeding.

Then he was by himself, in an enclave of shadow and comparative quiet. Just the tumbledown shacks on his left and a palm-frond warehouse piled high with dark crates on his left, and the memories of a past he was trying to forget.

What he heard then might have been a voice from the past: a woman's voice, young and clearly frightened, crying, "Somebody, please help me!"

In English.

"Domi!" he shouted. He drew his Glock 22 from its belt holster—not the flapped Cordura model he wore in the bush, but a Kydex combat rig, swift and hard-sided and donned especially for the trip to town. He wrapped his hand over the receiver and hauled back the slide just far enough to catch a reassuring glimpse of brass in the light of a crescent moon falling toward the Andes. Then he dashed down an alley between shacks that leaned toward one another like companionable drunkards for support.

He popped out into a little cleared space with a wagon, its mule unhitched and absent, parked on the far side of it. A woman stood there, small and slim but with all the right curves, and short haired.

"Domi?" he asked, confused.

A flare of yellow light as the woman lit a cigarette from a plastic lighter. The face illuminated, with its sharp angles and gaunt cheeks was, while striking in its way, none he had ever seen before.

"Sorry, mate," she said in a low-class English accent. "Never heard of her."

He sensed movement around him. *Surrounded!*

He brought up the Glock into a left-handed Weaver combat stance. "I don't know who you are," he said in a low, taut voice, "but you'd better call off your friends. Think of this as a hostage situation."

She laughed at him. "Go ahead and shoot. You think I'm afraid to die?"

Too late he sensed an impossible loom of shadowy mass to his left. He had been focused on the girl way too much; before he could either make good his promise and drop the striker on her or spin to engage the new threat, a foot swept up and knocked the handgun clean out of his hands with the force of a mule's kick.

"No need for guns, little man," said a voice like thunder echoing in an empty barrel. "Let's settle this man to man."

He spun and looked up at his attacker. And up.

And up.

"That's easy for you to say," he said, whipping out

his vintage Gerber Mark II combat dagger. "You're 'two man' all by your lonesome."

It was no exaggeration. Understatement if anything. His challenge had to be near nine feet tall. Reichert's eyes were on the level of his navel, or where his navel was bound to be behind the tunic of dark, stiff-looking material he wore. The man had a barn-door face that even in this light Reichert could see was dark in color, surmounted by a nimbus of wild black hair worthy of an animé hero.

"You've got balls," the monster said. "Too bad you don't have the loyalty to match it."

Reichert's brow creased in perplexity. "'Loyalty'? What the fuck?"

Belatedly he recognized his attacker. "You're with that ass-cheese Bates!"

He darted forward and to his right, tossing the Gerber from right fist to left, catching it blade downward and aiming for a hamstringing slash across the back of one of those redwood legs.

Reichert was fast, trained to an edge sharp as his steel, and had done this sort of thing before more times than once or even twice. But impossibly the monster's speed matched his. The left leg swung back and away out of danger—and a piledriver slammed Reichert onto his face; momentum carried him two full yards forward across the trampled earth to slam his head into a wood post upholding a roof of beaten-flat tin cans.

Ignoring the yellow sparks drifting behind his eyes,

he made himself spring back to his feet, snarling and spinning. A foot as long as his forearm took him in the center of the chest and squashed all the breath out of him as it propelled him back against the post. His head snapped back and cracked nastily into it; his brain filled with crimson sparkles.

He cut as fiercely as he was able at the vast shadow that rose up tall as a building before him. A hand as big as his head caught his wrist. Then he was being spun around like a doll, the wrist driven up between his shoulder blades. A second massive arm came around his neck and applied pressure.

"Time to go, little man," the voice said as Reichert blacked out.

Chapter 24

The mouth closed. From the bloated parody of a baron's face two yellow, slanted eyes regarded Brigid and Grant with malicious anticipation.

From the doorway Grant raised his Copperhead one-handed. Brigid clutched at his arm. "Grant, don't! *Kane*—"

"Forget it, sister," Grant said. His voice was raw as a fresh wound. "He's a write-off. Catching a quick slug'd be the kindest thing that could happen to him now."

The creature most resembled a monstrous caterpillar, from the little they could see of it. Beneath the folds of the swollen-seeming head the two humans could see comparatively little nubs suggesting caterpillar feet. Its body seemed squeezed into the space between floor and ceiling too tightly for it to move at all, much less with the horrible alacrity it had displayed in devouring Kane.

Suddenly the great yellow eyes went wide. A flash illuminated the monster's rubbery sides like a match struck inside a balloon. A muffled thud, like a distant door slam sounded.

The creature tried to rear up, eyes rolling, tears

streaming from them. It didn't get far, it didn't have far to get. A wild squealing skirled from distended nostrils each big enough to inhale a human head.

And then its head exploded in a wash of purple-and-green ichor.

The great body slumped in on itself as if deflating. From the steaming, dripping cavern of the neck stepped Kane. He was plastered in multicolored glop and chunks of flesh. Even in his full-body polycarbonate carapace his body language betrayed pumped and quivering rage.

"He did *not*," Kane said, "know who he was fucking with!"

"You shouldn't ought to use such language," a now-familiar voice said. "Not in front of a little girl."

Around the bend from the other direction—came Mary.

A little girl from her voice. And her manner. But there was nothing little about the creature that shambled into view. It stood taller than Grant on doughy, uneven legs, lopsided, hunchbacked, with a head that seemed to sprout out of the unlovely mass of it without intervention of a neck. The left side of the face looked almost normal, for a human afflicted with gigantism. But the right side looked like a wax model put in an oven and halfway melted, or perhaps a balloon with half the air let out: huge, distorted, flaccid, with slack rubbery lips and a terrible staring china-blue eye. A few tufts of sand-colored hair stuck out from the top and sides of the head, tied with scraps of cloth and twine in lieu of ribbon. An assortment of lab coats and shirts and towels and random swatches of cloth had been crudely stitched together into a parody of the black pinafore that the illusion-Mary wore, which fitted the body like an overstuffed sack. And a sack it might have been, of ill-associated parts and lumps and tubers. One bare mottled arm cradled a teddy bear, one-legged, with one button eye, long worn bald and white as a naked mole rat.

Without hesitating, Brigid stepped forward. "Mary?" she asked, her voice gentle. "Is that you?"

"It's me." Even Kane, hard man that he was and dripping with monster ooze to boot, winced at that girlish voice coming from that unlovely hulk. "I wish I could have met you under other circumstances, Ms. Brigid. I'd like to play with you."

"I'd like to play with you, too, Mary."

Grant looked at Kane, who shrugged.

"You broke my toys," Mary said, gesturing with a half-size stub of free arm to the still-steaming headless worm, "and saw through all my ghosts." She sounded very sad.

Brigid held out her hands to the grotesque being. "Let us help you. Let us take you out of here. We can get you…help. We want to be your friends."

"You mean that," the little girl said. "I can read it in your mind. But it's too late. You have to die now. So do I. All of us."

"What do you mean, all of us will die?"

Transferring the bald teddy bear back to the crook

of her elbow, Mary displayed what she held in a pink pudgy left hand: a small cylinder of plastic or metal with a button on one end. Her thumb rested on the button.

"Is that—?" Grant began.

"Remote initiator," Kane said. "Baptiste! Move it along, here."

"I'm trying, Kane!" The door began to slide aside with another hiss.

"Don't make me do it," Mary said. "Please."

A crack answered her, not just earsplitting but skull-splitting in the close confines of the ring room. The great mismatched head jerked back. A new eye, small and neatly round and black, had appeared alongside Mary's almost normal-looking one. Kane held his Sin Eater out toward her at the full extent of his arm.

The bent arm relaxed, falling toward the floor. The pathetic teddy bear dropped away unheeded, bereft of its last and long companion. As the great bulk of body settled toward the nonslick rubber matting on the floor, the hand opened and the initiator fell out, now harmless.

The three Cerberus exiles breathed a collective sigh of relief.

"We can't go any farther down," Brigid said.

"Back the way we came?" Grant asked, apprehension clear in his tone.

"There should be an elevator," Brigid said, scanning the corridor. "It will take us back up to the mat-trans unit." She pointed behind them, beyond the chamber they had just passed through.

"Now she tells us," Kane joked grimly as Brigid paused to examine the walls of the corridor. Recessed into the wall and hidden by shadows was indeed the elevator Brigid had promised.

As THE DIRTY-WOOL LIGHT of false dawn stained the lower hem of the eastern sky behind the defensive line, they came.

It was still as good as dead dark down in the trench when the crew of the Number 23 machine gun pit commenced to scream.

A searchlight powered by an alcohol-burning generator sent a blinding blue-white beam at a crazy angle into the star-encrusted sky. It swept down onto the emplacement.

Struggling figures were visible. Then one struggled up out of the rear of the trench. It was vaguely human, but seemed to consist of a strange yellow ooze. The figure waved its arms vaguely and screamed like a man afire. It staggered forward a few steps. As it did what appeared to be the right hand fell off, although it was hard to discern from the doughlike substance encasing it.

The screams and struggles dwindled. The figure pitched forward onto the ground. It continued to shrink, visibly…as if melting.

A storm of fire broke from the lines. The defenders were shooting at their fears, not visible targets.

After lingering as if unwilling to believe, the elevated spotlight swept forward onto the flat killzone cleared by the dozers. A patch of muddy soil perhaps ten yards wide and extending from the dark water of the river was covered by what looked like a thick carpet of the custard-like yellow stuff, pocked by the rupture of gas bubbles from within. It was alive, moving forward slowly as by some form of peristalsis.

Screams announced that similar living carpets of slime had reached the line, had begun to digest other defenders. A crank-driven siren began to whine an unnecessary alarm.

HAS ANYONE SEEN Sean?" Major Mike Hays demanded as he sat on the edge of a rude bed with crates for box strings and a big sack of some kind of vegetable husks for a mattress, struggling into his boots. As much as he had longed to be out of his sweat-stiff, evil-smelling armor-fabric battle dress he had declined to take it off while grabbing a few furtive but badly needed hours of shut-eye behind the lines in Esperanza. But he had insisted on shucking the boots. A man had his limitations. Even an old Marine.

Two negatives came back. From Reichert came the same silence that had greeted first the team leader's call and then an increasingly vehement series of queries and demands.

"Maybe he got lucky," Joe Weaver suggested laconically.

"He wouldn't stay out of the loop this long after the rocket went up," Hays said.

Neither of his hearers said anything. Nor did Hays

voice the logical next thing, the only apparent reason
the fourth and youngest team member would fail to respond. What that chilling fact might imply he had no
idea. And no time to contemplate.

"Then it's up to the three of us," he said. "Rally to
the river. It's showtime."

Chapter 25

The three rendezvoused in a little strip of woods that ran between the space cleared back of the defensive line and the shantytown. The identification challenge-and-response was carried out with hand signals and backed up by quick subvocalized calls on their comm channel. They were all bent under heavy packs and festooned with weapons.

They'd no sooner joined up than a blaze of light lit the scene. The alert crews upriver had floated down more flammables and torched the river. A horrific stench told the three that something had been caught in the conflagration.

There was a lot of aimless running and shouting going on. Shrieks erupted from various points along the line. Hays looked around for someone in a position of responsibility. To his utter astonishment Consuelo herself ran from the south with a pair of shotgun guards trotting in her wake, her heavy black hair waving like a flag behind her. Spotting the outlanders by their size, she turned and ran up to them.

"What's going on here?" Hays demanded.

"Monsters," she said. "Like living liquid, almost. They engulf their victims, and what they engulf, dissolves!"

Robison and Weaver exchanged a look. "I don't hear much commotion down toward the Marañón," Hays said. "Have Simón's men driven the stuff back?"

She looked at him, eyes as wild as her hair. "Simón's men have fled!"

"I beg your pardon?" Robison said.

"My people tell me they've been filtering back from their places in the line all night. Then when this new horror came, first devouring one of their machine-gun crews, the rest ran."

"How come we didn't encounter them coming from Esperanza?" Weaver asked.

"They went south, to the Marañón and then east along the bank. I was just there to see for myself. It's true! They've gone, and taken their guns and mortars with them!"

"Fucking great," Hays said. "Is *anybody* holding the line down there?"

"Some laborers and women. Apparently Simón took only soldiers with him. Some of my people went down there to fight when the remaining soldiers ran."

"Where the hell did he go?" Robison asked.

As if in answer a whistle blew from the makeshift docks half a klick or so away by Esperanza, where a pair of steamboats were moored. "That means they've got a full head of steam and are ready to roll," Weaver said. "There's your answer."

"Where're the boats going?" Robison asked.

"No time for that," Hays said. "We got to run with what we got right now or the creepy-crawlies are gonna swarm all over us."

He sent Robison left toward the Marañón and Weaver trotting north, barely seeming to notice his load, alongside Consuelo with her flying hair to see to the north end of their defenses. Hays moved right ahead to the center of the trench line.

He was in time to see a wave of pallid glop slosh over the breastworks and envelop a trio of Shuara warriors almost at his feet. They commenced to gyrate and wave their arms and shriek from dissolving mouths.

He chopped them down with a quick side-to-side burst of his MG.

"Fire! Somebody get some torches, here, dammit! Let's see how this man-eating carpet likes being on fire!"

Holding his FN-MAG at the ready—against the expectation they'd soon be seeing foes it would do a lot more against than animated saber-toothed tapioca pudding—Hays nodded at the warriors, who lit the twists of dried moss sap-sealed into the claypots with their torches and flung them into the midst of the living mass.

Where, naturally, they failed to break. Hays grinned and sprayed the ooze with a couple of quick bursts. The pots shattered; the huge blue-and-white muzzle-flame itself ignited their contents.

A great hissing laced with thin squealing rose from

the trench, accompanied by clouds of reeking smoke and steam.

All up and down the line bonfires were flaring up as the tribesmen fought back with the sole weapon effective against the walking mold colonies. More flames smeared themselves across patches of the death ground before the trench as more creeping colonies were spotted by light of the flames of the burning river.

Hays was just nodding in satisfaction at the discipline the Shuara were displaying in holding back their secret weapon—aided by the fact that only a few warriors, mostly subchiefs especially picked by Consuelo for seasoned steadiness, possessed the triggers—when a fresh chorus of shouts rose up.

Almost in front of where he stood a great dark shape erupted from the water. Shedding blue-and-red flames from a water-glossy hide, it clambered up the bank and trotted forward. Hays had a flash impression of a beast the size and general shape of a hippopotamus, with what looked like tentacles borrowed from a giant squid waving from its shoulders. Nearing the trench it opened a mouth lined with long curved tusks and charged.

Several Atshuara fired their single-shot break-action shotguns into the monster. It squealed in fury but wasn't slowed. Its hide was obviously enormously thick, almost certainly too thick to be pierced by pellets of shot.

Working the cigar to a corner of his mouth, Hays grinned. He clamped the buttstock of the machine gun against his ribs with his elbow and hosed copper-jacketed 7.62 mm slugs into that open mouth. Dark fluids and chunks of flesh flew out a mouth gaping wide enough to bite a man in two at a single chomp. A length of dark yellow tusk spun away, broken off by a slug.

The monster bellowed, voice now shrill with unmistakable agony. It dropped its broad haunches and squatted as if trying to brake, reared up halfway. Major Mike gave it another burst, aiming for the exposed throat and belly. It collapsed forward and lay still, close enough that the mottled dark skin of its snout began to blister in the flames of the toasting slime mold.

Hays looked around. The killzone between trench and river was dotted with dozens of the huge creatures. Comm-net reports from Weaver and Robison confirmed that the things were emerging all along the line.

"Fougasse," was Hays's one-word response.

Firing a long burst into the flanks of a monster that had gotten into the trench and was attacking tribal warriors, he ran to a wooden box half buried behind the line. He flipped open the splintery wood lid, reached down and by feel armed the command detonator within. Then he lit it off.

Five yards to his left a stream of orange fire erupted. It arced over the trench, raining down fiery droplets, to splash down in the cleared zone five yards this side of the riverbank. One hippolike creature was almost inundated by flaming fuel thickened by palm oil. Several others were splashed. The improvised napalm clung and burned fiercely, quickly defeating even the monsters' wet, thick skin.

To Hays's left and right other fire-fountains sprayed garish streams against the vaguely lightening sky. They were a devilish device for breaking up human-wave-style assaults, dating from the midtwentieth century if not before, which Team Phoenix called by their French name, *fougasse*. Big containers, in this case barrels with reinforcing earth mounded over them, were mounted at an angle. A bursting charge, here plain old black gunpowder, was sealed in the base of each. Then each barrel was filled with flammables, again a sticky mixture of kerosene, alcohol and palm oil. They were aimed to fall on attacking enemies and then detonated by command.

As the miniature volcanoes belched their sticky fire into the midst of the new attacking monsters, the Invaders faltered, as they had when the river had been torched several days before. They began to mill and bellow. Some even panicked and bolted back into the water. The Shuara's comparatively few rifles cracked, augmented by Weaver's heavy rifle to the south and Robison's full-auto shotgun, presumably firing slugs, to the north, taking their toll. Some of the monsters that had blundered into the trenches were isolated by the warriors and dispatched with lance-thrusts and axes.

Hays fired his machine gun into the huge beasts swarming in front of him. As the monsters already on fire .ran screaming in circles or stampeded in random directions, they bumped against their fellows, smearing them with that terrible flame that clung and bit without mercy.

Looks like we've stopped 'em again! Hays exulted to himself.

Suddenly a warrior standing to Hays's left emitted a terrible scream.

Hays spun. One of the fruit-bat-like flying Invaders had seized the man's head from behind with multiple clawed limbs, and was pumping the stinger at the tip of its scorpion tail repeatedly into his back. Then Hays saw something tubular emerge from the monster's lower abdomen and plunge forward into its victim. The warrior stiffened, and his shriek reached an ear-shattering crescendo.

Then his cries ceased. His eyes rolled up into his head, yellow foam slopped out over his lower lip and he dropped to his knees.

Hays blew him and his attacker apart with his MG.

Then he hastily retreated three steps from the trench and looked up. The demon air force had entered the fray, a dense black cloud of wings lit from below by the river's now-dying flames.

"Mechanic," Robison's voice said in his head. "Phone Man. The big ugly bastards have crossed the Pastaza north of the end of the trench line. We're flanked."

"Fuck," Hays said. "You copy that, Joe?"

"Affirmative," the former civilian said, for once

deigning to use approved military cant. "The flying foxes are all over us, and more of the hippos have started coming out of the water."

Holding his machine gun by both grips, Hays sprayed bullets into a swarm of the scorpion-bats descending on him. The bullets dropped several broken and flapping. The others shied away, apparently fearing the big bright muzzle-flame.

"Do we try to hold here?" Weaver asked.

"Negative. Damn. Our flank's turned. That's all she wrote. Time to go into *sauve qui peut* mode. If you'll pardon my French."

Chapter 26

With the sound of a slap by the back of a gigantic hand against his jaw reverberating among the tiled walls and floor of the little room, Sean Reichert reeled back. He fetched up against a wall. He let it prop him up by shoulders and splayed hands.

He gazed at the giant figure, blurry from one eye puffing shut. "Is that all you got?" he slurred through split lips.

Enkidu gazed down on him. He had taken off his tunic. His mahogany-colored chest stretched a gray sweat-stained undershirt almost to the bursting point.

"You have spirit," he said. His English was flawless, basically an educated middle-class American accent. "I have to credit you for that. If not originality."

"Yeah. Well, something about being hit in the head by the Jolly Green Giant tends to scramble my A material."

Reichert pulled himself upright and pushed away from the wall. His palms and the back of his own T-shirt tended to stick. He didn't like to think about that, nor the amount of his own blood already congealing in pools on the floor.

"What's this about, anyway?" he said. "You think you're going to get me to talk banging me around?"

He rubbed his cheek gingerly with the back of his own hand. "You're more likely than not to bust my jaw, big guy. Then where will you be?"

Enkidu smiled. He was the biggest human being Reichert had ever seen. Most of the extraordinarily tall men Reichert had seen were beanpoles. The others he'd seen pictures of were misshapen, with overdeveloped brows and jaws, victims of acromegaly that doomed them to abbreviated lives of pain and ill health, like the jovial wrestling star of Reichert's youth known as André the Giant.

Enkidu was no beanpole. Nor was he acromegalic. His proportions were if anything heroic. The closest mental comparison benchmark Sean had was basketball star Shaquille O'Neal, who was powerfully muscled despite being over seven feet tall. But this man was at least a foot taller, and muscled like a powerlifter.

Which, of course, confirmed Reichert's worst fears. Although he had never laid eyes on the man, during the months of intensive and eclectic training that preceded their cryogenic nap, Team Phoenix had heard rumors that Gil Bates's chief of security was just such a freak.

Then again, since the rumors also claimed he'd been an assassin, who fell clear into the gutter of skid row until he was fished forth and rehabilitated by Bates, Reichert and his buddies tended to discount them as mere talk. If an assassin needed one thing it was to be inconspicuous; and there was no way to make such a monster anything near that. There were a lot of improbabilities bandied around about Gilgamesh Bates. The man attracted them.

And a lot of them, Reichert realized, standing there in a haze of numbness he knew presaged a world of hurt later on, had turned out to be perfectly true. Only we found out about all that about two hundred years too late.

"We will use chemical interrogation to learn all of you that we require," the dark giant said. "Although my employer did suggest that I soften you up as a preliminary. This is more by the nature of recreation."

"You like the challenge, huh?" He raised his hands in a gesture of cartoon pugnacity. "Okay, put up your dukes!"

He saw a shadow flicker across that vast countenance. That one hit, he thought. Something about this setup bothers him— Fair play or compassion? Unlikely as either of them seems.

"I understand this is not perhaps strictly honorable," Enkidu said. "But I feel I owe it to you…or perhaps myself…to demonstrate to you the price of disloyalty."

"Loyalty? Ha! To that lying, backstabbing, murderous creep Bates? Are you fucking kidding me?"

Enkidu frowned. "Gilgamesh Bates is a great man. A visionary. A man of genius. A man of true compassion."

"Compassion? Possibly you haven't been keeping up

with current events, pal, but the jungles of the Upper Amazon are crawling right now with an invasion of critters that devour anything and everything natural they come across, especially people. And the very fact that you and I are both standing here—wherever the fuck 'here' happens to be—proves that Bates is in it up to his extra-high asshole. He's destroying the environment and getting people eaten alive. Don't hand me that 'compassion' shit."

"Sometimes harsh measures are taken," Enkidu said, "which are for the greater good in the long run. Like the amputation of a gangrenous limb to save a patient. Such is the true compassion."

"What an unmitigated crock of shit! You talk as if you know something, but if you really believe that, that great big barrel-sized head of yours is stuffed with fermented batshit."

Enkidu lowered the aforementioned head. "You are in a poor position to be insulting."

"What fucking position am I in, anyway? You're going to get your chickenshit kicks by beating the snot out of me anyway! What do I have to lose? So, come on, bring the whole load. Show what a man you are—all the steroids you probably been takin', it's gotta be a good half inch long!"

The already huge figure seemed to swell. Got him going, anyway, Reichert thought. An angry opponent was usually a vulnerable one. But this one was as much bigger and stronger than Reichert, as Reichert was bigger and stronger than a child and at least as well trained, judging by the way he moved. Would it be enough of an edge? Had to be.

He didn't think what might happen or what he would do even if, improbably, he happened to take down the monster. He couldn't afford to. He had to think not of himself, nor victory, nor defeat, but only of cutting and killing his foe....

The door opened behind Enkidu. His growing rage turning to annoyance, the huge man started to turn.

A woman came in. It was the same one who had lured Reichert into a trap—however long ago—with her counterfeit cries for help. She was pretty in the light, too, in an ultrapallid anorexic-waif kind of way.

Reichert hardly registered her presence before he moved.

At some point in his training he'd received extensive instruction in the rough-and-tumble Gracie system of Brazilian jujitsu. One thing his instructor had repeated over and over was that his system offered the best shot at overcoming major disparities in size and strength. The thinking was, if you took a larger and stronger opponent to the ground and successfully assumed the mount position, your legs pinning his hips, you had rendered him helpless and the fight was good as won.

Reichert wasn't sure all the skill in Brazil would make diddly-squat difference in the case of a foe three feet taller who probably weighed three times what he did, none of it fat. That made him no difference. He put his head down and launched himself in an all-or-nothing dive for those Sequoia legs.

He got nothing.

Enkidu turned his head to protest the intrusion. But his peripheral vision was excellent. He saw Reichert's charge begin.

Unfortunately Reichert had not had a chance to employ a lot of the feints or other tactics the Gracie system also taught. And unfortunately, the counter for the basic Brazilian-style, straight-in shoot for the legs had been known long before the war—known well enough it was even being taught to cops by the time the rockets launched.

Enkidu just dropped a dinner-plate-sized hand on Reichert's shoulder and pushed as he turned his hips. He needed neither his colossal mass nor strength to drive Reichert face-first onto the floor and then sliding into the wall. All it took was a little push to help him on his way.

Reichert's head cracked into the tile wall with a sharp, nasty sound. He tried to get up. Instead he collapsed, choking and puking.

"Terrific," Enkidu said. "If he's concussed, we'll have to wait to question him—the drugs would likely kill him before he told us anything. You should not have distracted me, Ishtar."

She shrugged. "He's going to die anyway. They're all going to die—Bates promised me."

She went to the sprawled young man, bent over him.

"If you're faking, and think to take her hostage," Enkidu called out, "don't bother. Nothing would please me more than for you to break her skinny neck."

"Prick," Ishtar said without looking back. She hauled Reichert's head up by his hair. His eyes rolled. "He's stunned, right enough. But both pupils are the same size. So maybe he's not working on a subdural hematoma, after all."

She let his head drop. His chin struck the floor with a thump. She straightened and turned to Enkidu.

"You should let me play with him," she said. "I'd get answers. I'd need some equipment, though. This room would be good." She pirouetted. "What is this place, anyway?"

Enkidu's laugh was like a manhole cover dropping back into place. "An interrogation room. Note the drain in the floor, the slight slope down to it. I had the appurtenances removed."

She smiled at him. "You could bring them back."

She approached him, as sinuous as a snake. "You're big and strong. I wonder, are you so gigantic all over? Worlds bigger than I. You could take me, you know. You could *make* me."

He turned his face away. "I don't do that sort of thing."

Her face registered genuine astonishment. "Then why in the world did you ever become an assassin?"

Chapter 27

"Say what?" Mike Hays said.

Standards within Cerberus had been relaxed since Kane, Grant, Brigid and Domi had first arrived there years before. Decam teams no longer came running to treat new arrivals like toxic spills. There were just too many people, too much traffic with the outside world. Nonetheless Reba DeFore had insisted on shucking the three members of Team Phoenix out of their filthy uniforms and herding them through showers of antiseptic chemicals before letting them roam free through the redoubt. They were all dressed in loose, spotless coveralls. But an aura of psychic grime seemed to hang on them, as if the dirt and blood of battle and the stink of fear were not readily sluiced away by merely physical cleansers.

They were also bone-tired from trying to keep the fallback from the Pastaza from being a total rout—not just of the Shuara warriors and their families but hundreds of civilians, laborers and volunteers, left likewise high and dry by Simón's midnight departure with all the troops. Another losing battle, by and large. They were too many, spread too wide, for Team Phoenix to contain them, even with Consuelo's help. Though they had found the element of calculation in her own character a bit of a disappointment, and had come to regard her, having learned of her shared history with Simón, as something of a ruling-class dilettante, she had a core of vanadium steel that showed when the flames roared highest.

But being outflanked, with an enemy pouring uncontested into one's rear, had routed many a more seasoned army facing far kinder enemies. In all probability stemming the rout would've proved beyond the resources of an entire twelve-man Special Forces A-team, just as stemming the Invaders' advance would've taxed a battalion of regulars. But for men whose life experience and intensive training had served only to reinforce their shared lifelong philosophy—that no task they undertook could ever be beyond their ability to accomplish—it was a soul-shriveling defeat.

For their part, Kane, Grant and Brigid didn't consider their escape from Abaddon redoubt a victory. They had jumped back to Cerberus alive and intact, but their investigation of the secret redoubt hadn't led to the discovery of the self-replicating assemblers they were searching for. It was, in Kane's opinion, a useless diversion, but Brigid and Lakesh were more sanguine.

"Gentlemen," Lakesh said, addressing Team Phoenix, "I must confess to you now that we have not been entirely candid with you."

"No shit?" Robison said. He raised his shaggy head enough to bring a bloodshot glare to bear upon the scientist. "That's not exactly front-page news.

"I don't know why you pulled us out in the first place," Joe Weaver said. "It's only prolonging the agony, waiting up here until the invasion reaches this far."

"But it need not come to that, friend Joseph," Lakesh said.

Suddenly all sixteen other eyes in the room were locked on to the scientist.

"I must first apologize further, I fear," Lakesh said with unusual tentativeness. Kane guessed he was far less confident of his ability to pull Team Phoenix's strings than he was those attached to the souls and psyches of the Cerberus contingent.

"We took more liberties with you than you have realized," Lakesh said. "Since charming Domi brought you back here, you have said nothing of your missing comrade, young Sean Reichert, the erstwhile Army Ranger and Delta operator."

The men looked at one another and shrugged. "We got time to mourn now," Hays said. "Before, it was all we could do to keep our minds on the people who were on the firing line with us. More than we could do."

The final words dripped with a bitterness none of the Cerberus group, except perhaps Domi, had heard from them before. They had spoken bitterly enough of Gilgamesh Bates when Lakesh had revealed to them months before how he had lied to and misused them. But now bitterness was tinged with the sour-vomit taste of futility.

"Do you not wonder what happened to him?"

"We didn't exactly have time to discuss it," Robison said. "The logical surmise is he either wandered into the wrong spot and got snarfed up by an unknown advance party of hoodoos, or maybe he stumbled onto Simón's little betrayal in progress and got silenced. Happens to the best, sooner or later. And obviously did. Although in either case, I'm surprised we didn't hear about it."

A corner of his mouth quirked up inside his beard, now grown out like unpruned topiary and shot with gray. "One thing that boy was always good at, was making noise."

"When the shitstorm's coming down we tend to let the dead bury the dead," Hays said. "It's not as if we haven't had six billion opportunities to practice that before. But I'm not so goddamned proud of leaving a man behind, especially when we don't know if he's even dead, thank you very fucking much for reminding me."

"Rejoice," Lakesh said. "Your friend is not dead. Or at least, we have abundant reason to believe he is still alive. He was kidnapped by the forces of your former master, Gilgamesh Bates, and taken to the secret subterranean stronghold from which he released and is controlling the Invader plague."

"How exactly," Joe Weaver said, his eyes unreadable

behind his round glasses, "do you happen to know that, Dr. Lakesh?"

"Because when you were first in Cerberus redoubt, I took the step of having subcutaneous transponders, like those borne by all our operatives, injected into all four of you."

The room was so quiet a fart would have sounded like a firecracker.

"Good thing these boys're disarmed right now, Doc," Grant said lazily.

"Please understand, my friends, that I did it entirely for your welfare," Lakesh said.

"That's what he always tells us," Grant said, "every time he does something snaky to us."

Lakesh shot him a pained look.

"Please believe me," he said, "when I say that everything I do, I do with the good of my people in mind. But I am also obliged to consider the greater good."

"So how did Bates's people get Sean into his fortress?" Robison asked.

"Obviously, through the use of some sort of light aircraft. It is unfortunate that more observation satellites do not survive in functional state—we have not nearly sufficient coverage for constant real-time observation, and so could only spot Bates's aircraft coming and going by lucky accident. Which has never transpired."

"Besides which," Joe Weaver said, "Bates undoubtedly knows when all the working spy satellites are overhead."

"Sadly, this is all but certainly the case."

Brigid roused herself. "But wait. If Bates's involvement is confirmed, and Sean Reichert was taken to a base in the affected area, it unquestionably means Bates possesses some means of controlling the plague."

"Or just turning it off," Kane said.

Lakesh was nodding and beaming. "You have recapitulated my reasoning precisely, my friends! Such flashes of genius give me hope."

Kane cocked a brow and looked sideways at Grant. "Was that a compliment to us, or him?" Grant shrugged.

"Forgive me if my neurons are a little bit depleted, here," Robison said ponderously, "but how do you reckon that, exactly?"

"Bates may be crazy," Major Mike said, "but he ain't nuts. He's just your average healthy megalomaniac. He wouldn't release the nasties without being sure he could stop them while there was still something of a world left for him to rule. And he wouldn't trap himself perpetually inside his fortress by letting them loose right over his own head, either. So he's got the cure we've been looking for."

"Admirably put, Major," Lakesh said.

"So all the cheese," Robison said, drawing it out, "is in this fortress?"

"Precisely yes."

"Then cut to the end," said Hays. "How do we get in, get Sean, turn off the bad bugs and stick Bates's fucking sheep head on a pole?"

"I must warn you, it will not be easy."

To Lakesh's blinking astonishment, his three fellow twentieth-century survivors burst into peals of harsh laughter.

"Forget 'easy,'" Joe Weaver said. "We don't even insist on *possible*. Just give us a shot and we'll take it, do or die."

Kane tipped an extended forefinger off his brow at the man. "Now that," he said, "is the spirit of the classic one-percenter."

Chapter 28

Sean Reichert lay naked on his back in a white haze of aching misery.

The haze wasn't an artifact of the highly professional beating the giant had thrown him. Rather he was locked in a small cell with white walls, relentlessly illuminated by fluorescents set flush into the ceiling, too high for him to reach even by springing with all his might off the low uncomfortable cot with the tubular steel frame. Undoubtedly the light fixture had a shatterproof polycarbonate cover in any event.

The room was scientifically designed to give him no scope to escape—even through suicide. There were no sharp edges. No brackets held the cot to the floor; its frame came straight up from beneath like an extrusion of the hidden fortress's steel skeleton. The bolts that held on the panels of the light fixtures, that secured the little polycarbonate shells protecting video cameras in opposite corners of the high ceiling, and the cover on a ventilation grate were countersunk. Both sink and toilet simply jutted from the vanadium-steel walls, impervious as an Abrams main battle tank. The tap in the sink was activated by passing a hand before it, and cut itself off automatically after a one-second flow. The toilet rinsed itself at intervals with a brief chemical spray from within the rim. There was a paper dispenser, flush with the wall, which dispensed single sheets; these dissolved instantly on contact with the flushing fluid, which was greenish with an acrid chemical smell. There would be no drowning, hanging or flooding the cell with wads of asswipe.

To be sure, had Sean Reichert *really* wanted to kill himself, he was by no means defeated, as far as he could see. There was neither pillow nor sheet to the cot to fashion into a convenient noose; it consisted of what seemed a single piece of some kind of hard but resilient foam. Perhaps he could contrive to tear or break pieces from it and choke himself on it. More promising was the frame itself. Without actually testing directly—since he didn't want to give his unseen watchers any ideas—he had determined that his head would fit between the frame and the floor. And then a quick death roll, crocodile-like, and he might send himself off with a snapped neck. Or he could employ an easier trick few people knew about, scissoring the vertebral artery with the very transverse processes of the cervical through which it was threaded, which would kill him in seconds regardless of medical intervention.

Or if I get bored, I can always just bash my head in on the wall. He'd seen a holding cell in Guatemala where a "guerrilla" prisoner—they were all called guerrillas, even they were drug-smuggler rivals to the drug smuggler the U.S. was supporting at the moment—had done that. Hell of a mess—blood and off-white clumps everywhere. But it worked.

He became aware of no longer being alone. He had not heard the door open. It was seamless, too. His nostrils, which had grown inured to all the sterile smells within the cell, easily detected intrusion: a smell of a female body, whose owner was none too particular about hygiene. And alcohol.

The crazy woman, he thought. She might conceivably serve as a hostage. He tensed his muscles.

And felt something bite into wrists and ankles. With a spasm of panic he tried to move. He could not. He was clamped to the cot by padded cuffs.

"You slept soundly, love," the woman said in her English accent. Her speech slurred ever so slightly. "I had you drugged and fastened down, not to put too fine an edge on it."

He opened his eyes. The thin redhead with sunken eyes and almost blue-white skin stood over him. She was wearing a dirty T-shirt and jeans. Her smile was a skull's.

"Drugged?" he managed to say. It was harder than he had expected; it felt as if his head was numb, including jaws and tongue, now that he tried to do something with them. "How?"

She shrugged. "Bit of gas slipped in through the vent. Odorless and colorless, of course. Not that it matters." She turned to address someone over her shoulder. "Bring it in and set it down here. Carefully!"

A man in a gray uniform came in the door carrying a sort of pedestal table. When he set it down beside Ishtar and the cot its surface seemed to be covered with trays of gleaming surgical instruments.

She glared at the sec man. He turned and left without waiting for a tip. The door slipped noiselessly shut beside him.

Ishtar stripped off, kicking out of her jeans and leaving her garments in a careless pile on the floor. Smiling, she bent over Sean.

She caressed his forehead. Her fingers were cold as he imagined the implements on her tray to be. But not near as hard. "Ah, you're perspiring. You're beginning to be afraid. That's good, love, very good. A proper appreciation of the situation, as my old man would say. The bastard."

She bent, suddenly, and seemed to inhale his penis, which lay understandably flaccid between his thighs, into her mouth like a piece of spaghetti. His scrotum tensed as she applied brief, intense and thoroughly professional oral suction. Despite himself his cock sprang instantly to attention.

She had moved around to look him in the eyes. She smiled—then bit down.

Not hard. Not even enough to cause real pain. But his coccyx came up off the hard pad and the breath blew out of his body in a desperate yell.

"See?" she said, raising her head from his manhood. "This is the game we're going to play. I am going to teach you about pleasure, and helplessness."

Her eyes gleamed like poison stars. "And of course pain. Mustn't overlook that."

Somewhere an alarm began to blare, rising and falling to the beat of Reichert's yammering heart.

THE SKY ABOVE THE WOODED Montaña highlands east of the Andes foothills was a dome of aching blue, decked with just a few clouds so bright they seemed polished around the edges.

Death came from a clear sky.

As Joe Weaver had discerned, Bates's people kept careful track of when functioning spy satellites had his base in view, whether overhead or oblique. So their stealthy tilt-rotor scout and recon craft had been able to leave the subterranean facility, fly their brief missions and return without detection. When distance or the mission required longer-duration sorties, the craft were grounded and concealed under special camouflaged thermoinsulative Mylar sheets; their construction, made up largely of polymers, ceramics and nonferrous metals, was intrinsically hard for magnetic-anomaly detectors to sense.

But with its wingtip motor pods tilted vertically to "hover" regime, lifting it helicopter like from an underground hangar whose stressed-concrete roof, covered over with live growing local flora, was already sliding shut beneath it, the verti was unmissable. In any sense of the word.

Like lasers from the very heart of the early-morning

sun appearing over a forest-covered wall of the valley, twin eye-searing yellow beams stabbed to the center of the craft. An answering globe of yellow simply devoured its fuselage, save for the tail and the snout. Unjoined, the wings, tail assembly and the aircraft's nose, with Lexan windscreen still incongruously intact, fell back into the brush atop the now-sealed door in a rain of burning fuel and aluminum as a fireball was pushed skyward on a growing stalk of black smoke.

Two curious shapes swept low over the concealed facility: streamlined black lozenges. The two Manta Trans-Atmospheric Vehicles, braking themselves with retro rockets, made a complete circuit of the base skimming the very tops of the trees that sprang from it. Invisible clouds of death streamed from beneath the down-curved wings.

With a groan and creak of disused mechanism a popup turret thrust itself from what appeared to be an undistinguished patch of ground. Its top still covered in grass and bushes, it pivoted to track the two intruders with its 20 mm Gatling gun. It was a Phalanx emplacement, quite similar to those deployed to protect the baronial villes of North America.

Its compound barrels spun, emitting a bright dragon-breath of yellow flame and a shrill roar. It was unable to traverse fast enough to catch the black diamond craft; its shells arced out to explode far in the forest beyond.

A second tower rose, ahead and to the left of the low-circling TAVs. The lead, left-hand craft braked itself fu-

riously with blue-hot retro flares, skidded sideways.
Rockets lanced from beneath its wings and struck the
Gatling emplacement before it had fully risen. The top
of the tower erupted like an unblocked volcanic vent.
Smoke and fire continued to jet from it as the 20 mm
ammunition went off in a train of secondary explosions.

The lead Manta had inevitably slowed. The first
tower swept its scythe of explosive projectiles rapa-
ciously toward the now-vulnerable craft.

Then went silent, as the invisible VX-derived aerosol nerve agent the twin craft had dispersed had its brief
and violent way with the gun crew.

The slowed Manta waggled its flying-wing fuselage
tauntingly, then straightened and rejoined its wingman,
now flying lead, in completing the laying of its invisible death-blanket above the facility and the surrounding forest.

They were little concerned the nerve agent would
penetrate the facility and kill the occupants. Of course,
with the sole exception of Sean Reichert, that would
have delighted them, except that the unseen and silent
killer would have deprived them of the pleasure of killing their treacherous megalomaniac of a former boss
themselves. But the agent was of low persistence and
only just heavier than air, so that it would sink only
slowly. Nor would it penetrate far into the base itself,
and anyway, Team Phoenix already knew the ventilation system was hardened against chem attack, as

against a great many threats. It was just the Phalanx-tower crew's suck luck that their pop-up emplacement deployed itself beyond the coverage of the base's special ionic air scrubbers....

Team Phoenix knew a great deal indeed about the erstwhile Bennett Redoubt.

"THE FACILITY WAS BUILT secretly in the late 1990s," the thin, slight, gray woman with the round glasses like Joe Weaver's said. Her voice, which on introduction to the Team Phoenix trio as Sally Wright had been almost inaudibly faint, grew noticeably in volume and confidence when she was in lecture mode, as now.

She stood barely visible in the dimness of the briefing theater on Cerberus redoubt's third level, her form and features limned by glow from the giant LCD wall panel display. It showed an elevation cutaway view of the facility, which appeared to incorporate seven levels including subterranean garages and hangar facilities— and, of course, various pop-up defensive systems.

"It was ostensibly intended to aid the War on Drugs, which was extremely active in that area of what was then Peru. I say 'ostensibly' because there was clearly something else going on."

A chamber on the fourth level flashed yellow and then expanded to fill the screen. Rotating, it proved to have six sides.

"A mat-trans gateway?" Kane said. He, Grant, Brigid and Domi were in the briefing room, as well as the three Team Phoenix men. They were all getting this information for the first time.

"Who doesn't have one?" Grant said.

"Why hasn't our traffic-detection system shown the existence of the gateway before?" Brigid asked.

"Because it has apparently never been activated," Lakesh said. He was seated up front with one knee crossed over the other and both hands clasped over it. "At least since we acquired the capability of monitoring gate activity."

"Why didn't we know about this place before?" Grant asked.

"I'm afraid that is a matter of some embarrassment to us," Lakesh said. "The answer appears to be simply, we didn't look."

"You mean all this time a diagram of Bates's secret base has been in our data storage?" Kane demanded. "That whole time we were wading through Abaddon—"

"As well as all the time our allies spent enduring brutal conditions in South America—" Brigid said. She often took the part of her old mentor. This was not one of those occasions.

Lakesh held up his hands. "Yes, yes, my friends. It is true. I can only offer my apologies."

Several people began talking at once. Heatedly.

"Excuse me." Somehow Sally Wright's timid voice managed to make itself heard. The incipient riot was put on hold as heads turned toward her.

"The base is not listed among the standard known

Totality Concept facilities, any more than Abaddon was. Indeed, the search criteria that revealed its existence in the records we have recovered—I should say, *you* recovered, since I'm such a recent arrival and didn't have anything to do with collecting the information— were the latitude and longitude coordinates of the place where we lost the signal of Sean Reichert's transponder. It was simply hidden, nor did Dr. Lakesh or anyone else here in Cerberus have any reason to suspect its existence."

Kane realized he'd been holding his breath. He let it go in a long, ragged sigh. "All of the shit we've been crawling through has been totally unnecessary."

"That's about typical," Grant said. "Are you surprised?"

"No," said Kane, "but it would be fair to say I'm pissed."

"Cut to the chase," Major Mike said, in a growl not unlike Grant's. "How do we get in?"

"Several possibilities," Sally Wright replied, "suggest themselves."

BENT UNDER HEAVY PACKS a pair of unearthly figures trotted through the scrub and sparse trees concealing the buried redoubt. They were humanoid, bulky, camouflage patterned in brown and green. Their faces were all curved plastic and snouts. They carried longblasters in gloved hands. A third figure lay on its belly in the scrub, tucked behind the receiver of a modified FN-MAG machine gun with its bipod down.

The three free members of Team Phoenix were kitted out in MOPP gear: Mission Oriented Protective Posture, Level Four, the level used during actual chemical or biological attack. The MOPP gear would protest them from the nerve agent dispersed by the Mantas to target the monstrous Invader bioforms that swarmed all around. Computer god that he was, Bates had been too canny to release his life-forms directly from here, thereby pinpointing his base to geographic analysis. But he had released them, or instructed Ishtar to, so that they would shortly overrun the area and serve as additional security—which he neither had to house, feed nor pay, and whose morale never, ever faltered, even a little.

Whatever you could say about Gil Bates, he was a man who thought.

The gun tower shattered by the Manta's rockets was a no-go: the wreckage of the weapon itself blocked entrance. Larry Robison reached the second gun tower first. Curling around his Saiga combat shotgun, he knelt next to it. Joe Weaver was shedding his pack as he came up. He popped open the top, pulled out a prepared satchel charge and swarmed right up his partner's back. He wedged the charge beneath the Gatling's barrels, keyed the initiator timer with a gloved thumb and jumped back down. After grabbing up his pack by a strap, he and Robison scuttled around to the far side of the gun tower.

The charge had been intended to bust open one of the carefully baffled ventilation intakes. That the Phalanx had emerged only to have nerve gas chill its crew was purely bonus. This was an easy way in.

The charge went off with a crack. "All clear," Hays radioed, watching from a safe distance off. "Good shot."

His two companions went back around the tower. The results of the blast were very gratifying: the front top of the tower had been knocked open, and the Gatling itself hung out of the emplacement like an eyeball dislodged from its socket.

Once more Larry Robison boosted Weaver up to the top. Weaver had doffed his pack again and was only carrying a suppressed MP-5 machine pistol.

"Clear," he said shortly. "All dead in here."

Hays stood, picking up his FN-MAG up by the carrying handle. "I'm coming up," he said. "Let's get in quick, and maybe we can get out of these damned monkey suits before the bad guys climb up our assholes!"

"Right," said Robison. "I'd hate to die uncomfortable."

SLOWLY THE FOG of jump nausea subsided.

This time, at least, there had blessedly been no dreams. Or visions. Or whatever. "Arrggh," he heard Grant's voice croak as he pried his eyes open to turquoise-tinted gloom. "For being turned inside out and used to beat a Tartarus slagjacker's carpets, that wasn't so bad. But my head hurts so hard I can hear it throbbing."

"That's not your head," Domi said. She was sitting up with her hands braced behind her on the floor of the hexagonal chamber with the blue-green armaglass walls of which Kane was slowly becoming aware. "It's alarms."

Kane squeezed his eyes shut. She was right. He had taken the pulsations for the throb of his own pulse. Even at its best a jump was disorienting.

They were taking a big bet that the occupants would not expect intrusion via the gateway. It was a bet doubly hedged. First, Brigid's and Sally's biographical research suggested, and Team Phoenix went far to confirm, that you were unlikely to lose big wagering on Gilgamesh Bates's balloon-headed overconfidence. He habitually believed no one else was nearly as smart as he was. He would take for granted that, since Cerberus hadn't found his hidey-hole before, they wouldn't now.

And second, Hays, Robison and Weaver were giving themselves up in an all-but-suicidal attempt to storm the fortress from outside to provide the Cerberus group a diversion.

"Big strong men." Domi stood over Kane with hands on hips. She was dressed in short boots, baggy khaki shorts and a camou blouse, and over that a ballistic-weave vest with steel-ceramic trauma plates, lighter and more pliable than Kevlar. Armor notwithstanding, it wasn't Kane's notion of a sensible way to dress for battle, but any notions he'd had about reforming Domi, or taming her to any version of what he considered sense, had long been leached out of him. God knew the girl had shown she could take care of herself, in her own bizarre way. He accepted the surprisingly strong white hand she extended to help him to his feet. He looked out through the turquoise armaglass walls: the chamber beyond was empty.

He and Grant both wore gleaming hard-contact armor. Brigid wore the same armor as Domi over considerably more subdued garments, long khaki pants and a tan shirt. Kane unslung the weapon he carried in place of a Copperhead: an MP-5 with integral suppressor from the Cerberus armory, like the one Joe Weaver had taken. There might be need for stealthy killing. The MP-5, firing from a closed bolt, had a tendency to overheat in a firefight, especially the shrouded-barrel suppressed version. But if he needed to just blast, he had his good old Sin Eater.

Now he jacked back the machine pistol's charging handle far enough to confirm a round was chambered. A gleam of silver—he slammed the mechanism locked.

"Let's go," he said. "Who wants to live forever?"

"I was hoping to make a stab at it," Grant grumbled as he moved to put his back to the door frame to cover his partner's—the eternal point man—exit.

Chapter 29

"Compromised!" The mogul's screech of fury rose even above the ebb and flow of the alarm in his master bedroom-cum-command center. "Explain how this is possible, Enkidu! Explain this *total* fucking incompetence to me if you can!"

His big mahogany mask of a face cast in grim lines, the bodyguard picked his master up off the giant bed of maroon satin and set him on his feet.

"Would you rather I explain," he said, opening a closet door, "or help secure your safety?"

He tossed an assault vest from the closet at his employer: a bulky, heavy but simple construction of ballistic-weave fabric and Kevlar, with overlapping steel-ceramic plates hung down the front to protect the wearer's vital centerline from collarbone to crotch. It was hot, heavy and uncomfortable, and didn't do a lot for agility. But it would stop most things short of a big-bore Magnum rifle round. Bates shrugged it on over the gold-trimmed maroon silk robe that encased his gangly torso.

A scattering of heartbeats earlier the big display on the far wall had shown a vision of a lunar landscape, black and silver-gray. Now it showed a schematic of the fortress with two of the pop-up turrets flashing red and apparently stuck in the extended position.

"What about Ishtar's fucking pets?" Bates raged as Enkidu helped pull the vest the rest of the way down. "They should have torn any intruders to pieces by now."

Enkidu's dark eyes flicked to the displays. "External atmospheric samplers indicate an aerosol nerve agent has been deployed across the top of this base and environs. All the horrors are dead, probably for a half-klick radius."

Bates's long ovine face immediately lost whatever little color it had left. He began to hyperventilate. "Nerve gas! My God! My God! We're—"

"Safe," Enkidu said. "From that, in any event. Remember, our air intakes are designed to filter out any possible airborne threat—biological, chemical, radiological. And we have internal sensors that will selectively shut down blocks of the ventilation system should any gas infiltrate through the damaged turret."

He checked the displays again. "Real-time analysis of air samples indicates toxicity is already dropping rapidly outside. They used an extremely nonpersistent agent, it appears."

A chiming sounded: the first bars of Beethoven's *Für Elise*. Enkidu and Bates froze momentarily, then turned as one to the screen. The chimes signified a special direct-channel call incoming for Gilgamesh Bates; a rectangular yellow cursor blinked in the lower right-hand corner of the big display.

"Accept," Bates commanded mechanically.

A face appeared: big and grinning, with a brush of silver hair and a luxuriant silver mustache. Eyes of piercing pale blue stared out at Bates and his enormous henchman.

"Gil," the display said. "Mike Hays. A blast from the past. Remember me?" Behind him was visible a scene of destruction: twisted metal wrapped around twisted bodies. Past Hays's left shoulder half a skull hung over a jagged lip of metal. The major was wearing some kind of bulky camou coveralls with a belt of linked .308 cartridges slung over one shoulder.

"Major Hays!" Bates said. He split his pink beard with a smile of spurious delight. "How excellent to see you. I've been hoping against hope for the opportunity to set right certain painful misunderstan—"

"Cut the catshit, Bates," Hays said. "We've come back from the past to kick your ass. Just thought I'd be neighborly and give a little warning to you and your giant sock monkey there. And if anything's happened to Sean, you'd better hope we're *this* merciful when we catch you."

He raised his full-sized MG one-handed to point directly at the vid pickup. The screen filled up with a flare of flame. Then snow: visual static.

Enkidu chuckled, a noise like fist-sized rocks jostling each other inside his great tumbler of a chest. "They've got courage," he said. "Have to give them that."

"They've got *in!*" Bates shrieked, spittle flying from his mouth. Enkidu stood out of range. "Don't you see that's all that matters, you imbecile? Now go and kill them! Do you hear me? *Kill them!* Or I swear I'll let Ishtar give you to her pets!"

Enkidu frowned. The corners of his mouth sagged. "You don't have to threaten me, Gilgamesh. You know that."

Bates raised both skinny arms in the air. "Just do it! Now!"

Enkidu nodded. Then he grinned. "I will. In the meantime—stay in this room. Please. I'll leave a guard. You'll be safer here than anywhere else."

As the Cerberus team had gambled, the room immediately surrounding the mat-trans chamber was not secured. Grant and Kane quickly confirmed it before Brigid and Domi stepped out. Brigid carried a 9 mm USP in a shoulder holster. Domi had her Detonics and, of course, her knife.

Aside from some unusual fixtures mounted where wall met ceiling, which the intruders had neither time nor inclination to inspect, the room outside the gateway chamber was fairly standard: consoles, a few chairs.

Outside in the corridor a pair of guards in stiff gray uniforms stood flanking the door. They nervously eyed a red light set high on the opposite wall flashing in unison to the brain-piercing alarm. They had received orders via the headsets both wore to stay at their posts no matter what. Each fingered the M-4 carbine he held. They were to hold position and do their assignment: keep anyone from trying to use the mat-trans.

Neither responded at once when the door slid open between them. It was impossible: nobody was inside, nor could be. Everyone within the fortress knew the gateway was a secret, long hidden by the master, Bates himself. No one could jump into it because no one outside the redoubt Bates called New Ur knew of its existence.

While their minds were trying to process sensory data leading to an impossible conclusion, a tall figure encased completely in gleaming black armor stepped right out between them. Its left gauntlet whipped up and around in a back-fist that smashed the mouth of the guard on that side and dropped him to his knees gargling his own blood and teeth. The other hand pressed the pierced-shrouded muzzle of a machine pistol beneath the right-hand guard's short ribs and fired a triburst.

As the man fell sprawling, the black figure aimed the pistol at the temple of his gagging, choking comrade and fired a single shot.

Kane stepped forward, scanning the corridor and the widened area before the door. His MP-5 was slung beneath his right arm. "Clear," he called.

Letting his Sin Eater snap home and taking up the MP-5, he stepped forward to cover the right side of the corridor. Grant came up on his left. The two women emerged behind, keeping carefully behind the heavily armored males. Ahead of them the corridor turned sharply right and curved away on the left. There were no signs of sec men.

"Looks like they were more concerned with people gating out than gating in," Grant said. "Just like Lakesh suspected. Much as I hate to give him credit."

"He's earned plenty blame," Kane said. "We can afford to be generous this once."

"Just don't make a habit of it."

"No danger there."

The redoubt's mat-trans chamber lay on the third of seven levels. The command center, their first objective, was a level above.

"What about Sean?" Domi asked as the four moved cautiously forward.

"What about him?" Kane asked, never looking back. "He's not our lookout. Let his friends worry about him."

"Their job is to provide a diversion for us," she said.

"Yeah. And they all know they're likely to get used up doing it."

"But what if Bates's people kill him before they get to him?"

Kane looked back over his shoulder. His face was mostly blanked by the concave red visor, but his mouth was set in an exasperated line. "What if the others die before they get to him? What if *we* die before we save the world?"

"We fight. They fight," Domi said. "Fighting gives a chance. Prisoner got none."

"Domi, shut it," Grant said. "The kid's not our concern."

Domi looked to Brigid for support. The taller woman looked unhappy, but she shook her head. "Domi, they're right."

Kane found the doorway to the stair. The facility's command center should be right above. The builders of the redoubt seemed to have wanted a convenient bolt-hole.

He opened the door as quietly he could and spun quickly inside, covering with his MP-5. To his surprise there was no sign of anyone in the whole well, not even the sound of voices or footsteps. Grant was right behind him, covering. Brigid slipped in next.

He had reached the next level up, the command level, when he realized Domi was no longer with them.

THE BLOWN-OPEN POP-UP turret had a door at its root, which gave into a corridor. To the right of that doorway another door opened onto a ready room for the Phalanx crew.

The eight-man security squad cautiously approaching along the corridor from around a bend reckoned the whole turret crew of four was dead: nobody was responding by intercom in either turret or ready room. They themselves had been delayed by the necessity of shrugging into their own baggy containment gear, complete with hoods and masks, before pulling on assault vests over the lot. It was hot, stifling and altogether uncomfortable, and it made them feel clumsy and clownish.

The squad was split into two teams of four. Each team had two men armed with 5.56 mm M-4 carbines—baby M-16s—and one man armed with a Benelli auto-loading shotgun. In addition each fourth man carried a curved tactical shield of steel-ceramic laminate, four feet tall by two broad, with a little polycarbonate Judas window to peer through. The shield bearers, leading the way side by side, each held a 9 mm Beretta M-9 pistol in a bulkily gloved right hand.

Like everyone else currently inside the redoubt—so far as they knew, anyway—they were freezies, chronically displaced twentieth-century survivors. They had been picked for, among other things, a certain lack of imagination. Team Phoenix, on the other hand, had been composed of men selected in major part because Gilgamesh Bates's psychological evaluators deemed them possessed of such extraordinary toughness and mental resiliency that despite high levels of intellect and imagination they would not be driven mad by their temporal dislocation. Or at least before they had served their purpose, which was as far as Gil Bates cared about any other being than himself.

Despite their essential dullness the New Ur sec men were creeped out. They weren't just two hundred non-rewindable years remote from the world they had known, but on another continent—all were North Americans—and a whole hemisphere away, buried underground in a vanadium-steel bubble, with all the surrounding terrain for klicks in all directions infested with bizarre life-forms instantly lethal to them. The only woman resident in the facility on a permanent basis was a certifiably mad scientist who alternated between treating them with visible loathing and attempting to seduce them. Since the penalty for taking her up on such offers was being tossed naked out of the facility to the tender mercies of the monsters she herself had been responsible for creating in the first place, that avenue of release was closed.

Women from the increasingly distant areas not yet affected by the Successor bioforms were periodically captured and brought back as comfort girls. For security reasons they could never be returned, and so were used up and discarded like tissues. The sec men hadn't been picked for their sensitive and compassionate natures, either, but since Bates was way too canny to rely on sociopaths, however functional, for his personal safety, it bothered them, however dimly.

So they would have had to be not mentally stolid but defective not to get the weirds, all things considered.

Add to that the inevitable boredom and monotony, despite the availability of literally millions of hours of videos and computer games, not to mention Enkidu's frequent and merciless training, and they were not on the steadiest ground, in morale terms. And now some enemy had not only found their hidden fortress but, impossibly, broken through their guardian monsters and their impenetrable shell to get in at them. That didn't encourage them, either.

It did mean the sec men didn't need the threat of Enkidu's harsh but fair discipline—nor their employer's cruel but capricious vengefulness—to keep them moving forward to the fight. Anybody who'd gone through all that to get into New Ur had to be mightily pissed. Even the least imaginative had to figure that mercy was not high on the intruders' agenda.

But nothing had prepared them, as they drew within five yards of the ready room, for the metal corridor to fill with hideous pealing screams, nor the figure of a man totally wrapped in flames to fly out from the side door and right up in their faces.

Chapter 30

As naked as a lizard, Ishtar darted back and forth between her captive and the door. Reichert quickly realized she had no more idea than he did what was going on: even had the rising-and-falling blare of the alarm not been piped into the cell at head-splitting volume through concealed speakers, making it hard to hear even his thoughts, a firefight could have been raging right outside the doors utterly unheard because of the room's soundproofing. Which ironically had been created to keep loud noises *in*.

By sheer bad luck, the frantic microbiologist was near the door when it opened and Domi stepped through with her Detonics in hand. Whether Reichert or Ishtar was more surprised was a nice question. But the scientist reacted with blinding speed, seizing Domi's gun wrist with both hands and slamming it into the wall.

"Fuck!" Domi said, and slugged Ishtar with her left fist. Her gun hand, however, opened, and the compact but heavy handgun fell free to clatter loudly on the tiled floor. Reichert winced, in part because he hated to see a fine firearm mistreated, and also because the weapon was on full cock and the thumb safety was off.

If anything, Ishtar was smaller than Domi, and not in nearly such good shape. But she had the strength of the well and truly deranged. She screeched at Domi like a rabid wildcat, alternately buffeting her and ripping at her like one. Domi, seasoned little scrapper that she was, was trying either to get a grip on her opponent or drive a compact, powerful blow into her. But Ishtar thrashed too wildly to allow either.

Despite himself, Reichert watched in fascination. Under other circumstances he'd pay to see two such attractive women, one naked and the other not that far from it despite a bulky obvious armor vest, engage in a catfight like this. In fact he had, on a few rather guilty occasions. But those had been staged and comparatively friendly affairs, though tempers did tend to flare a bit, leading to black eyes and bloody noses.

These two, on the other hand, were utterly dedicated to and focused on incapacitating or killing each other as expeditiously as possible, with mere maiming and disfigurement done only as by-products, in passing.

The murderous panther speed and fury—and intent—should have robbed the spectacle of all erotic content, even for a lad who'd knocked around the places he had. Or so Reichert told himself. But the fact was, it didn't, exactly.

In the middle of the whirling ball of rage Ishtar bit Domi's left arm. Squalling furiously, Domi yanked it free, leaving white skin between Ishtar's less-white teeth. Domi head-butted her opponent, breaking her fine, narrow nose. Blood streaming freely down her mouth and chin, Ishtar broke free and staggered back, blinking furiously.

She backed against the cart the sec man had wheeled in. Her hand darted out and snatched up a scalpel with a wickedly curved blade. With a hawk scream of triumph she gathered herself and sprang.

Right onto the serrated nine-inch blade of Domi's knife.

It took her about half an inch to the left of her navel. The pain cut through the insulation of Ishtar's hyperadrenalized state. Her eyes snapped wide, and with a scream more of anger than agony she flung herself backward.

The knife ripped free, doing more damage on the way out than it had going it. Ishtar's bare heel lost purchase on bloody tile. She fell straight over backward and slammed the back of her skull against the stout metal-tube frame of the cot to which Reichert lay bound. She lay motionless, blood trickling from her head where her scalp had split open.

"Whoo," Domi said, rubbing her left eye, which was swelling rapidly shut. "She sure fused out."

Then she looked at Reichert, and paused to smile at his utter helplessness before she bent to free him.

WHEN KANE STEPPED through the door of the redoubt's command level a gigantic hand dropped on top of the MP-5 he was holding out before him and simply took it away from him as if he had not more strength in his fingers than a child.

He had emerged into a wide spot in the corridor. A blank metal wall of what had to be the command center itself loomed ahead. Kane pivoted toward the figure that loomed over him. His Sin Eater sprang from its holster. The great hand flipped aside the machine pistol in time to intercept the handblaster in midtrajectory. It wrenched the Sin Eater free and tossed it away, as well.

Grant came out fast, raising his Copperhead. The giant swatted Kane aside and grabbed Grant by the left forearm. His blaster went off, a shattering sound in the metal-walled confines, as Kane slammed against a wall. Unfortunately none of the screaming ricochets found a home in the red-leather flesh, abundant a target as it was.

Roaring in surprised anger, Grant tried to snap a shin up between the giant's oak-trunk legs. Enkidu pivoted his hips and took the kick on the inside of a thigh. His great slab face registered nothing as the black polycarbonate greave bit like a blade. Unhurriedly he plucked the Copperhead from Grant's gauntleted hands as casually as he had the Heckler & Koch from Kane's, then wrenched the Sin Eater, power holster and all, from the armored forearm.

Kane was having problems catching his breath. Little yellow lights still danced around in his skull. He felt an inclination to just sit and enjoy the show for a while.

But his partner was not faring well. Dangled by one arm like a child being reproved, Grant drove two punches into the great gray-tunicked chest, producing no visible effect. He raised his right foot, planted the corrugated sole against the monster's flat belly and ran up Enkidu's chest and threw himself into a backward somersault.

Laughing, Enkidu let him go. He stepped back as Grant landed in a crouch with a fist down on the floor.

"I hate guns," the giant said. "They're not honorable."

Kane had got his mind sorted out and straightened. He rubbed the back of his right gauntlet across a mouth exposed by his visor, saw dark liquid gleam against the darkness.

"We're not honorable, asshole," he said. "We're Mags."

Enkidu laughed again. His teeth were big and white. Each looked to be the size of one of Kane's thumbnails. "It's a lot more interesting this way, don't you think?" he said.

Kane and Grant turned visors briefly toward each other. As of one accord they hit Enkidu from both sides, Kane high, Grant low.

Or tried. Enkidu served Grant as he had Sean Reichert back in Esperanza, flopping a hand on his shoulder and slamming him to the floor to go skittering along the neoprene runner on the metal floor for four yards, banging his limbs off the wall. Kane meanwhile hit the giant with a forearm shiver under the left arm; Enkidu accepted it, then caught Kane in a front bear hug with both arms, one hand locked on the other wrist.

Kane found himself in air with his boots flailing. He

tried to head-butt Enkidu in the face but couldn't reach. He settled for trying to smash the huge man's collarbone with his armored forehead but couldn't get there, either; he just slammed his head into a great wad of pectoral muscle and kicked futilely at the sec chief's legs.

"Do you know what the crush strength of your armored suit is?" Enkidu asked. He spoke conversationally, with no evidence of strain. "It's not really built for this, you know."

He was right, Kane realized. Creaking loudly, the armor was giving way beneath the man's superhuman strength. His own arms were pinned to his sides.

The usual escapes taught in Magistrate training for a front bear hug were, like all Mag Division combat techniques, brutal and effective. But they were also predicated on facing an opponent of at least approximately the same size. Enkidu was as much bigger than Kane as Kane was than Domi, and proportionally at least as much stronger; he had to have outweighed Grant and Kane together.

Kane's vision began to blacken around the edges. In his failing peripheral vision he saw Grant lunging forward with a long-bladed Magistrate combat knife in hand.

Laughing, Enkidu brought up his right leg and slammed a forward thrust kick into Grant's chest. Grant flew backward. Hit the wall hard.

Slid down and lay without moving.

THE CITADEL'S tactical-response team shield men recoiled from the flaming man. The terrible screaming went on. The hall filled with the stench of a barbecue gone terribly wrong.

The burning man struck the wall across from the door from which he had emerged. Beyond him a figure appeared from the stairs at the foot of the wrecked gun tower, reaching the corridor floor in a long, low dive. Before the tactical squad could respond a full-dress machine gun roared, adding its muzzle-flare to the hideous glare illuminating the hallway.

The tactical shields were designed to stop handgun fire, although they were also effective against shotgun pellets and even .223 rifle bullets. The machine gun fired full-sized .308 rounds. The shields were unlikely to turn those.

But the canny gunner wasn't leaving anything to chance. He fired straight along the floor, ripping the flesh and shattering shinbones and thighs of legs protected neither by the shields nor by body armor.

In moments the eight-man squad lay thrashing and screaming and spurting on the ground. The flickering muzzle-flash ceased, and then the thunderous hammering sound subsided.

So had the screams. The burning human figure slumped against the wall to the machine gun's left. The flames had mostly died. The smoking corpse was fastened by duct tape to a television cart; a broomstick up the back of its uniform blouse had kept it upright for its brief pyretic journey. It was in fact a man's body, but the man had never felt the flame. The nerve gas had thoroughly killed him a while back. And a few incendiary-gel pencils stuffed in his pockets had kindled him.

Larry Robison pivoted from the ready room door and knelt by the wall, covering with his Saiga shotgun. Joe Weaver came out next, unbowed by the heavy pack on his back, MP-5 at the ready. He moved forward quickly among the fallen security troops.

"You scare me sometimes, Robison," Major Mike Hays said, lying down behind his FN-MAG.

"I thought it was a bravura performance," the ex-SEAL said. His voice was raw. He'd spent the past minute screaming his lungs out to provide a soundtrack to his improvising horror show.

Six muffled shots, irregularly spaced but close together, sounded from farther down the corridor. "Clear," Weaver said.

"You do that pretty handily for a lifelong civilian."

Weaver's mouth grinned beneath the circular lenses that masked his eyes. "Quickest form of anesthetic," he said. "I left two for questioning."

"Why two?" Robison asked.

"In case the first doesn't want to answer."

Groaning slightly, Hays picked himself up, then picked up the machine gun by the handle. "Damn, I need a vacation." He waved a hand at the smoke trailing from the corpse. "Christ, this guy stinks! Let's get the skinny and get the fuck out of here. We've got a computer tycoon to kill."

KANE COULD FEEL blood pressure build in his skull. His rib cage caved slowly inward. He strained with all the force of his powerful muscles. It might have been some kind of a machine that held and slowly constricted him, and not human arms. If the giant sec boss could really be called human.

The stairwell door opened. Brigid stepped forth, her handblaster held out before her. "Put him down," she said.

Enkidu looked at her and laughed. "You won't shoot," he said with Jovian certainty.

He squeezed tighter. Kane's last breath came out as an agonized gasp.

Chapter 31

Without changing expression, Brigid fired the USP until the slide locked back.

"Yes, I will," she said.

Enkidu dropped Kane and staggered back against the wall as Brigid pumped sixteen 9 mm copper-jacketed rounds into his cavern chest. He put a hand to the front of his tunic, which was dark and sopping. He stared at the red wetness on his fingertips, then slid slowly to the floor. He painted a smear of scarlet down the wall.

"Sorry to have taken so long," Brigid said, replacing the magazine in the grip of her H&K. "Some sec men tried to come up the stairs. I had to discourage them."

Grant was helping Kane to his feet. "Does that mean she missed seeing us get our asses kicked?"

It felt to Kane as if he were inhaling shards of broken glass. "No good," he croaked. "She saw the aftermath."

They picked up their scattered hardware. "Damn," Grant said. "Have to wait till we get back to Cerberus to fix these holsters."

"When did you become an optimist?" Kane asked.

He stuck his Sin Eater into his belt, checked the chamber of his MP-5. "Come on. And thanks, Baptiste."

"I wondered if you'd get around to that," she said.

"So I'm going soft. Don't mean nothin'. We're probably all going to die down here anyway."

Although they moved cautiously, if purposefully, they saw no one—not even guarding the door to the command center, when they approached it.

"Could it be a trap?" Brigid asked, crouched around a metallic curve of wall.

"Nothing's ever this easy," Grant said.

"Mebbe it is," Kane said. He strode to the door. Reluctantly the others followed.

The control-room door swung open when he hit the contact panel outside. Holding his MP-5 ready, he swung around and inside.

More than a dozen people huddled inside. The occupants seemed divided evenly between technicians and uniformed security troops. As Grant stepped through the door and to the other side, covering with his Copperhead, the sec men ostentatiously raised their hands.

"Who's in charge?" Kane asked.

A short, stocky man with a shaved head, wearing glasses with heavy dark plastic frames, stepped up. "I guess that's me," he said. "I'm Dr. Cornell."

Brigid came in and sidestepped to clear the entrance. "Guard the door," Kane told her without looking back. He turned to Cornell. "Where's Gilgamesh Bates?"

The hairless head shook. A large green-gray mole

seemed to throb on the right forehead, right where the hairline might have been. "We don't know."

"We don't care, neither." It was one of the sec men, with blond hair cropped close to his head and prominent jug-handle ears. "We had enough of his crazy-ass shit." That elicited a general murmur of agreement.

"Where're your weapons?" Grant asked.

The sec men stepped to either side to reveal a careless firewood stack of arms against the foot of a console. "Great morale in this place," Kane said.

"Does anyone know what means Bates had of controlling the Invader bioforms?" Brigid asked.

Cornell blinked. His eyes were murky behind his glasses, the color of stagnant pond water. "She means the Successors," another tech said.

Cornell raised his head. "Ah. The Successors. Ishtar's diabolical little playmates." He smiled. There was a gap between his front upper teeth. "Yes, indeed. Tanks and tanks of the stuff. Down in the garage level."

"It's a self-replicating assembler," explained another technician. "It'll spread on its own once released. But we've been growing as much of it as we could, so it wouldn't take so long—"

Kane held up a black-gloved hand. "Save the explanations," he said. "Right now we just need answers. How many people in this facility?"

"Eighty-four," Cornell said. "Forty security and forty-three technical personnel. And one prisoner."

The door opened. Standing closest, Brigid jumped and swung, bringing up her handblaster.

Domi entered, helping Sean Reichert. He wore a pair of gray sec-man trousers that didn't fit and carried a Beretta. He looked beat to shit. Domi didn't look much better, but seemed to be glowing all the same.

"I guess you won, huh?" Grant said.

"Domi?" Brigid said.

"Woulda been here sooner," the albino said, "except he had to scavvy a pair of pants. Men are such babies!"

Shaking his head, Kane turned back to Cornell as Domi and Brigid helped the young man to a chair. "Where is everybody? The corridors are deserted."

"Most of our personnel have locked themselves in their living quarters," Cornell said. "Once it became apparent the facility had been breached, it seemed the most prudent course."

Kane turned to Grant in amazement. He was grateful the visor masked his expression. "We buffaloed the whole damned outfit," he subvocalized for the benefit of his own microphone patch, so that only his comrades could hear. "Seven of us took this whole damned place down."

"Not everybody's locked in their bedroom," Reichert said aloud, responding to Cornell's words, since he had not heard Kane's. "That big bastard's still on the loose. Enkidu, his name was."

"What do you mean?" Kane demanded. "Baptiste chilled him. You must've had to trip over his body getting here."

"No body," Domi said, shaking her head. Despite a shiner and a swell assortment of gouges and multicolored bruises, she was feisty as always. "Big smear of blood on the wall. No chills."

STAGGERING, HER PALM PRESSED flat to her belly to contain the burning pain in her guts—and possibly her guts themselves—Ishtar grunted in triumph as she reached the door to her lab on sixth level. Her head was a pulsing bag of pain. When her head struck the frame of the prisoner's cot, the blow had split her scalp at the back of her skull and quite possibly caused a fracture to the bone. She was in a bad way.

But she had grown up with pain. Each step down from the holding cell to the lift and then down to the entrance to her lab had been like a fresh stab to her gut. It wasn't the worst pain she had known. When her rockstar father had raped and beaten her for the first time when she was five, it had hurt far worse.

And unlike then, she now had the means of striking back at her tormentors. Oh yes, she did. Against all humanity. Against the cancer cells who infected the world, who had raped it as her father had her.

Like the anonymous U.S. Army officer in the longago Vietnam War—about the time of her own birth, in fact—who had famously said, "We had to destroy the village in order to save it," she saw no irony in the plan she had created and launched, with the aid of Gilgamesh Bates. She meant to destroy the natural world precisely in order to preserve it. For the world as it was had been irreparably damaged by Man, the ultimate evil—the ultimate pathogen. Even before the unimaginable devastation wrought to the environment by the nuke-caust, humans had ravaged the Earth with their industry, their pollution, their commerce. And their science.

So she would use science, the weapon of the enemy, to destroy the current order of the world—in order to make it anew. *Better.*

Without any trace of humanity. Even her.

Except, of course, for that brief, inconsequential sequence of her own unique DNA she had incorporated into the stuff of the basic Successor genotype, and which was carried by every bioform. So that she, and she alone, would be the mother of the new world.

The biometric reader next to the door recognized her palm pattern and opened the door to her. Only she and key members of the staff had such access: Bates was not eager for accidents, nor for the ever present possibility that one of his stolid thugs or the venal or frightened technicians and scientists he had brought with him through the cryo vats might have second thoughts about the magnitude and permanence of what they were doing.

Ishtar stepped inside. The door shut behind her with a soft squeal, like a small, frightened animal. Inside it was dim, cool, tiled. The smell of cleansing agents tickled her nose.

At once her pain began to diminish. She was home.

Returning to her children.

She knew Bates had undisclosed plans. He wanted to rule the world; he made that abundantly clear to her. He had made it clear from the very outset, when he had recruited her back in the 1990s. And while he claimed to her that ruling over a world inhabited solely by her Successor forms, and his personal retainers, would gratify his full desire, she knew better than to believe him. He loved power over people too well. He could not do without his underlings to dominate, to use—to rape.

But he was a fool. He thought no one was smart enough to use him as he used others.

And now he had been outsmarted. Someone had successfully penetrated his impenetrable secret stronghold. And that wasn't all.

Ishtar was about to show him how wrong he was, when he thought he could use her and her creatures for his ends—and dispose of them when he had no further use for them, like some kidnapped village girl.

She had, unwillingly, created a self-replicating assembler designed to attack and destroy organisms bearing the distinctive signature of the Successor genotype, and no other organism. Fool though he was, Gilgamesh Bates was a shrewd fool; he had forced her to demonstrate that the characteristics he demanded of the anti-Successor assembler were in fact in place before he ever permitted the release of the Successor forms into the forests surrounding the precipitous upper Marañón.

Her assistants—her intellectual jailers, she thought

of them—were of course far less brilliant and capable than she was. She scarcely had to remind them of it, although she did more than occasionally. But they were capable enough in their way; Bates was almost as clever as he thought he was about picking subordinates. Specifically, they were more than competent to check the characteristics of her counter-Successor assembler. And Bates himself…was able to spot anomalies even her staff had missed in analysis of the assembler's performance.

His punishment had been to threaten to withdraw her from the project. To imprison her, using his clod of a monster of a bodyguard he had dubbed Enkidu, after the legendary Gilgamesh's wild-man sidekick, to deny her access to her children, her heritage. If she tried to double-deal Bates again, she would be removed permanently.

Ishtar feared death far less than she feared pain. She knew there were still limits of agony she could not bear to be pushed beyond. But her own death meant nothing. She was, after all, just another cancer cell.

But *failure* was intolerable. Not to be borne.

So she had in the end given Bates what he wanted. But she had laid her own plan. Gilgamesh Bates and his henchmen would never be permitted to disperse the counter-Successor. And no more would the mystery invaders, like the albino freak bitch who had spoiled her game with the captive traitor and set her guts to flame.

She reeled. Blackness gathered between her eyes,

and she fought against the agony, nausea and dizziness. But her will was chilled titanium. She made herself totter across the outer office, gain access to the holding chamber with the armaglass window where her children could be put on display to the unappreciative eyes of Bates and his ilk, as if they were mere specimens, not superior beings who would purify and inherit all the Earth.

Her children would embrace her. They loved her. She knew it. They would accept and nurture and heal her.

And even as they were doing that, they would be scouring all of New Ur of every remnant of that intolerable contagion known as human life.

Chapter 32

The door to Gilgamesh Bates's personal command center-cum-bedroom was as heavy as the armor of a main battle tank and every bit as adamant.

The shaped charge Joe Weaver carried in his ruck, the approximate size and shape of a flower pot, was designed specifically to rip open a late-twentieth-century MBT like a paper sack. The door fared no better.

Weaver with his MP-5 and Robison with his shotgun went in fast. His machine gun not ideally suited for room-clearing operations, Hays held outside in the corridor, securing their backsides.

After anticipating a foot-by-foot fight they were unlikely to survive—a pure diversion to allow their Cerberus comrades to get to the goal and do what needed to be done to stop the plague—what they met was all but anticlimax. They had encountered little resistance on the way to the stairs and down to the fifth level, where, Bates's sec men had told them without any persuasion whatsoever, the master's bedroom headquarters lay. The scattered pockets of resistance had been wiped out or routed by quick volleys of full-auto fire and a few grenades.

Nobody, it seemed, was eager to die for the man who would be king.

In what seemed just a few seconds and was probably little over a minute Robison radioed, "Clear."

"Whaddaya mean, 'clear'?" Hays said.

"Even a Marine should know what that means," Robison came back, "sir."

"Nobody here," Weaver said. "No fugitive billionaires, no nine-foot bodyguards. Not even a Shuara bedwarmer. Nobody."

"Well, fuck me," Hays said. "Where is the son of a bitch?"

"I've never been a billionaire megalomaniac, although it sounds like interesting work," Weaver said. "But if I was Gil Bates, I'd be running as far and fast as my skinny old spider legs would take me."

"YOU MEAN Major Mike, Larry and Joe are here, too?" Sean Reichert said. He sat lolled on a bench with his stolen Beretta loosely held in his hand.

"You think they leave you in a cage?" Domi asked.

The young man shook his head, more in befuddlement than denial. "He's had a rough time, Domi," Brigid said. "I don't think he's tracking too well."

Reichert held up a hand. "I've been alternately drugged and beat up," he said. "But I'm okay now."

He belied his statement by standing up, swaying, and only preventing himself from falling by bracing himself with his gun hand on a console. The Ur techs tensed at this, but Kane noted his finger was outside the Beretta's trigger guard and the slide safety engaged.

"Don't try this at home," he said.

"Sit back down and rest," Brigid said.

"Gotta help 'em," he said doggedly. "They came for me. I gotta go to them."

It wasn't a tight syllogism, but none of the Cerberus four questioned it. "What say you and the ladies hold the fort here," Kane said to Grant. "I'll take the kid and help find his pals."

"You were ready to leave Sean in the lurch before," Domi said. "Now you want to help him?"

Kane shrugged. "We got the control room now. If you three can't hold it, why would four of us be able to?"

"Two," Domi said. "I go with."

"Fine with me," Brigid said. She had moved to stand over the sec men's piled weapons, just in case. "Grant and I should be able to hold."

"I'd say it sucks," Grant said. "Why do you go and I stay?"

"Because I'm the point man."

ISHTAR'S FINGERS FELT COLD and fat as they punched out the code for the special containment. The heavy door opened.

Her masterwork stepped out.

It was the climax-form Successor—the *true* Successor, the intelligent form meant to succeed the evil and fallen Man. Not even Bates knew of his existence.

Her prince stood no more than an inch taller than the minute scientist. He was vaguely humanoid in shape, in that he had one head, two arms, two legs. The eyes were insectile, jewel-faceted compounds as big around as Ishtar's palms. His mouth was a complex assembly of palps and shredders. His neck was a thin stalk. His body was colored in shades of yellow and brown, slender, gracile, though clad in an exoskeleton covered with short spines. His arms were thin, and ended in claws of four talons opposed by pairs. His waist was wasp narrow. He showed no external genitalia. His legs were thin and grasshopper-like.

He looked at her with his eyes glittering like emeralds. She stood nude before him and spread her bloody hands wide.

They embraced. He held her tight.

"I knew it," she sobbed. "I knew that you would know me and love me."

His arms locked together behind her back. From his frontal carapace sprang a dozen spikes, piercing her breasts and ribs and belly, pinning them together.

She screamed.

Her scream rose in pitch and volume as his ovipositor, as chitinous and spiny as his thorax, drove up between her legs, and the Successor bioforms made final communion with their creator.

LARRY ROBISON BELLOWED hoarsely as a 5.56 mm bullet broke his right upper arm as he leaned around a doorway to fire his Saiga. He fell back. With alacrity surprising for his bulk Mike Hays jumped out to replace him, firing his FN-MAG from the hip like a submachine gun. Sec men in body armor staggered as his heavy, high-velocity bullets hammered them.

On the far side of them Enkidu hurried his master down the hall. The giant had absorbed far more damage than Ishtar. But he had a great deal more mass to absorb it. Although temporarily rendered unconscious by the shock to his system of having Brigid's magazine emptied into him, he awakened shortly. He was weakened, and certainly suffering massive internal bleeding. But his endurance was as mighty as his musculature, his will perhaps mightiest of all. He had roused himself, willing himself to ignore the pain, and gone and rousted Bates from the bedroom where he had left his employer. Clearly the situation was going to hell in a hell of a hurry; it was time to activate the escape plan.

In Bates's bedroom the tycoon had already discovered that most of his foot soldiers were barricaded in their dorms and declining to budge. They had the impression the facility was already full of enemies, that they were hopelessly outnumbered and it was best to offer no resistance and hope the invaders offered terms.

But they were fighting men, of sorts, and Enkidu was a fighting man par excellence. By example and sheer force of personality he had chivvied another squad in tactical armor out to help cover as he helped Bates, in his gold-and-purple robe and tactical vest, to retreat to the mat-trans unit.

It was good he had them to shield his boss—and himself, for that matter. Because the three erstwhile employees of the Bates empire who had invaded the fortress from above caught them up from behind as they scurried toward the mat-trans chamber. And Team Phoenix immediately commenced to simply try to butcher its way through the guards to get at Bates.

Lacking much choice—caught, as they were, between the three invaders and Enkidu—the security troops fought with trapped-animal desperation.

Joe Weaver swung his MP-5 left as a head poked around the far corner of the corridor extending that way. The head was encased in a gleaming black helmet with a red visor. The mouth and chin beneath were pale.

"It's Kane," the mouth said unnecessarily. "Don't shoot—we're reinforcements."

Weaver let out a wordless cry of joy as Reichert limped around the corner, with Domi sticking tight beside him. Reichert ran forward unsteadily to embrace the older man. Then he and Domi knelt to help Robison bind his wound.

Hays stepped back into cover around the corner. "Got 'em on the run, but we gotta press or they'll get away."

"I know," Kane said. "Baptiste got the control center crew to work the video surveillance system for her." He tapped the side of his helmet to indicate that the fiery-haired ex-archivist was providing guidance over their comm net. "Looks like time to let a hard-contact Mag lead the way."

"You got it, big guy," Hays said, grinning fiercely beneath his mustache.

With his Sin Eater in his right hand and Larry Robison's autoloading shotgun in his left, Kane swung around the corner and advanced upon the sec men. They cringed at the sight of him, imposing in that black armor so cunningly designed for maximum intimidation. Their bullets rocked him but did not penetrate. His answering bursts smashed arms and legs and sought out weaknesses in their body armor.

They were quickly joined by the even more potent fire of Mike Hays striding right behind him to his right. The big .308 machine gun's power was awesome: the muzzle blasts slapped Kane like Enkidu's own hands.

The guards died or fled. Then they died anyway, shot in the back. Neither Kane nor his companion was willing to leave them the option of standing up and fighting on.

"Come on," Kane said, breaking into a run, "they're into the outer chamber."

Weaver, Sean and Domi came around the corner to follow them, leaving the injured Robison to guard their rear with the MP-5 Kane had swapped him for his Saiga. Kane hit the door and plunged recklessly inside; if Enkidu was there he'd fill him full of even more holes.

But Enkidu stood behind a quartet of nervous-looking guards, looming above them, as the door to the mat-trans chamber itself slammed shut.

"Step aside, big man," Kane said as Hays came in to stand shoulder to shoulder with him. "It'll take too long for Gil to gate out. We'll get him whether we have to come through you or not."

Enkidu laughed and held up a pair of M-4 carbines. Apparently duty to his master overrode his distaste for firearms. "We'll see, crayfish."

And Brigid's voice screamed into Kane's ear, "Get out! Get out now!"

Though Kane and Brigid Baptiste disagreed over how to handle almost every situation, in the crunch Kane had learned to trust his *anam-chara* implicitly. When she cried her warning he turned and drove the others out by sheer vehemence. Then he slammed the door behind them.

"What the fuck?" several voices asked him at once. He asked the same of Brigid.

EXACTLY WHY Bates had had the system installed no one in the command center knew. He claimed it was to preserve a line of escape in case Ishtar's horrors somehow got loose. Everyone more or less took that to mean, when she got fed up and *let* them loose. But at that they were skeptical: the weird insensate animals, much less the slime molds and aggressive plant forms Ishtar was using to remodel the Upper Amazon and, in her dreams, the entire Earth, could scarcely get through the steel and armaglass into the mat-trans chamber itself, for all their claws and stings. Then again, nobody put it altogether past her to try to create a Successor form that knew how to open doors....

Or perhaps it was to keep humans at bay in the event of a mutiny—which to Bates's mind had to be an infinitely likelier expedient than what was happening, this impossible invasion.

For whatever reason he had commanded nozzles to be installed near the ceilings, attached to tanks filled with nitric acid under extreme pressure.

Entering the jump chamber, Gilgamesh Bates had triggered the system. Then jammed the door latch from within with an ancient Boy Scout pocketknife he carried with him always for obscure sentimental reasons.

The realization of the fate his master, whom he had served so loyally, had condemned him and his remaining men to at last broke even mighty Enkidu.

Watching from the vantage point of the command center, Brigid and Grant could see what Kane and the rest could not: Enkidu pounding his mighty fists on the armaglass windows of the chamber as his master abandoned him, and he and his men blistered and smoked and dissolved slowly in fuming clouds.

Chapter 33

"Eminently satisfactory," Dr. Mohandas Lakesh Singh said, peering at the big display, so like the one back at his own fortress of Cerberus, in the New Ur command center.

It showed a satellite map of the Marañón area, showing the eerie blue-green of the Invader-seized areas. Mapped onto it was a green hatchwork showing the areas over which the counter-Successor assembler had been sprayed by the Ur aircraft. A yellow fringe around it showed in false color where the satellite sensors had detected a die-off of the artificial life-forms.

"Amazing," Grant said. "It's working."

"We knew it'd work," said Kane, standing beside him and behind Lakesh. "It sure cleaned out the lower-level labs for us."

From a review of the surveillance video they had learned that Ishtar, sorely injured as Domi had left her, had made her way down to her laboratories on the sixth level, with the evident intention of releasing a swarm of her hideous offspring throughout the redoubt itself. She had made the mistake of closing the doors behind her.

Mistake because her creatures had turned on her before she had a chance to open the doors again. Her ace-in-the-hole creations, faintly humanoid Successors with hands, had not been instructed in how to open the doors, and weren't quite human enough to figure them out in the limited time before the doors opened in their faces and they were blasted backward by shotgun and machine-gun blasts. A handful of incendiary microgrens had followed. The doors had been shut again while those did the work. Then, with the outer chambers cleansed of Successors, the doors had been opened again and the anti-Successor nanomachines released into the labs.

When they peered through the armaglass window into the interior recesses of the lab, Ishtar's body—bloated with the Successor young whose bodies expanded as they dined on her flesh—had still been moving. So they threw in more incens, and afterward flushed that area too with the assembler.

Grant rubbed his long chin. "Things don't usually work out. Not this neatly."

"With all respect, friend Grant, I beg to differ," Lakesh said. "Quite often things to which we turn our hands turn out for the best. Even including this case, in which—quite against all odds—we managed to save the world."

"For the moment," Grant said. "From this."

"And despite our best efforts Gil got away," Kane said.

"Our friends from Team Phoenix will resume the hunt for him with redoubled vigor," Lakesh said, "once they finish supervising the destruction of the Invader bioforms."

"I still can't believe his destination didn't register on your wizard mat-demat tracker in Cerberus," Kane said.

Lakesh looked thoughtful. "Gilgamesh Bates seems to be a most unfortunately resourceful individual, it must be admitted," he said. "Still, we have successfully thwarted him. Sooner or later he'll slip up again, and we shall have him."

"Is that 'slip up' as in letting us put a stick in it for him," Kane said, "or 'slip up' as in almost letting that crazy woman wipe him out, along with the rest of the world? We almost had a pretty big accidental discharge here."

"Still," Brigid said, "Lakesh does make an excellent point—Gilgamesh Bates has displayed a strong and consistent tendency to outwit himself."

Kane looked at Grant. "And who does that remind you of?"

The door opened. Brewster Philboyd, tall, skinny, blond, with heavy dark-framed glasses and receding hair, came in with emphatic swings of his long arms and legs.

"The laboratory cleanup progresses most splendidly, Doctor," he said heartily to Lakesh. He ignored Kane and Grant.

"Marvelous news," Lakesh said. "I have every faith that you'll be able to restore this facility to full functionality in short order, Brewster."

"I shall certainly give it my best."

Arms folded, Grant leaned his head down toward Kane's. "You really think it's a good idea putting this guy in charge?" he asked sotto voce. A leading figure among the refugees from Manitius Moon base, Philboyd had a marked tendency to try to run the show—wherever and whatever it happened to be.

Kane shrugged. "Who cares? He can name himself emperor of South America and the Greater Hebrides for all I care. As long as it keeps him out of our hair for a while, I'm all in favor of it."

Philboyd either didn't hear the exchange or did a fine job pretending he hadn't. Still without acknowledging either man, he turned a toothy smile on Brigid.

"And you, Brigid," he said, "perhaps you'd care to stay down here and help us? Your quite remarkable skills would come in very handy. Very handy."

Kane looked down at his fist and mentally told it to unclench.

She smiled. "Thank you, Brewster. But no. For my part, I'm more than ready to get back home. We're finished here. It's done."

BUT IT WASN'T DONE.

Three days later, with reports streaming incessantly into Santa Caridad that the Invader bioforms were dropping dead in windrows, Simón the Liberator decided the time had come to hold his triumphal parade, confirming his status as President for Life of the Marañón Republic. After betraying Team Phoenix and fleeing

Esperanza under the cover of darkness, Simón had invaded Santa Caridad and usurped his uncle's position as president. Not only would he celebrate his new status as president, but he would also announce the final, guaranteed-victorious campaign against the savage Jivaros, who had been scattered and mortally weakened by the monsters.

And so, in the bright light of a perfect morning, he rode forth on his white stallion at the head of marching files of his troops in polished steel helmets, toward the cathedral in the center of town where the archbishop would affirm him as president and bestow the blessings of the Church. The streets were duly thronged with citizens, it having been made abundantly clear that attendance was mandatory. Yet the crowds were subdued, despite the scores of soldiers armed with truncheons who preceded the Liberator, scowling to encourage the masses to show their approbation. Perhaps it was emotional exhaustion from the just-averted threat of extermination by legions of unnatural beings.

And then as Simón approached the plaza as his career neared its apex, his head exploded.

Just like that, with no warning. Out of a clear blue sky, as the citizens told one another afterward; one moment he rode in triumph, the next his torso was toppling from the saddle with blood fountaining from the stump of its neck as what sounded like distant thunder rolled across the plaza.

Just what struck down the glorious hero at the apex

of his triumph was something of a mystery. The city police were not exactly advanced in their forensic techniques, at least by the standards of the world that had vanished two centuries before. But they could do geometry, or in any event could consult with experts from the university who could. The learned professors were able to project a straight line from a statue that had shattered at the same instant as the Liberator's head, through the estimated position of that selfsame noble head, and so established the flight of the bullet that killed him.

Except the line pointed directly and only to a villa on a hill a mile and a half distant. And everybody knew no rifle would make such a shot; and even if one could, surely at that distance no rifleman in the world could hit a moving man in the head, even a slow-moving one.

The confusion attendant upon the champion's mysterious death was enormous. In the midst of it all a small junta of influential citizens put forth a remarkable candidate to replace the stricken leader: the previous president's illegitimate but acknowledged daughter, Consuelo Vásquez. Since the Liberator's right-hand man, the one-eyed de la Sombra, had been tragically found only the previous dawn hanging from a lamppost—an apparent suicide—there was no organized opposition, especially after the junta moved with commendable dispatch to round up Simón's surviving officers and extract loyalty oaths from them. Or, well, else.

Of course, all this meant that the war of final extermination against the Shuara was postponed indefinitely, to say the least. The citizens of the Marañón Republic did not seem unduly disappointed. They had bellies full of war, if nothing else.

And no one spoke, or at least not too loudly, of the fact that until very recently indeed Consuelo had been leader of those very Jivaros in opposing the republic. Because, after all, it was always unhealthy to criticize the president for life, even by implication.

One city constable, perhaps more credulous than the rest, and perhaps something else altogether, took the trouble on the day following Simón's fall to pay a visit to the abandoned villa the professors had pointed out, and to examine the attic. There, lying upon the floorboards—which he noted were altogether free of dust— lay a curiosity: a single playing card. It was a joker, in fact, and scrawled upon it was, "Payback's a bitch."

Being a prudent man, as well as a curious one, the constable slipped the card into his pocket. As a memento.

Then it was over.

TAKE 'EM FREE

2 action-packed novels plus a mystery bonus

NO RISK

NO OBLIGATION TO BUY

PROMISE TO DEFEND

The elite counter-terrorist group known as Stony Man has one mandate: to protect good from evil; to separate those willing to live in peace from those who kill in order to fulfill their own agenda. When all hell breaks loose, the warriors of Stony Man enter the conflict knowing each battle could be their last, but the war against freedom's oppressors will continue....

STONY MAN ®

*Available
October 2005
at your favorite retailer.*

SKYFIRE

Wind of a grim conspiracy comes to light, and the levels of treachery go deep into America's secret corridors of power. When the Cadre Project was created decades ago, it served to protect the U.S. government during the Cold War. Now it's a twisted, despotic vision commandeered by a man whose hunger for power is limitless, whose plan to manufacture terror and lay a false trail of blame across the globe may find America heading into all-out world war against the old superpowers.

DEATH LANDS®

Ritual Chill

**Cursed in fathomless ways,
the future awaits...**

STRANGE QUARRY

A cold sense of déjà vu becomes reality as Ryan's group emerges from a gateway they'd survived before—a grim graveyard of lost friends and nightmares. The consuming need to escape the dangerous melancholy of the place forces the company out into the frozen tundra, where an even greater menace awaits. The forbidding land harbors a dying tribe, cursed members of the ancient Inuit, who seize the arrival of Ryan and his band as their last hope to appease angry gods...by offering them up as human sacrifice.

In the Deathlands, the price for survival is the constant fear of death.

Available September 2005 at your favorite retail outlet.